KILLING SHOW

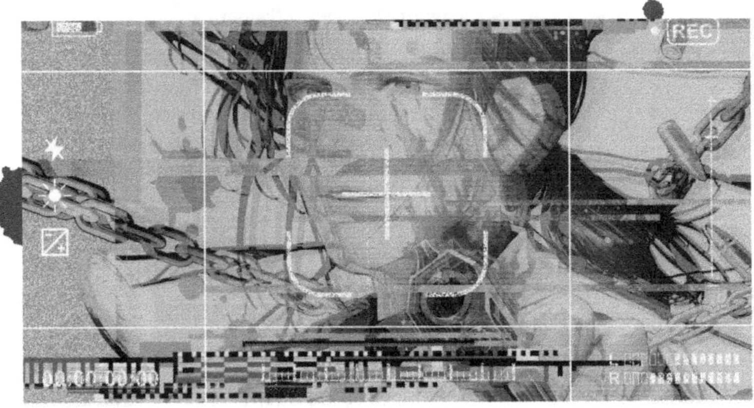

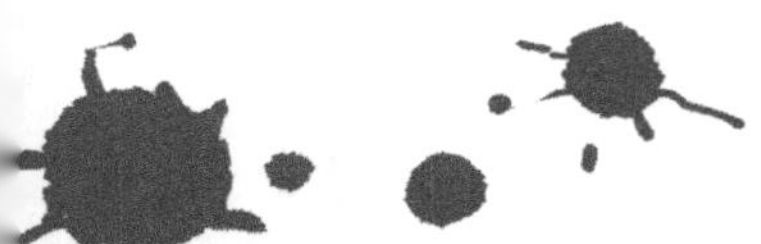

Killing Show
An imprint of Via Lactea Ltd.

Copyright © Fox

No part of this book may be reproduced in any form or by any electronic or mechanical means, including information storage and retrieval systems-except in the case of brief quotations embodied in critical articles or reviews-without permission in writing from the author.

This book is a work of fiction. The characters and events portrayed in this book are fictitious or are used fictitiously. Any similarity to actual persons, living or dead, is purely coincidental and not intended by the author.

Author: Fox
Translators: XiA; Pengie
Editor: Viv
Layout Designer: Elizabeth Z

CONTACT:
Customer Support: info@vialactea.ca
Wholesale & Distribution: market@vialactea.ca
Other Cooperation: https://vialactea.ca/pages/cooperation
Discord Channel: https://discord.gg/vialactea

Follow us on X/Instagram/Facebook: @ViaLactea_Ltd
Official Website: www.vialactea.ca

ISBN 978-1-77408-524-0 (pbk)
Printed in Canada

LOCATION:
Shops At Waterloo Town Square
#27, 75 King Street South, Waterloo, ON
Canada
N2J 1P2

Via Lactea and Via Lactea Logo are trademarks of Via Lactea Ltd.
ALL RIGHTS RESERVED.

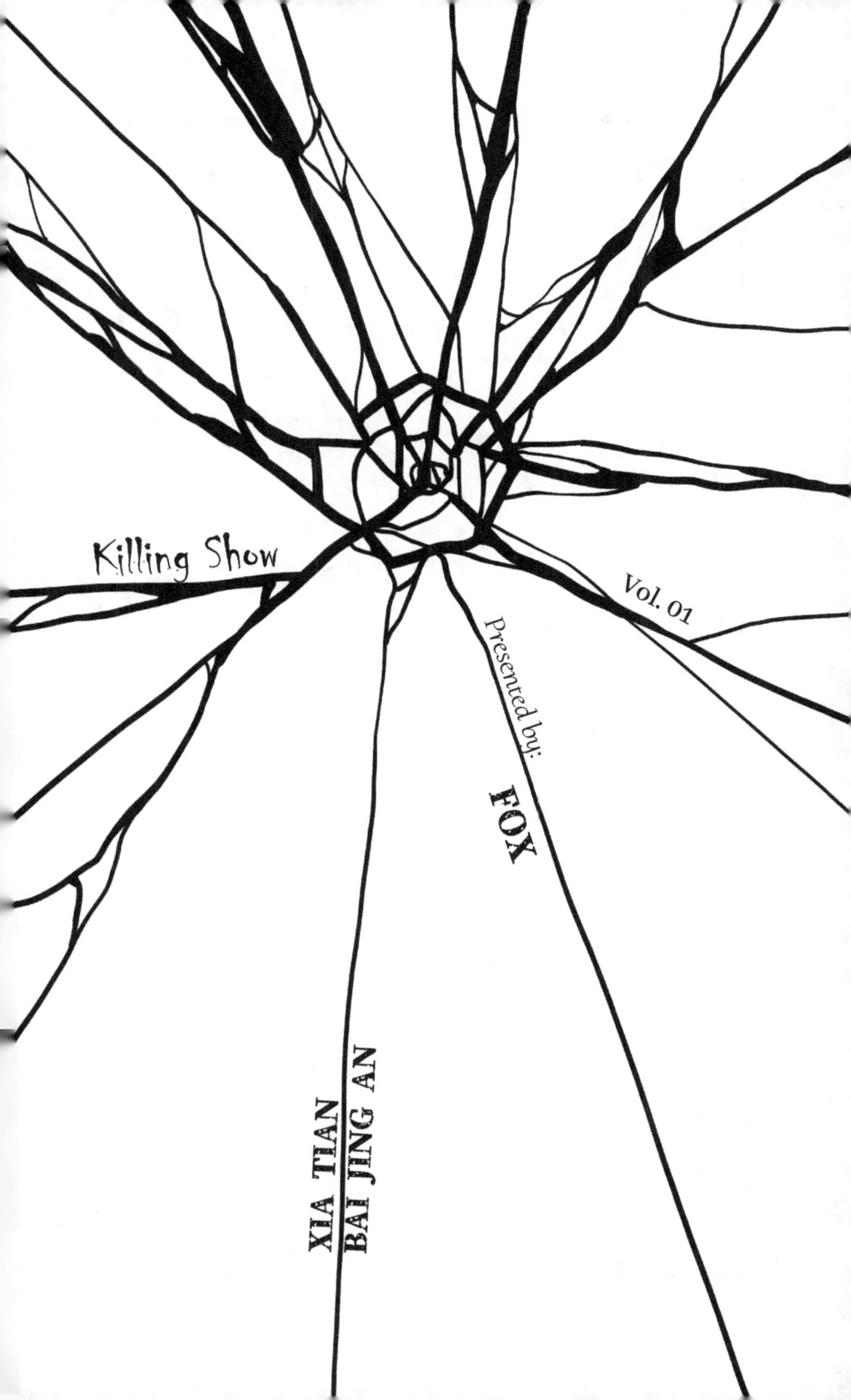

Killing Show
Vol. 01
Presented by:
FOX
XIA TIAN
BAI JING AN

CONTENT

CONTENT

CHAPTER 01

COVER-UP

Xia Tian stood on the Upper City hotel's balcony in his rented tuxedo, staring at the stars.

Specks of starlight dotted the horizon, which the Milky Way spanned. It resembled a huge jewelry box.

It was too windy on the balcony, and a little cold too, but he felt good. Although his circumstances were not any better, he'd finally left the abyss of darkness that was the Lower City and had come to the Upper World, where he got to see real sunshine and the starry sky.

And now, he was at the celebration dinner party for the second round of the Gilded Broadcasting Corporation's 199th Asaijin Team Tournament.

Three months ago, the Upper City had recruited him—a felon from the Lower City—to participate in Gilded Broadcasting Corporation's Killing Show: the grandest entertainment event in the Upper City, with a long history of requisitioning criminals. This was also the one and only chance Lower City residents like them got to see the real sky.

Xia Tian had been ravenously stuffing food into his mouth

from the moment he arrived. For the first time in his life, he ate his fill of cakes, cream, chocolates, and candies, feeling satiated like never before.

He snuck some food into his pockets and swiped a participant's wallet while he was at it. The guy had ostentatiously left it out in the open; it'd be Xia Tian's own loss if he didn't take it. He looked around again to see what else he could swipe; Gilded Group wouldn't miss this bit of stuff, anyway.

As a mega corporation, Gilded Group's floating cities were everywhere in the sky. Even the person among Xia Tian's acquaintances who had traversed the farthest had never once walked out of their shadow.

The moment he entered the Upper World, sunlight seemed to pour down like a bright, clear yellow liquid, blanketing the earth and sky. Xia Tian had been so badly injured at the time that he couldn't even sit still, but he pulled himself together to stare at it for a long while, thinking that dying here wouldn't be too bad. But he'd survived, and had now been living in the Upper City for three months as a Killing Show newbie. He'd narrowly survived the first two rounds with passable performance—he'd killed a total of four people, barely getting through the stage. That was only because Bai Jing'an believed that they should stay where they were and not move around willy-nilly. That guy really was annoying.

Through random lot-drawing, Bai Jing'an and Xia Tian had been selected to be on the same team on this show. While Bai Jing'an was a tactician whose addition to a team could level the playing field, he was a boring coward. Xia Tian hadn't seen him since the dinner party started; that guy couldn't ever wait to disappear from the light—as if the bright lights of the Upper City were some kind of lethal toxin.

Xia Tian was admiring the stars on the skydeck when a

young man with red hair approached him. Smiling at him with a trippy expression, the latter scanned Xia Tian's data on the virtual screen and cut to the chase without bothering to address him by name.

"Hello, I'm the assistant to Mr. Zhi Leng, chief show producer of the current Killing Show."

According to him, industry bigwig Mr. Zhi Leng had noticed Xia Tian's potential to become the star of the Killing Show. And so, he'd like to meet him *alone* to map out a plan for his road to fame and glory.

It had to be known that in the Upper World, the stars of the Killing Show were the real kings of the entertainment industry, the ones who had the world wrapped around their little fingers. Once you made a name for yourself, not only would you have money and bed partners at your disposal, all of Upper City would prostrate themselves at your feet. You'd be the god on the summit of Mount Olympus.

Xia Tian was over the moon. No matter what he saw now, he'd be beside himself with joy.

He went into the lobby with the assistant and made his way to Zhi Leng's suite. Before entering, he glanced back again at the starry sky that twinkled cold and cheerless in the far distance. It was a price and privilege that those in the Lower City could never imagine.

Zhi Leng was impeccably dressed, though he looked gaunt thanks to the prolonged weight loss program he was always on. His suite was located on the top floor of the hotel, with a spacious skydeck and observatory. His living room was large enough to hold a fashion show or some other small-scale team battle games any time he pleased—allegedly, he did indeed engage in such entertainment from time to time. Xia Tian sat as relaxed as he could be on the sofa with a wine glass in hand, pretending to

be part of the crowd that frequented such events.

Xia Tian was tall, with long, slender limbs. As a member of the Lower City District where brutality was the prevailing custom, he was long used to this way of life; killing without batting an eye. He'd been a bona fide dangerous individual ever since he was young, and it was because of this that he went to prison and was later recruited by the GBC. They believed he would be a good candidate for the Killing Show.

He was all smiles, and his smiles were gentle and polite. He was pretty good at pretending to be sweet-natured, just as he was good at pretending to be docile, to like something, and to show tact—this was basic survival skill. He even had the darling face of a well-behaved child, and when he smiled, he could be deceptively convincing.

His profession in the Killing Show was a "Warrior," but they didn't even refer to it by that title these days—instead, they outright called it the "Killer." Reality shows do like sensational names.

"I saw you on the surveillance program earlier and thought you had an excellent image," Zhi Leng said. "The current Asaijin Team Tournament needs a hero, and you're a pretty good choice."

He walked back and forth as he talked, and when he came to this point, he walked behind Xia Tian and put his hands on his shoulders.

"Th... That's wonderful," Xia Tian said. "I'm very grateful..."

Zhi Leng's hands touched his hair, then he untied the leather cord that bound it. Xia Tian's hair cascaded down. He didn't finish the rest of his sentence.

Xia Tian lived in District N21 in the Lower City, where men had the habit of keeping their hair long. He wanted to cut it short when he came up here, but a third-rate image consultant told him he needed to have his own distinctive characteristic if he wanted to be noticed. That distinction could be one's place of residence, religion, ethnicity, or personality, but the most important thing in this line of work was to *not* conform and blend in to the masses. And so, he'd never cut his hair, but it really was in the way during fights, so he always pulled it back and tied it up tightly behind his head.

Zhi Leng picked up a lock of his hair and stroked it in his hand. "Opportunities are something for which you must personally strive."

It took Xia Tian five seconds to finally realize what Zhi Leng had in mind. He sat still and let the guy play with his hair, thinking to himself about how he had heard about this sort of thing happening in reality shows. It was inevitable in authoritarian places. No big deal; he didn't mind selling himself. His mother did it too, and so did his elder sister. He was a criminal himself. Everyone around him had always thought he'd be lying dead on the streets sooner or later, turned into protein feed.

It was just sex, no? He could totally make that sacrifice.

"I'm more than willing to strive for it," he answered. He turned his head to smile as agreeably as he could at Zhi Leng.

Zhi Leng smiled too, seemingly satisfied with how sensible Xia Tian was. He put the leather cord into his pocket. "Come with me to the bedroom."

"Sure," Xia Tian said.

He stood; he was a head taller than Zhi Leng. He really couldn't understand what this guy saw in him, but rich people had strange tastes.

With his hair hanging loose over his shoulders, he walked into the bedroom with Zhi Leng, finding it rather awkward to present himself before others like this. *But when in Rome, do as the Romans do,* he told himself. The opportunity to be here was rare. Nearly a thousand people had died in the first two rounds of the tournament, and most of those deaths had been thanks to the whims of the producers.

It was a rare opportunity to have a bigwig willing to take him under his wing. No matter what, he had to grab hold of this opportunity.

Xia Tian entered the bedroom and swept a glance around. Other than noting how astoundingly luxurious it was, he also subconsciously determined his potential escape routes, hiding spots, and weapons he could use to kill—this habit was an occupational hazard of those in his line of work.

Zhi Leng lifted his chin to the bed. "Take off your pants, then kneel and lie prone on the bed."

Xia Tian felt himself smiling—a smile later described as predatory, or "sunshine bright, icy cold," or something. They said he had the smile of a true Killer.

"Sure," he answered.

As Zhi Leng began to take off his own pants, Xia Tian turned to look at a golden sailboat sculpture on the table. It was the prize for a sailboat race. The floating cities, also known as the Upper World, were initially just a small anti-gravity zone where the wealthy lived in hopes of being closer to the sun and pure air. The zones increasingly grew in number and size, spreading across the sky like cancer as the rich built houses up there one after another until they covered the entire expanse of sky.

The wealthy lit up their cities' lights, as if they were the sun. Below, countless civilians lived, unable to ascend to the sky— like livestock reared in the basement.

His parents had never seen the sky their entire lives, and the same went for his siblings. Meanwhile, these people built a huge lake in their anti-gravity city to hold sailboat races. Such a luxury would have been simply unimaginable had he not seen it himself.

"I want you to pretend to be afraid," Zhi Leng said. "And call me 'master' while we're at it—"

Xia Tian picked up the sailboat, weighed it in his hand, and slammed it hard against Zhi Leng's temple.

The chief show producer of the Killing Show instantly lost consciousness and collapsed. Xia Tian kneeled on him and smashed the sailboat in his hand down again and again on his head.

It took just an instant to work out the modus operandi for the murder, but the process was too fast to recall, so much that it morphed into the instinct and impulse to crush everything in sight.

He nearly pulverized the man's head. Brain matter splattered everywhere from the bashing; his eyeballs even popped out. Truly a masterpiece. There was even a specific term for this in the Killing Show—overkill.

Some said it was the result of adrenaline overload, while some said it was a stunt, but Xia Tian felt it to be human nature. Sometimes anger would just course through your veins, and like gasoline, there'd be no controlling the aftermath when it came into contact with a spark.

He'd only left his hometown to join the Killing Show because someone had slapped his elder sister and called her a whore—just who was she trying to fool? He'd walked over and shoved that guy, and things had gotten ugly... Actually, what the bastard said wasn't entirely wrong, but he just couldn't stand it. He didn't know why the heck he couldn't endure this sort of thing. Most people put up with it, and they all seemed to do fine, no?

With a frosty expression, he used his blood-covered hand to fish his hair cord from Zhi Leng's pocket and pulled his hair back to secure it in place.

When he put his hands down, he realized he was trembling.

His hands were covered in blood, blood that had soaked through his cuffs and stained him almost up to his elbows. At his feet was a pants-less corpse with its head smashed open and splattered all over the expensive carpet.

He stood up, walked into the bathroom, and washed the blood off his hands.

Throughout the act itself, his face was expressionless, and his demeanor calm. Now that the adrenaline had worn off, he realized his hands were trembling.

His body reacted first. Something—probably reality— washed over him like icy water. His stomach lurched, and he felt like throwing up.

That was fear talking, along with a feeling of doom.

He was no stranger to it.

As Xia Tian stared at the person in the mirror, the gears in his head turned rapidly.

There was no way he could get away with this; the assistant knew he was here. Besides, the one he'd killed was Zhi Leng, for god's sake—the chief show producer of the GBC's Asaijin Team Tournament!

The best outcome he could hope for himself was to be killed on the spot, but perhaps it'd be worse. These people could sell him to some shady, underground channels on the dark web, where his death would be a source of entertainment. Hell was like that, too.

He subconsciously reached for his nape. In order to prevent the criminals from going berserk and destroying the world or something, the Upper City implanted all of them with punish- ment devices during enlistment. His district administrator was itching to test it out on him and make his life a living hell.

He should have listened to Zhi Leng and stripped, turned his back, lay prone on the bed, and called him master or whatever he so desired. It would've been over soon. The rules were the same everywhere if you wanted to survive... Suddenly feeling like throwing up, Xia Tian rushed to the toilet bowl and puked out the stuff he had eaten today.

Following that, he washed his face, folded his sleeves to cover the bloodstains, and took a towel to wipe away all the fingerprints he might have left behind. Without looking at the corpse again, he opened the door and walked out.

He couldn't stay in this place, not even for a minute longer.

I'll have to steal a car, Xia Tian thought, *and drive all the way down the Lower City's highway before selling it off at the second or third scrapyard I come across. They'll have a way of making sure no one recognizes the vehicle.*

Then he'd use the money to trade for a car from the Lower City. It'd be a piece of junk, but the good thing was that it'd be inconspicuous. He'd drive north and find a decent black-market doctor as soon as possible to remove the thing in his nape. It'd likely leave some neurological damage, but no big deal. Afterward, he'd sustain himself for the time being by stealing with whatever bit of thievery skills he had.

But they'll find me, he thought. *I can hide out for a while, but they'll be able to find me. That was the chief show producer of the Asaijin Team Tournament!*

Right then, he saw Bai Jing'an.

Every floor of the hotel had an observation deck that could be accessed via the stairs. Some banquet attendees were chatting on the largest skydeck on the top floor. Bai Jing'an was talking to a few people who looked to be bigwigs at first glance.

He didn't look particularly striking, although he was so prim and properly dressed that it didn't seem like his clothes

were rented. Instead, he looked like he was born to wear such attire. He was listening to them with a smile on his face. His hair was neither long nor short, and he looked neat and cultured. Just like Xia Tian's impression the first time he met him, he was like a glass of plain water—lukewarm, boring, and nondescript. He repeated what everyone else said and did nothing out of the ordinary, and he just watched as the others fight, never once getting a drop of blood on his hands.

Just then, Bai Jing'an looked up and saw Xia Tian.

His expression went cold when he took in Xia Tian's appearance. He turned around, said something to those people, and left them to walk over to Xia Tian.

Xia Tian stood by the elevator and looked on as he came over.

The closer Bai Jing'an got, the colder his expression became. He looked like a teacher who'd just seen a student who was always getting into fights and didn't want to give him the time of day, but had no choice since the party in question was standing in his path, crying with blood all over his face.

"What happened?" he asked.

Xia Tian glanced at Zhi Leng's suite, and Bai Jing'an's expression dropped a notch colder. But even so, only his eyes appeared colder and harsher; the rest of his expression made it look like it was no big deal, and that he was only having a not-so-pleasant chat with his teammate.

Bai Jing'an turned around, pushed the door open, and walked in. Xia Tian stood at the entrance for a while before he followed him in and closed the door. When he entered, Bai Jing'an was standing at the doorway to the bedroom, staring at the badly mangled corpse. Blood was all over the floor, and soaking in it was the sailboat sculpture, like a boat sinking in a sea of blood.

Bai Jing'an looked expressionlessly at it for a moment, then turned around and pulled the wardrobe open.

Xia Tian looked on in bewilderment as Bai Jing'an rummaged through the wardrobe and dragged a large, high-end suitcase from a luxury brand from deep within. He opened it up and shoved the clothing in it back into the wardrobe, then he turned to look at Xia Tian.

"Stuff him inside."

Xia Tian arched his eyebrows. This development was not quite what he imagined, but he walked over immediately and helped stuff Zhi Leng's corpse into the suitcase. The man's legs were bare, and his penis had shriveled into a tiny ball; a pitiful lump of soft flesh.

Bai Jing'an closed the suitcase and zipped it up. It now looked like a perfectly typical luxury suitcase.

"Perfect," Xia Tian declared.

Bai Jing'an threw him a dark look and turned his head to survey the room. His eyes were gray and as plain as water like the rest of him, and the way he looked at the room was just as detached and vapid as he acted while live on the Killing Show, where all he did was make charts and assess the finer points of tactics at their disposal.

Without so much as a word, he walked over to the wall and found the built-in network interface. He used his cell phone— they tried to call it a "portable data terminal" these days, but the term cell phone still circulated around—to connect to the network. The interface of the security program popped out, and he hacked his way in without even batting an eyelid.

He was a tactician, but owing to the imbalance of professions, he also concurrently took on the role of a cyber support specialist to hack and harvest data and the like. Hacking into the public network of a hotel was child's play to him. He kept

his hands busy as he hacked past the hotel's firewall. The pervasive stench of blood in the suite meant nothing to him.

"He called me into the suite," Xia Tian spoke up behind him. "Then—"

"I know what he did," Bai Jing'an cut him off.

Xia Tian shrugged. Rumors about Zhi Leng doing this sort of thing were everywhere, and Bai Jing'an looked like someone who knew everything.

He watched as the guy retrieved the data, methodically breached the entry point, cleared the records, deleted the cache, and modified the details of the video of the corridor. He did it all with unhurried order, like he was having a formal meal that called for impeccable etiquette. Bai Jing'an was also like this the first time Xia Tian met him, and it didn't look like he had changed much as he stood in a bedroom with the chief show producer's corpse.

"He had his assistant call me over," he continued to tell Bai Jing'an.

"Assistant," the guy parroted, his tone indifferent and flat. A tactical keyword.

As he spoke, he coded the program to intercept the video and overwrite the original footage. Without even looking up, he said to Xia Tian, "Clean yourself up."

He was proficient in his work, and there was nothing much Xia Tian could do to help here. Thus, Xia Tian shrugged and walked into the bathroom. Bai Jing'an was right—with the way he looked now, he could still make a quick escape, but if he wanted to blend back in at the banquet and play at being the gentleman, he'd be exposed in the blink of an eye.

The bathroom was large, with heated floors and cleverly arranged lightning that made it look like a brightly illuminated dreamscape. Xia Tian looked at the man in the mirror, dressed in a tuxedo with his hair tightly tied back. His features, refined and dashing, carried a hint of a newcomer's shyness and bashfulness, making it easy to leave a favorable impression on others. But just ten minutes ago, he'd cracked open the head of his "promising future." That guy's corpse was still lying out there like the wrecked aftermath of a disaster, no longer able to use his ultra-luxurious bathroom anymore.

This thought inexplicably made him laugh. His smile bloomed on his genteel, innocent face like a gaping wound, revealing the smell of fury, hunger, and blood from the darkness of the Lower City. He suddenly wanted to know Zhi Leng's expression at the moment of death. A shame he couldn't see it from that angle.

He turned on the faucet and cleaned himself up. He gingerly ran his fingertips across his nape. It'd once hurt like crazy, but the skin was now smooth with no trace of a scar.

He cleaned off the blood splattered all over him. Even the leather cord used to tie his hair was stained through, dirtying his hair.

After cleaning up, he looked a lot less guilty. Facing the mirror, he drew in a breath and flashed a smile again. This time, his smile was innocent, wholesome, and even a little childlike, ready to mingle with anyone any time.

Not bad, he thought. He left the bathroom and returned to the partially cleaned-up murder scene.

Bai Jing'an was still on the program port, erasing all traces of entry. His skill in destroying evidence was top-notch. No surprise there; the weapons and ammunition used during battles on the Killing Show were the real deal. Regardless of how beautifully packaged they were out of the arena, they were all essentially first-rate killers, villains with blood on their hands, or skilled hackers. Whenever the need arose to kill someone, wreak havoc,

or destroy evidence and cover up a crime, their techniques were also the best in the world.

On hearing him emerge, Bai Jing'an spoke without looking up, "Wipe up the blood."

Xia Tian looked at the gruesome scene on the carpet. It was truly... brutal.

"I'm not particularly good at cleaning," he said to Bai Jing'an. "You're almost done anyway, so why don't you wipe down the carpet while you're at it..."

"Then don't bash his head in until his brain splatters everywhere," Bai Jing'an retorted. This was the longest sentence he'd said since he got here.

Xia Tian swiped a rose candy from the table at the side and put it in his mouth. He shrugged, indicating that this was a special situation, yes?

"But if he disappears, the police will surely come here to investigate. A little luminol spray can make this place light up like it's New Year's Day. There's no point in cleaning at all—" he said.

"They won't find anything," Bai Jing'an cut him off. "It's cleaning day tomorrow."

Xia Tian was momentarily taken aback, then he smiled. As one would expect of a tactician, his reaction was swift when it came to flouting the law. There was a grand banquet today, so of course there'd be a big clean-up tomorrow. Considering the "needs" of the rich these days, the hotel would do a thorough cleanup at the end of each month, or the day after a large-scale gathering event. For "special cases," all it took was a phone call for service to be rendered at any hour.

Xia Tian had heard of at least two dozen unlucky fellows who disappeared from the bedrooms of powerful personages, and it was through the "private cleaning service" that these fellows vanished off the surface of the earth. Back then, he found the rich people from the Upper City unbearably repulsive, but now he felt this service to be simply made for Mr. Zhi Leng.

He picked up the tools, whistling as he began to wipe the blood and brain matter off the ground. Bai Jing'an threw him a frosty look, and Xia Tian ignored it. And so it was to the hum of a cheery tune that the carpet quickly became as clean as new, as if the mess he'd made earlier had never existed.

Tomorrow, it would thoroughly vanish.

Xia Tian proceeded to wipe off the fingerprints next. Bai Jing'an turned around to drag the suitcase and set it upright.

"Use the service elevator," Bai Jing'an said to him.

Xia Tian nodded and took over the suitcase. Bai Jing'an had already hacked into the service elevator, and Xia Tian put the suitcase inside and sent it right to the parking lot.

Nobody noticed them. Everyone was busy eating, drinking, laughing, taking drugs, and finding someone to bed. The death of a person was nothing worth paying attention to.

Both of them kept their cool as they passed through the banquet area and made their way to the parking lot. This was a magnetic levitation zone. All the expensive cars here belonged to the rich people attending the dinner party, as well as other big names from reality shows. However, most of them took the sky-train—case in point, Xia Tian. He still had to take a ride back after the banquet. Bai Jing'an, on the other hand, looked more like he belonged to the privileged elite class with a house and a car to his name.

His teammate walked right into the parking lot, looked around, and then hacked into a black hovercar with a common naked body symbol painted on it. Meanwhile, Xia Tian went to the pickup area to retrieve the suitcase containing the body.

When he went back, Bai Jing'an had already started the

car. He opened the trunk, and Xia Tian put the body in with a neutral expression. They carried out this series of actions with simplicity and efficiency, soundlessly and in perfect tandem.

After all, they were both pros in this field.

Xia Tian sat in the passenger seat and scrolled through the photos of the vehicle owner on the in-vehicle display screen. Said person was having fun with a group of naked men and women. Xia Tian browsed through them all with great interest.

People like this who participated in dinner parties probably wouldn't be clear-headed before afternoon the next day. He wondered if Bai Jing'an had noticed the guy before, and that was how he knew before he hacked into the car that no one would realize if they used it overnight. Even if someone were to inquire into the records, tracing the trail of this kind of car would be a disaster.

He turned to look at Bai Jing'an. The first time Xia Tian saw him, he thought he was a local from the Upper City; maybe because he didn't look as restless and wretched as the rest of them. Instead, he seemed to be a detached and composed individual who didn't ask for much—like he already knew what was going to happen.

At the time, Xia Tian thought that although the Upper World was inhabited by a group of deranged perverts, there was no denying that they were sometimes very handsome when dressed in formal suits.

He sized up Bai Jing'an again. The guy in the driver's seat ignored his probing gaze and drove the car onward. Although he was driving a stolen car to dispose of a body, he looked like nothing was out of the ordinary. His eyelashes cast shadows on his face, and his expression was as calm as ice, betraying no hint of emotion.

The guy turned a corner and drove through a park with luxurious stretches of green expanse.

Xia Tian felt hungry again—possibly because he'd thrown up the food he had at the party earlier in the bathroom. He fished a chocolate cupcake from his pocket. He went hungry so often as a child that when he grew up, he'd stuff his pockets with snacks whenever he had the chance—it gave him an inexplicable sense of security.

Xia Tian pulled out even more cupcakes as well as some marshmallows, planning to replenish them later when he returned to the banquet hall. The organizers were so rich that they wouldn't mind. He generously handed a piece to Bai Jing'an, who politely turned down his offer.

Xia Tian leaned back comfortably in his seat and dug into the food. The suitcase containing that dude was in the car's trunk. All was quiet and pleasant.

The car roared out of the city, and the landscape beyond gradually grew emptier and more rundown. Bai Jing'an turned another corner, taking the hovercar path that stretched downward in the direction of the Lower City.

However, they did not go all the way to the Lower City, but to the transit hub below the Upper World. Located here was a protein-feed plant that turned corpses into pure protein, which would be fed to the fast-growing genetically modified animals raised for food in the Lower City. The citizens from the Lower City sometimes consumed them too—a trend that was now gaining momentum.

Greenery couldn't grow in the Lower City, other than in greenhouses, and half of the limited food available had to be handed over to the Upper City as "technical service fee." The crops in the Upper World, on the other hand, were decent, but they would never be sent downward. Feeding the people

underground with corpses was the most economical way to deal with hunger.

The plant was completely automatic. It was already extremely rundown, with a battered but lit advertising billboard at the main entrance that said, "Professional, Sanitary, and Reusable."

They parked their car at the back door, and realized the plant was secured with a physical lock when they attempted to open the door. Xia Tian took care of it easily with a piece of wire before dragging the high-end suitcase in.

The inside of the feed plant was basically a horror movie, which was why it was never shown to the public on television. However, as a resident of the Lower City, Xia Tian was very familiar with this sort of place. There was always a large number of corpses stacked here all year round; a mix of human and animal corpses that machines slowly pushed onto conveyor belts, which then carried them into sealed machines.

No one knew what went on inside, but the end product was a clean, purified, creamy, milky-white beverage that bore no resemblance to its origins at all.

What he was more familiar with was the reception desk in the lobby, at which was a dirty reception droid that would purchase corpses at low prices. The entire process was automated. Sometimes, the citizens from the Lower City would kill people and sell their corpses to make a little money. Those people would size up others with calculating eyes; Xia Tian knew some of them. It was all very normal.

He tried to haul Zhi Leng onto the automatic scales to weigh him for sale, but Bai Jing'an grabbed ahold of Zhi Leng's leg and threw Xia Tian a stern look.

"The money from the sale is enough to treat us to a good meal," Xia Tian said.

"You'll leave a record," Bai Jing'an warned.

"I can erase the records," Xia Tian said. "Just one stealth program, and this place will be like your wife's..." He swallowed an expletive he was used to saying in the Lower City and continued, "Uh, anyway, it can be easily modified."

Bai Jing'an looked at him without the slightest inclination to compromise and dragged the corpse inside. Xia Tian could only follow after him. Comforting himself, he thought, *All right then, it's not like he can be sold for much with all that weight loss.*

Naked corpses were piled up high in the raw material staging area; the clothes that had been stripped from them were placed on the other side. The clothes should be destroyed according to regulations, but most would be looted and later circulate into the black market.

Xia Tian always found this place to be horrifyingly creepy. It was like the end of the line—here, your entire life turned into a pile of gleaming white trash.

When they stripped Zhi Leng of his clothes and threw him into the heap of corpses, the chief producer looked no different from any of the other corpses from the Lower City. It was then that Xia Tian felt this place wasn't too bad after all—at least it and the former chief producer were made for each other.

Xia Tian flipped open Zhi Leng's leather wallet, swiped the cash in one practiced move, and threw the rest on top of the corpse. He noticed that Zhi Leng's ring and cufflinks also weren't too shabby and crouched down to take them, but he sensed an icy gaze on him and looked up. Bai Jing'an was glaring at him.

"What?" Xia Tian asked.

"I hope you can exercise some basic common sense," the guy said icily.

"Do you know how much these are worth?" Xia Tian said.

If Bai Jing'an knew, he certainly wasn't interested. He held out his hand with a frosty expression, and Xia Tian locked eyes with him in a standoff for ten seconds before reluctantly handing over the gems. The guy's expression was a bit agitated, so it was better to not argue with him.

Bai Jing'an picked up Zhi Leng's clothes and the blood-stained suitcase and put them into the incinerator along with the gems. Xia Tian went back to rummage through the pile of dead people's clothes to see if there was anything he could take. But this place had already been looted; all that was left was the stuff that nobody else wanted.

There was a pretty decent tuxedo in the pile, and Xia Tian wondered to which unlucky guy it had belonged. It was covered in blood; the poor guy had been stabbed with a not-so-sharp knife more than a dozen times before he died. The tuxedo was no longer worth recycling, and taking it would only bring him trouble.

He felt that his way of killing Zhi Leng was the recommended method of killing rich fellas—the clothes could remain flawlessly intact and be reused. A shame Bai Jing'an had mercilessly burned them.

He picked and chose, eventually finding just a little doggy button with worn-off ears that was worth recycling. He thought his little sister back at home would love it. He'd ended up in the Killing Show right after a harrowing stint in prison, so he'd never even gotten the chance to take a last look at her before he left.

Given her IQ, it was hard for Xia Tian to imagine just how long she could survive in the darkness. He felt a wave of distant pain and anxiety, though his face betrayed none of it and he still looked as relaxed and merry as he always did. He put the button into his pocket. He was used to this sort of feeling.

Xia Tian had no clue why Bai Jing'an would help him. Of course, chaos would ensue if something happened to Xia Tian—

Bai Jing'an would have to draw random lots again for a new comrade-in-arms for the next round, and improvise on the tactics and the like at the last minute, but those were all unknown variables. If someone found out what Bai Jing'an was doing now, he'd be an accessory to murder, and it'd be game over for him just like it'd be for Xia Tian.

Even if he asked, Bai Jing'an would most likely not pay him any attention, or throw him a random bland answer—the kind of meaningless words said for the sake of saying. Xia Tian himself could spontaneously shoot off two or three dozen such words, too. But he decided not to ask anything in the end. What if he asked, and Bai Jing'an suddenly changed his mind?

It was like when you finally rose to the Upper City and saw the sunlight cascading down. It was best not to shout and make a din, and just let it shine on. Otherwise, what if it reacted to the ruckus and disappeared? What would he do then?

Xia Tian didn't know what that guy was thinking. He could only guess that since he was a tactician, he'd do whatever he felt to be the most beneficial course of action. And besides, Xia Tian was in such a terrible situation right now that he'd accept any help from anyone, no matter the price he had to pay.

Xia Tian didn't find anything else worth recycling, but that had always been the case for the feed plants. Bai Jing'an activated the machine and incinerated the clothing, then sent Zhi Leng's corpse deep into the machine. No matter what sort of big shot the deceased had been, the machine would quickly and tidily ingest them and render them into clean, purified protein form.

With practiced ease, he went through the entire process for destroying the evidence to cover up the crime before he turned to leave. He walked up to the car, locked the back door with an indifferent expression, and started the engine, looking much like

he had just gone on a boring outing and could finally go back home now.

"What about his assistant?" Xia Tian asked.

"He's at the dinner party," Bai Jing'an answered impatiently.

Bai Jing'an drove the car all the way back to the hotel and parked it in its original spot. No one noticed. They slipped back into the evening dinner, and Xia Tian watched Bai Jing'an walk briskly into the hall. It was as if he'd never left. Xia Tian couldn't at all tell that he'd just disposed of a corpse.

Bai Jing'an greeted one of the producers with a smile and casually took a glass of champagne from a waiter before he continued to make his way into the crowd. There, he casually took two hallucinogens from the "candy box" on the table and put them into the glass. Fancy candies laced with soft drugs were placed everywhere at these dinners to keep the merrymaking at the party sufficiently high.

Xia Tian watched with interest as Bai Jing'an put on a show of holding the glass while he made a joke no one would remember to another player. At the same time, he slipped a green pill into the glass. By the time he'd walked to the center of the hall, the glass of champagne had already turned into a wild carnival.

Looking preoccupied, he passed by the assistant who had approached Xia Tian an hour ago and told him to go to the penthouse suite. Right now the guy was engaged in a lively conversation; he was quite drunk and gesticulated wildly as he talked.

Without batting an eyelid, Bai Jing'an handed him the glass. The guy downed it all in one gulp and continued with his conversation, looking like he had no idea what he was talking about or what he had just drunk. In a place like this, everyone was always reaching for a drink, eating, laughing, and having sex—like they were living in a world without a future.

Xia Tian knew the stuff in the glass would give him a few

happy hours. When the next day rolled around, no one would be able to dig up a thing from his memories.

He turned his head, took another sip of his drink, and smiled at a pretty chick next to him. Maybe he could find himself some company tonight.

The people of the floating cities lived in an endless game, without any reservations whatsoever. All that mattered was having a blast. Meanwhile, his crime soundlessly melded into the opulent debauchery of the Upper World.

CHAPTER 02

OPENING CEREMONY

Zhi Leng's disappearance was discovered a week later.

At first, no one was concerned; it was all too common for big shots to disappear for a few days at a time. They'd sometimes lose themselves in some dim, raunchy environment for a spell before resurfacing, claiming that the city was too noisy and they needed a change of scenery to draw inspiration for a new round of badass exhilaration.

Someone only realized he was actually missing after the third round of the tournament had kicked off. The police must have conducted an investigation at the hotel, but Xia Tian couldn't be sure; no one approached him for questioning. Every day, he went to the free immersive simulation platform the organizers provided for combat training, counting on his old savings and stealing to get by so he didn't go hungry again.

He would never go hungry again.

He saw the police coming in and out of the hotel, but he didn't ask around or discuss anything about the incident; he kept a low profile, even coming across as particularly endearing and likable.

As for Bai Jing'an... Xia Tian thought an incident like that would surely bring about a shift in their relationship, but this was clearly a misconception. After that night, they didn't see each other in person. Bai Jing'an only sent him a text message with a long list of training he needed to do; the guy truly never forgot his professional duties.

It wasn't until half a month later that they had two coordinated training sessions on the immersive simulation platform. Bai Jing'an didn't say a word about the incident at the dinner party; it was as if he wanted all too much to keep his distance from Xia Tian after that risky business. Even when he had to say a few words, he sounded like he was trying his best to keep their conversations to a minimum.

Xia Tian had trouble understanding this development. To him, interpersonal relationships had always been simple: once you went through adversity together, you'd form a bond and be on friendly terms; enough to go out for a drink. Of course, you also had to be prepared to be betrayed at any time, but everyone would still be willing to have that drink.

However, Bai Jing'an was obviously not that kind of person. He was a foggy mystery hiding behind his teammates, his tuxedo, and his official responses. The only thing Xia Tian could be sure of was that that guy didn't really like him... Which was, of course, understandable.

Perhaps there was a time Bai Jing'an had been high-spirited, guileless, and childish, but Xia Tian hadn't made it in time to see it for himself. When he'd finally encountered him, the guy was already buried deep underground. He would no longer laugh heartily or cry bitterly, and he would only keep quiet and say nothing. He wouldn't get chummy with anyone and join them for a drink.

Xia Tian had always kept his distance from this type of

guy, but... This was the Asaijin tournament system where team-mates were determined by random draw, stressing the "collision of odds" and the "concurrence of both bad luck and pleasant surprises." You'd never know what kind of teammates you would encounter, what abilities they were masters of, and how the two of you would get along; thus, it was full of fricking "suspense" and other such vexing shit. To date, he still could not be sure what type of person Bai Jing'an was.

But no matter what either of them thought, it was clear neither of them could shake off the other for the time being.

The police did not make any headway with their investigation in the case of Zhi Leng's disappearance. Public order and security in the main Gilded City had always been terrible, and Zhi Leng had countless enemies. Anyone who'd climbed their way to that position was bound to have a little blood on their hands. What's more, the vast majority of people didn't have a decent alibi on nights like that.

Xia Tian didn't know how the police investigated it, but in any case, the topic was quickly forgotten after a short period of online discussion. This was the Upper World, where dead people were all too common. You had to keep up with the trends.

Georg, the chief show producer of GBC Channel 7 *Piquant Sky*, and Qi Xiashang, the chief show producer of GBC Channel 3 *Deviant Lab*, had a PK match. The former eventually took the champion crown, replacing Zhi Leng as the boss of this team tournament season.

Piquant Sky was a survival reality show, the kind where everyone was on an island and wore very little clothing. Although Georg had quite a number of deaths under his belt, he'd never before helmed a show as wild and insane as the Asaijin Team Tournament; the epitome of reality shows.

The new show producer came from the fashion industry.

Georg was the type who liked to be innovative and produce dramatic scenes, and was burning with ambition. Ready and raring to go all out and make a splash, he of course he wasn't the least bit interested in Zhi Leng's disappearance. He wouldn't cooperate with the investigation, his mind solely set on starting the tournament as soon as possible. He demanded the police wrap up the case quickly, and also ordered all personnel involved in the reality show to get back to work immediately so they could move on to the next round. They couldn't waste time on trivial matters.

The case was quickly closed, and the police found someone to randomly convict and execute to close the book on the issue. The unlucky target was a show producer from the Asaijin Team Tournament Storyline Subdivision. He hadn't even been at the party that night, but a storyline he'd devised in the last Killing Show tournament killed off a star that one of the bigwigs liked, and so he became the scapegoat.

The 199th Killing Show Pay-to-View match hosted in collaboration with GBC Channel 9 moved into the pre-launch teaser phase, and topics of relevance dominated online headlines and trending search lists. It didn't matter how much power and influence Zhi Leng had once wielded that let him do whatever he pleased. When he died, the war chariot of the Killing Show mercilessly steamrolled over his corpse and departed with a roar. Everywhere the Killing Show went, everything else had to make way.

Soon afterward, the third round of the 199th GBC's Asaijin Team Tournament's Killing Show officially began.

The lot drawing ceremony was held with lots of pomp and ceremony at the Skystone Square in the main Gilded City. The big screen first played a collection of highlights from the previous Gilded Team Tournament Match, followed by a trailer with majestic, rousing music, calling on everyone to participate in the great cause of the Killing Show; to test their wisdom and strength upon this world-renowned stage on which everyone had their eyes.

Nearly two thousand Killing Show contestants—criminals, deviants, and other unlucky devils—stood at the foot of the stage in formal attire, like an army awaiting inspection. Hundreds of cameras were pointed at every corner, recording their raring-to-go or heavy-hearted expressions, and the dreams that would soon be shattered. The footage would become the talk of the town.

Xia Tian looked around absent-mindedly. Bai Jing'an stood to his left, dressed in a black tuxedo. He actually was quite handsome, but was expressionless as he stared fixedly at a certain spot in the air. He was lost in his own world and didn't want any contact with the rest of them.

Latte stood to his other side, watching the big screen intently with the expression of a man full of hopes and dreams. They'd gotten this guy from the first round of lot drawing. Their team's luck was average—they'd gotten three warriors and one tactician, and consequently, in the first two rounds Bai Jing'an had to double as a cyber support specialist while Xia Tian had to double as a sniper. There also used to be a guy named Jian Kui in their team, who was an idiot just like Latte. He'd died in the second round, and Xia Tian really wished Latte would've too. Unfortunately, he hadn't, so he was still in the team doing stupid things.

Xia Tian stood among the teams of players and fiddled with the little doggy button missing an ear in his pocket, wondering why he hadn't thrown it away yet. He didn't like bringing these trinkets onto the battlefield. In places like these, all you want to bring are guns, ruthlessness, the resolve to face death, and grim hope tainted with blood.

But he still thought of the younger sister he'd left behind in his hometown. She was still a child, and her life was a complete mess. Her best skill was hiding, and any day now she would become just one of the countless victims who came to a tragic end in the Lower City.

As he was leaving, she had tugged at the corner of his clothes and made him promise that he'd come back for her. He'd promised her that he would return a rich man, and when that time came, he'd weave her a super pretty flower crown to wear on her head. But how would that be possible—

Xia Tian's stomach lurched as he was hit with the familiar sense of nausea he could never shake off. Fear and fury blazed like fire inside of him, giving him the urge to kill something; the more violently, the better. He suppressed the feeling, telling himself that it was all too common. No one cared.

He looked around restlessly. Everyone had on a solemn expression, looking like they were about to wage a holy crusade. He abruptly left the neat formation of teams. Several people beside him stared at him, but he ignored them and passed through.

He hadn't gotten far when a staff member in comical yet serious-looking battle armor came over with a frosty expression and sternly asked him to return to his position.

"I gotta go to the restroom," Xia Tian said.

"But the ceremony isn't done yet," the other man said.

"You wouldn't want me to relieve myself right here."

"Before the ceremony ends, the formation of players must remain in line—"

"Are you asking for a fight?"

The other guy glared at him for a moment, seemingly caught in an internal struggle with himself, but eventually he gave in and made way. "Please be quick."

Xia Tian gleefully made his way to the restroom. He didn't feel like throwing up anymore after tormenting the staff. He dawdled for a bit and pocketed a handful of candies before he swaggered back to his original position. Bai Jing'an threw him a glance, and he flashed him a dazzling smile in return, even offering him a piece of candy. Bai Jing'an shook his head to turn it down, so Xia Tian ate it and even threw the wrapper on the ground. He noticed the staff member from earlier glaring viciously at him, and he gave him the same dazzling smile.

Also worth a mention was a pointless, trivial incident that took place at the lot drawing ceremony. The promotional trailer on the big screen was taking too long, so Xia Tian was looking around while still in a pleasant mood. It was then that he saw a lock of Bai Jing'an's hair sticking up in the breeze. He reached out and pressed it down.

Bai Jing'an waved his hand away, and Xia Tian said, "It's sticking up."

The other guy said nothing, but gave him a warning look.

After a while, the lock of hair stuck up again. Xia Tian pressed it down again and even smoothed it down to keep it in place. Bai Jing'an sucked in a breath, as if telling himself to stay calm and put up with Xia Tian.

The lock of hair stood up again three more times, and each time, Xia Tian pressed it back down in all earnestness. Bai Jing'an looked like he was struggling to put up with it, but he didn't resist anymore.

This was only a frivolous interlude in the ceremony—it was because the promotional video was too long, and Xia Tian had always been someone who couldn't keep his hands to himself—but this segment was captured by the cameras and posted to the official website under the category, "Interesting Rookie Players This Season." In the comments underneath, someone roasted

Xia Tian, asking, *"Just how old is he?"* Another person gushed, *"So cute."* A few discussed his performance in the qualifying round and called Bai Jing'an, *"That guy who looks bored."*

These people later formed a discussion group to follow Xia Tian's performance in the Killing Show. Small groups like these would pop up every time the Killing Show was on—some long-lasting, some short-lived like the bubbles in fruit juice, but nothing out of the ordinary.

No one particularly noticed, but it was the first time Xia Tian had his own fans. This fanbase would continue to expand until it became a monster shaking the colossal foundation of the floating cities.

The long commercial and trailer finally came to an end, and the lot drawing began. Their squad welcomed a new teammate for the next round: a doctor.

Their lot-drawing luck really was *meh*.

The so-called doctors joining this sort of tournament only knew how to do basic wound dressing and first aid, which were things anyone participating in the Killing Show already knew how to do. It was one of the least useful professions.

The organizer would often pull stunts like these to mislead the audience, create chaos, and increase the death toll. Xia Tian swore when he got the results of the lot, and a guy next to him told him with a bitter expression that he should thank his lucky stars he didn't get a chef or a tailor.

The main hall of GBC's Asaijin Team Tournament building thronged with seated contestants who were resting and having their meals. Testosterone pervaded the room, and the entire building was like a powder keg, with fights and scuffles erupting everywhere.

Xia Tian's group sat on one of the sofas in Hall 3, drinking

the free supply of alcoholic beverages. It relaxed the contestants, but also made them more prone to losing control, providing the GBC with sensational footage with which to make headlines.

One guy at the table beside them had a breakdown, shrieking something along the lines of "*This game is rigged!*". Their team was originally comprised of a sniper and a chef, and now they had a tailor and a cleaner. Truly, it was a scene straight out of a comedy show.

The guy flung his wine glass and started crying in the middle of the hall, totally throwing his image into the bin. One of his teammates tried to console him, but he'd also had too much to drink, and in the end, they were hugging and wailing together.

The hall was brightly illuminated and clean, with battlefield-themed decoration. Everyone was drinking, talking, and shouting, indifferent to what was happening on this end, though there were some who gloated over the group's misfortune. Either way, no one stepped forth to console them. GBC loved scenes like these. Heck, once someone even passed out from crying live on the scene.

Latte downed his twelfth alcoholic beverage and said aloud that they should take out the doctor first once they entered the arena. It'd make it easier for them to act, and they could save resources too. That was what everyone else did.

Xia Tian felt like he should be bawling in despair with those at the table beside them; everyone's lot-drawing luck was really too terrible. What this guy said was so stupid he didn't know how to respond.

"Killing a teammate counts as murder. The organizers have rules about that!" he said.

"But he's getting in the way!" Latte retorted.

"Of course he is. Why else would he be here?"

"I don't understand why the organizers have to do all this

shit. The Killing Show is all about courage and the glory of fighting, so why not just fight it out?"

Xia Tian sighed and decided not to say another word to him. If he continued the conversation, his own intelligence would take a beating for sure. Who knew if stupidity was contagious?

Latte was quite intimidating-looking, perfectly fitting the bill for a "scary-looking killer" on the Killing Show. He was big and tall, and his head looked like it'd been hacked into five or six pieces before being assembled back together by an unprofessional hand. Something terribly brutal must have happened at some point in his life, and even now, this brutality was still entrenched in his flesh, bones, and expression, making him look a little off-kilter. His mind couldn't keep up with the average person's train of thought, either.

These injuries came from his stint in the battle arena in the Lower City, where Xia Tian had also spent some time. A deep meter-long scar was still embedded in his back. Those really weren't sweet or pleasant days.

"Thanks, I-I won't hold you guys back," the doctor stammered. "I've been working out lately, and I have a degree from Gilded Third University of Medicine. I never thought I'd participate in the Killing Show, but there have been some issues at work lately..."

Gripping a glass of some alcoholic beverage, he smiled tentatively at Xia Tian, trying to spark some semblance of a friendship, but Xia Tian ignored him. Compared to Latte, who looked like a warrior in all his glory, this doctor huddled up in the corner was another version of tragedy.

His name was Xu Peiwen. He had neatly trimmed black hair, and was so thin and fragile that he looked like the tender stem of a plant that would snap with just one jab of the finger.

He was here due to the additional clause in his loan contract.

Such contracts were prevalent in the Upper City, and came with an assortment of rules attached regarding on loans, guardianship, immigration, and enforcement of criminal laws, among other things. It was all to ensure an abundance of bloodshed and many feasts for the eye for the entirety of the Killing Show. They were another breed of offenders in the city, who, having failed in work, money, competition, and life itself, were reduced to stepping into the arena, never to crawl their way out again.

With a frosty expression, Xia Tian took another plate of desserts and focused on tackling them. The tables elsewhere only had wine glasses on them; their table was the only one filled with a bright and colorful array of snacks.

He wished the guy would shut up, but the man just kept going. "They wanted to repossess the house, saying that if I didn't comply with the additional clause, my wife and daughter would end up in the Lower City. They'd never survive that place. Mr. Li...the executor of my contract, said I only had to fight ten matches. Anything more than that would be overcompensation, and I could sue them. As long as I can survive ten rounds, I can keep the house..."

He sounded like he had arrived at the realization that his situation wasn't all that bad after meticulously working it out, and that the organizers' contract had been fairly accommodating—that the future was pretty bright.

Xia Tian was sure he wouldn't survive the first two rounds of the pay-to-view match. The person who negotiated the contract with him must have known that, too. Xia Tian, however, wasn't planning on saying anything, just like the person who negotiated with him must have not said a word about it either. If anything, he had probably even encouraged this dream with a smile.

Dr. Xu continued to ramble on and on. Meanwhile, the

table next to them was discussing how to kill their new tailor teammate with efficiency and without breaking the rules—even as the person being discussed was cowering in the corner without saying so much as a word.

The third round was a survival match. About a hundred or so random teams would enter different arenas with enough resources for them to survive six or seven days—however, the match would only end after fifteen days had passed. After that, the gates open up and the bountiful sunlight of the Upper City would shine upon them. The winners could then feast, drink, and make merry, while the bones of the losers would rot within.

This year was the men's tournament. The Killing Show initially held three seasons of mixed gender matches, but it was called off because the scenes were way too perverted. Now, the team matches were held separately for men and women, but it did little to prevent rape, sexual abuse, and the like. To outlaws, gender was never a barrier.

That place would be hell.

Beside him, Bai Jing'an was writing something in a small notebook he was holding, looking like he was filling out a boring user survey. Still primly dressed in his tuxedo, the loose lock of hanging hair added an air of childishness to his face, but it was still a face frozen over by ice—the face of one who knew not to put his hopes on anything. If he was devising a plan to kill someone—and of course he was, that's precisely what tacticians did—then he was definitely the most depressing, dullest schemer that Xia Tian had ever seen.

Xia Tian asked the waiter for another glass of wine. The doctor was still yapping on and on, while Latte had struck up a conversation with the people at the table beside them, asking for tidbits of information through the grapevine—such as the death count last round, the stars who had died, the ordinary folks who had died, the NPCs who had died...everyone who had died.

Xia Tian and Bai Jing'an sat on opposite ends of the sofa. One with a notebook in hand and one with a plate of snacks in hand, both were silent, their expressions somber.

Both were waiting for the killing to begin.

By the time the drawing for the type of match had ended, Xia Tian began to think that the doctor wasn't so bad after all. The Asaijin tournament system also drew lots to determine the match type—it could be themed to post-apocalyptic survival, gunfights, a bizarre power struggle in a mansion, or a battle of the cold weapon era.

This time, they drew the lot that called for a medieval age theme. In other words, there would be no firearms, no cannons, and no explosives in this part of the show. No airplanes or cars, either. Everyone had to return to the cold weapon era of blades, spears, and arrows.

Looking at the notification on the big screen, Xia Tian gloated, "I really want to see the expressions of everyone on teams that drew cyber support specialists."

"The *Pre-Show Warmup* will film them for you," Bai Jing'an responded without looking up.

Xia Tian laughed. Bai Jing'an was talking about a trailer preview, which captured the contestants' expressions when they read the notification. They selected the most interesting footage to make a special compilation of clips, seeking amusement at the expense of these tortured contestants. These people had nothing better to do, and there was no telling just how far they'd go.

He walked around the room again. The pre-show scene was boisterous, but he always got edgy and overwrought with nervousness, his stomach twisting tightly into a knot.

Wanting to watch something to distract himself, he looked

up at the screen in the battle preparation zone, on which the Killing Show commercial was broadcast with no breaks. Now, it was showing a wide-angle shot of the massacre in District N—a spectacular disaster stretching over a vast expanse as far as the eye could see.

Xia Tian shivered. He jerked to his feet, rushed to the bathroom, and vomited violently.

No matter what kind of lens or shot was used, he could always recognize that disaster. Some things, once experienced, could never ever be expunged from the soul.

When he emerged from the bathroom, damp-haired and grim-faced, the map had already been issued. Bai Jing'an's expression was cold as he turned over the map, which was made of paper—presumably to echo the medieval theme. As the tactician, he had to commit all the routes to memory within half an hour and devise a rough plan.

However, the map could also be incorrect; this was a medieval map, which meant inaccuracies were unavoidable. It was all a matter of luck. Despite its tendency to mislead, the official map would still single out one or two resource supply points, so everyone still had to painstakingly memorize it.

Latte paced the room restlessly. Meanwhile, the doctor sat in the corner calling home, as if he couldn't survive if he didn't talk. At first, he touched on some commonly asked questions before death, but then he unexpectedly started chatting about the new drama series on air.

Xia Tian sat in the corner, biting his fingernails. After a while, he said, "I still feel like throwing up."

"The bathroom's to the right," Bai Jing'an said coldly.

Xia Tian went to the bathroom again, looking rather ill. He could still hear the doctor chatting about the drama series. In fact, Xia Tian knew that series—it was a nightmarish serial about the romance between Bai Lin—the leader of the Lower City Resistance Forces—and the daughter of an elite from the Upper City, and how he healed her hurting heart or whatever.

Why do those people from the Upper City always have to stick their hands into anything halfway decent those down below have?

Vexed, he sat on the lid of the toilet bowl and stared blankly at the tiles. The doctor was speaking in an urgent tone, his voice quavering, as if he would crumble into a heap of debris the second he stopped chatting.

Xia Tian vomited again before stepping out of the bathroom. He thought he resembled a mentally incapacitated stray dog waiting to be slaughtered after being caught in a tiger's jaws. Bai Jing'an threw him an irritated look, and he couldn't even muster a smile in response.

He sat down gloomily in the corner. He couldn't stomach anything after having just thrown up, so he picked up the match schedule introduction and flipped through it. They would be entering a large forest next. Everyone would go in with just a dagger and a canteen of drinking water, nothing else. Want to make a fire? Make one yourself by chopping wood, then.

There was basically no prey in the forest. You might capture a hare, and open it up only to find sophisticated electronic instruments in it. There was not even a shred of meat in sight, and you'd have to pay triple to compensate for the official losses. They had to pick a resource supply point and get something out of it.

From the information released so far, there were a total of three resource points, and all participating teams would assemble at them when the time came. This segment of the Killing Show was commonly known as the "opening ceremony." Many players would die in the battles here; sometimes hundreds of people. It was a veritable meat grinder.

He looked up and saw the back of Bai Jing'an's head. That lock of hair was sticking up again—what an eyesore. Xia Tian stood up and walked over to him, feeling vexed as he pressed the hair down and smoothed it to ensure it stayed in place.

Bai Jing'an sucked in a breath, but said nothing—although he was probably telling himself to bear with it.

CHAPTER 03

PLUNDER AND KILL

Xia Tian and his small team stood in the dense forest, wearing their medieval garments.

The scenery around them was beautiful; no doubt the props team had spent a lot of time on it. This could be tapped in the future for the development of various kinds of games, or sold as holographic models. There were mini cameras all around the forest, but they were so artfully concealed they weren't visible.

Xia Tian's hair was still damp when he came in. He'd been worrying about making a disgrace of himself on entering the field, but when it really started, he was so engrossed with the thought of finding someone to kill that he didn't feel like throwing up all that much anymore.

He looked up and saw a squirrel on the treetops. Having seen him too, it took flight in fright. It didn't look like a machine. Sometimes GBC would provide real animals too, so perhaps it was edible?

Xia Tian was wearing a black linen tunic. There was a large tear on the back, which looked like it had been crudely sewn back together after someone slashed it with a blade. He didn't

know if someone really had died wearing it, or if the organizers had made it deliberately so it looked that way.

Bai Jing'an, wearing a white tunic, exuded the air of a detached, cold-hearted military adviser. The colors of their clothes were randomly determined to prevent anyone from figuring out their professions based on them. Even so, there'd still be a large number of cyber support specialists active on the field, and whenever Xia Tian thought of them, he felt like bowling over with laughter. They were definitely easy pickings, sure-win points for the taking.

"Wow!" Latte said as he looked around. Xia Tian didn't care what he was wearing. "I've never been to a real forest before. Those groves in parks are all private property that require passwords to enter."

Xia Tian said nothing. He'd never seen a real forest either, but he wouldn't make a hullabaloo about it in front of the cameras.

Bai Jing'an walked up to the small hillslope at the side and surveyed the terrain. The destination to which they were teleported was random, so they had to determine their location from the surrounding terrain, then pinpoint the resource supply points from there and figure out how to make their way over.

The slope of the hill wasn't steep, but it was enough to make out the size of the forest, as well as the nearby vegetation and rivers. Bai Jing'an took two looks, made a noise of affirmation, and walked back down.

"We're about two kilometers northwest of the third resource point."

"Let's go there now!" Latte hurried a step in an unknown direction and looked back. "Hurry! The others will snatch up all the stuff if we keep dragging our feet!"

"We're not going to the resource point." Bai Jing'an turned

and walked off in another direction.

Latte was momentarily floored. He looked wistfully in the wrong direction he'd picked, reluctant to leave. Bai Jing'an surveyed the surroundings as he walked, looking like he was taking a stroll, which he definitely wasn't.

Then he continued, "We will plunder from the others."

On television, tacticians would usually make some signature gestures when assessing the situation and formulating a plan. From pushing up their glasses to stroking their chin, or even emphasizing their points without letting up... They'd put on an appearance that said, *"I'm doing something very cool and tough right now,"* lest the audience out there couldn't tell. But there was no commercial appeal whatsoever when Bai Jing'an did his thing. He didn't look like a participant in the Killing Show, but a tour guide who hated his job as he took tourists to the crummy attractions he'd seen a thousand times. He looked the very picture of a vexed, bored-stiff person who'd completely given up on life, so much so that others would start to feel bored when they saw him.

This jaded tour guide quickly led them through a grove of trees and across a small river to seek a suitable ambush spot. Xia Tian sized up the place. It wasn't so strategically situated and treacherous that it'd make others wary enough to take a detour, but it was enough to give those who lay in ambush here plenty of advantages. In a few more days, someone would surely occupy this place. The match, however, had just started, and everyone was running towards the resource point ready for a big battle—which was why this place was so quiet, peaceful, and unnoticed.

According to Bai Jing'an, they'd be able to wait it out for a small team that not only carried supplies with them but were also a cinch to overpower and plunder clean. He calmly laid out his tactics to his fellow looters and set the signal to attack. Xia Tian sized him up with fascination. Bai Jing'an's eyes were lowered, and occasionally, his gaze would meet his, each time cold and flat.

"I still think we should go to the resource point. Everyone is heading there," Latte said. "I think...we should consider the issue of honor."

That is, the Killing Show's propaganda of valor and struggle as witnessed by millions of people, and all that shtick.

"Every move we make will be displayed on the terminals before the eyes of countless audiences," he said. "We must defend our honor before the whole world!"

No one paid him any attention as they followed Bai Jing'an's lead to check the ambush points. Xia Tian had the urge to say "*Can you not be stupid?*" when he twisted his head to look at the end of the trail. Bai Jing'an turned to look, too. Several seconds later, they heard the faint sound of jumbled footsteps and grumbles.

Latte picked up his short sword and made to charge forth, but Xia Tian grabbed hold of him and covered his mouth as he dragged him into the shrubbery. Bai Jing'an gestured for both of them to be quiet.

Twenty seconds later, a small, unsuspecting squad passed through the ambush zone, grumbling to each other as they did. They had no idea where they were, and they didn't have a tactician in their team either, which was why they had yet to figure out their location. What an unprecedented streak of bad luck.

Saying things like "*We're goners this time,*" they left the area without even realizing something was amiss. All this while, Xia Tian's team lurked silently behind the shrubbery.

Three more squads passed by next—some were a motley crew, and some with more troublesome figures. However, every-

one was empty-handed, given that the match had just started. In a rush to look for resources, they had no plans to get into conflict with anyone.

Latte was burning with the desire to charge out, but Xia Tian held him tight in place. Latte was not suited for this arena—he didn't know that no matter how he preached about valor, this was ultimately a game where you went all out to survive through various kinds of machinations. They weren't attacking because there were no benefits to be reaped, and the reason they were waiting was for the battle to end. When that happened, some would perish on the spot, while some would return with a full load.

And that would be the time they make their move.

Xia Tian didn't know how the battle at the resources point was going. There were no explosions and flying cars on a medieval battlefield, nor were there large-scale holographic projections; it was only the most primitive hand-to-hand combat. He could only judge the intensity of the battle by the respective fleeing teams.

The organizers had the third resource point set up next to a lake. The scenery there was beautiful, and once the battle started, blood would dye the lake red. Once they started the sale of spin-off merchandise, they'd give the lake a bloody and dramatic name.

At first, most of those who emerged victorious only passed by them from afar without getting close. It was not until half an hour later that the first team passed through the ambush point.

It was a three-person team. Bai Jing'an didn't give the signal when they passed. Xia Tian took a look and knew that this team would be a tough nut to crack. All three were professionals. They carried with them a large number of supplies, evidently winning big in the battle earlier. They had blood on them, but a closer look revealed that the blood was splattered on them. They had barely sustained any injuries themselves.

They came closer, and Xia Tian lay low without moving. The group of people was talking about the battle at the resources point, their tones relaxed. Xia Tian heard a familiar voice spring out.

"All right, we should unite—"

It suddenly occurred to him he had heard this voice before.

Near the end of the second round of the tournament, Xia Tian—having gotten into a quarrel with Bai Jing'an, who'd told him to get lost—had fallen behind. He'd then wandered near an abandoned building. His ears had been ringing no thanks to a rocket launcher, so he'd only spotted them when he was close. Those people had been arguing while standing behind the ruins of a wall.

Xia Tian had dodged and hidden himself behind the wall. The people had been making a racket, interspersed with someone's piteous wails. From the sounds of it, someone named Luo Qingtian had found a young man in the closet, and the guy had handed over the score counter and announced his intention to surrender.

Luo Qingtian had made the guy crawl out of the closet, strip, and dance for him. The guy had been surprisingly obedient, but Luo Qingtian had felt that his "dancing was horrid," so he had shot the guy in the lower body.

The gunshot and screams had drawn the other companions over, and one of them had yelled at Luo Qingtian, "What's your freaking problem, man? His screams might draw the others over. And who the hell knows just how long this match will last?!"

"He must have danced badly because he was nervous," another one had chimed in.

Then another one who had sounded like a newcomer said in

a slightly shaky voice, "H-He's still a kid. Since you've already taken the score counter and maimed him, then...let's just drop it?"

The others had disagreed. Who knew if he would bear a grudge if he were rescued? Men who had suffered sexual humiliation were the most vindictive. Then they had even started chatting like the guy wasn't there. Meanwhile, the kid had already screamed himself hoarse.

This kind of thing was all too common in the Killing Show. This was a fenced-in land of lawlessness, where the players would do all sorts of deeds for fun and amusement. The production team would edit the footage before releasing it; sometimes, they would cut it because it didn't fit with the player's style.

The newbie who hadn't known the rules was still trying to salvage the situation. "We don't have to do this. He's already—"

Xia Tian had then heard the "bang" of a bullet penetrating through a skull.

The other side had finally quietened down, and then Luo Qingtian had said in a serious tone, "Stop arguing. We're a team. We should be working together."

Three seconds of silence had followed, and right at this time, the match had ended.

The ending scene of the Killing Show was well worth watching; it was like stepping out of hell into candyland.

The gloomy, doomsday-like sky had suddenly changed as laser light displays and fireworks blossomed in competition with one another in a dazzling array of colors. It had been all very grand and festive. Majestic music had slowly started playing, as if the whole world was impassionedly singing.

A holographic projection of the host had then appeared in the sky, his smile radiant and his hair beautifully coiffed. He had been dressed in the full formal gear of a medieval warrior, looking a tiny bit pretentious.

"Heroes, you've proven your courage and strength!" he'd proclaimed.

Everyone on the ground who had been hiding, killing, and fleeing had stopped in their tracks and looked up at the sky.

The host had continued, "Injured parties, please stay put. Medical personnel will arrive shortly to begin treatment. The St. Gold Medical Supply Co. will be providing their services to the heroes this time—"

He had then gone on to talk about courage, as well as the celebration party and the like, peppering his speech with plenty of sponsors' names. Under this display panel sky, the killing had come to an end. Those who had been still alive at this moment were considered to have survived the round, and next there would be time for revelry. Killers and victims would gather together in a hall to guzzle alcohol, get high on drugs, have sex, and eat their fill.

Someone from the team ahead had exclaimed, "Finally!"

And someone next to him had cheered cooperatively. These people had then departed.

Xia Tian had walked out and looked down at the corpse. It was indeed a kid. He had probably just turned sixteen, the minimum age to participate in the tournament; he was a lad still wet behind the ears.

He had collapsed among the ruins, sans his clothes. Luo Qingtian had not only maimed his lower body but also given him a hole in his head. Blood had soaked the ground. No one had given him a second look.

Someone's cries had echoed in the distance, but Xia Tian hadn't had the energy to turn around to see who it was. This kind of thing happened all the time and everywhere.

He'd turned his gaze away and trudged wearily toward the exit, beneath the rainbow effect on the horizon.

Halfway there, he'd spotted Bai Jing'an, who was similarly coming out of hiding. That guy, not noticing him, had merely swept a glance across the trail of devastation on the battlefield, the lights from the fireworks reflected on his face and eyes. Hair disheveled and clothes filthy, he'd looked dispirited, cutting a forlorn sight amidst the gorgeous scenery under the sky—like a specter who had lost his way.

And now, Xia Tian had once again encountered this team just as the match of the new round kicked off.

After the battle at the resource point, their team only had three people left... The one who died was the newbie who was kind with his words. This was normal; he was the only guy on the team who wasn't professional enough and didn't fit in with the others. That kind of person always died as dictated by circumstances and at the discretion of others.

They walked up the path, discussing their next tactics and talking about looking for a spot to lie in ambush and finding someone to "play" with. Being the experts they were, they trod with caution and vigilance.

Xia Tian stared at the one walking in the middle of the group, heavily protected. That was Luo Qingtian. His hair was dyed a fashionable hue of silver that looked pure under the overcast sky. No doubt he must have spent a lot of money—that was one of the top three hairstyles in the last Killing Show season. It was said to fully demonstrate a tactician's cold-blood, arrogant, and unfeeling demeanor.

That face of his was equally beautiful and exquisite enough to satisfy any nitpicky viewer. In the Killing Show's official portrayals, he was depicted as a player who was ignorant of worldly affairs, had no secular desires, and was capable of handling every matter rationally. As for the sadistic killing that happened that day, GBC never broadcast it.

The sky bore down on them gloomily, turning the entire world into an expanse of drab, lifeless gray. Those people's voices drifted over faintly, advancing steadily like mold spots on bread.

Xia Tian later looked up Luo Qingtian's data. The man was born in District T9 of the Lower City, but he wasn't really considered a local because his father was the local district administrator. When he was nine years old, his father got a transfer and moved the whole family back to the floating cities. He excelled in school and scored extremely high on intelligence tests. However, he'd shown great interest in the Killing Show from an early age and joined the trade soon after becoming an adult.

Initially, the Killing Show was nothing more than a game for the rich in the Upper City to watch death row inmates kill each other for amusement, but as the entertainment industry developed over the years, the wealthy class also began to participate in the games. In show business, adoration was piled on to those with villains' charm and appeal, and people worshiped those with blood on their hands in this drug-addled fool's paradise in the sky. They put a crown on evil, like it was something legendary.

And Luo Qingtian seemed to have found his homeplace. Unlike the majority of the rich who only joined the game once for fun, he stayed in this blood-soaked land for the long term.

His background reminded Xia Tian of the little brat of his hometown's district administrator. He had a tireless interest in cruelty, and was extremely nimble at wielding the whip. Just the thought of it made Xia Tian's entire body ache. He'd once sworn to kill him, but...he'd never found the time.

Xia Tian stared at Luo Qingtian's long, pure-as-snow hair from where he was behind the bushes and felt a tingling sensation that burned deep within him.

This is definitely fate, he thought.

The small team cautiously made their way through the ambush site, continuing their conversation about finding someone to "play with."

Luo Qingtian was saying, "...We'll be safe as long as someone likes to watch."

Xia Tian thought that if he could grab the timing and land right in front of this guy in one leap, he'd be able to kill him before anyone could react. He could cleave into his body, and blood would spurt from his arteries. The guy would have a second or two before he realized he was beyond saving, then he'd die.

Xia Tian clenched his fists, relaxed them, and clenched them again. The desire to burn him to ashes engulfed him. He really, really...didn't like Luo Qingtian's hair. That long, ice cold, snow-like hair, that handsome face, and those apathetic eyes. In those eyes, everything in the world was reduced to a series of blood-soaked plans. No agony. No death. No retribution.

Just one blow, and that face would disappear. Blood would stain his silver hair, and there'd be no beauty to speak of... *No, maybe it'd still be pretty.*

Xia Tian gripped the hilt of his blade. Body taut with tension, he was all but ready to pounce when someone behind him grabbed his shoulder.

He turned his head. Bai Jing'an, who had come up behind him at some point, was staring at him.

For a fleeting moment, Xia Tian wanted to wave his hand away and tell him to go about his own business, but Bai Jing'an's grip was strong, and he looked like he wouldn't let go if Xia Tian didn't explain himself.

Xia Tian never had a habit of discussing with others before doing something, but time was limited, and no doubt he couldn't do shit being held back like this.

Thus, he quickly flashed a dazzling smile at the guy and made two battle signs: *Kill Luo Qingtian first. End the battle in one minute.*

It was a crazy plan. Bai Jing'an looked at him expressionlessly, but the gears were obviously turning quickly in his mind. He replied to Xia Tian with a few concise gestures to make some corrections to his plan.

Within seconds, the cold and detached tactician had already factored in the desire to kill into his calculation of the plan's efficiency. They quickly exchanged a few details, and then Bai Jing'an pointed down to indicate, *Strike now.*

Xia Tian pounced, and the assault began.

Behind him, Bai Jing'an looked down. His expression belied an iciness and killing intent that was so focused under the dark clouds, it was as if all the light was concentrated on him. A flash of something from his past nature materialized indistinctly, disappearing as quickly as it appeared.

Like a carnivorous predator, Xia Tian moved swiftly and landed steadily on his feet before Luo Qingtian.

Before anyone realized what was happening, Xia Tian swung the short sword in his hand the very instant he landed and hacked into Luo Qingtian's neck.

Luo Qingtian reacted quickly and reached for the crossbow at his waist, but his fingertips slipped on it for a split second. The single strike from Xia Tian was incredibly swift and powerful; it had severed the artery in Luo Qingtian's neck and nearly slashed his head completely off.

He died almost instantly.

At the same time, the person behind him realized what had happened and whipped around to strike with his sword.

There was no dodging this move. Grabbing Luo Qingtian by the collar, Xia Tian rushed a step forward and reduced some of his strength. The sword cut through his crudely sewn linen tunic and tore his flesh, but his bones were unscathed, and he could still continue.

He was still gripping the hilt of the sword. The blade was wedged deep into Luo Qingtian's bones; the force of the blow had been so great that he couldn't extract it for a moment.

In those two seconds, he stared intently into Luo Qingtian's eyes. The latter's face was awash in fury and disbelief at the realization of his imminent demise. Xia Tian started to laugh. His face was splattered all over with blood, but he gloated and laughed with abandon.

That guy wouldn't look pretty anymore, would no longer mastermind and control the fates of others as he pleased. That self-satisfied face would be forever frozen in agony.

The warrior behind him, having struck out with his sword all the way, couldn't pull back in time. Xia Tian took a step back and turned aside to the left, revealing Luo Qingtian's corpse to the guy while he elbowed him hard in the face. He heard bones breaking and glanced at the guy's face. Blood had stained his chin red, but the guy just stared disbelievingly at that silver-haired corpse.

As corpses went, he really was quite pretty.

Latte, who'd been hiding a little farther away, immediately rushed over when he saw the fight breaking out here. He'd been lying in ambush far away to prevent anyone from escaping after the attack was launched, but now it was clear that wouldn't happen. All the fighting was taking place right there, and in thirty seconds, it'd be over.

Xia Tian grabbed Luo Qingtian's corpse by the collar, keeping it upright to block the guy in chain-mail armor at the end of the squad. That guy was completely stunned as he stared at the corpse, at a loss for what to do. With their tactician's abrupt death, everyone on the team had been thrown into confusion—especially since the one who'd died was a highly intelligent, handsome, and refined tactician who managed and handled everything.

But they wouldn't be stunned for long. The guy behind Xia Tian stalled for just a moment after taking an elbow, then raised his sword at him once more.

Xia Tian turned to the side to dodge the blow and yanked the corpse in his direction. The other guy's sword pierced diagonally into Luo Qingtian's body from the right rib.

The guy shuddered. Any warrior knew the sensation of a blade cutting into a human's body, and you'd never forget it for the rest of your life if it came from someone like Luo Qingtian, who was also your teammate to boot.

He stared blankly at Luo Qingtian's corpse, looking utterly flustered and at a loss. Xia Tian spun around, coming up behind him to catch the guy in a chokehold with his arm. The lapse of control was momentary, but to someone like Xia Tian, that was enough.

Securing the guy's neck with one arm, he clasped the back of the guy's head and gave it a violent twist. It was a standard textbook killing move, skillfully and ruthlessly executed. In his last moments, the guy even subconsciously tried to make a grab for Luo Qingtian's falling body. And then, it was all over.

The second one, Xia Tian thought. Then—

He suddenly reached out and grabbed the blade of a bloodstained sword that was inches away from his lower abdomen. But he was still a fraction too late, and the tip of the sword pierced his body.

He looked across the two corpses and saw the one and only surviving player.

For a moment, he couldn't recall his name. All he remembered was a pair of eyes teeming with murderous intent. In just the blink of an eye, this was all that was left. No points, advertisements, or money.

Only one of them could be the last man standing.

After realizing what was happening, the guy had stabbed his sword through his teammates' bodies from behind, and then into Xia Tian's lower abdomen.

Xia Tian grabbed the blade of the sword tightly. Blood flowed between his fingers. From this angle, he could see Luo Qingtian's filthy hair and battered corpse.

He flashed a brilliant and dashing smile at that pair of furious eyes across the dead body, then said, "As it turns out, your lives aren't that valuable after all."

By this time, Latte had finally reached them. He raised his dagger to slash at the last person standing—Xia Tian suddenly remembered that his name was Flint. Flint drew the scimitar at his waist with his left hand and blocked the blow. At the same time he parried Latte's blade, he thrust his sword in Xia Tian's direction without so much as a pause. *Truly a fricking desperado*. Xia Tian suddenly tightened his grip, and more blood spilled to the ground. Fortunately, the quality of this sword was not that great.

But he forgot one thing—there was no one else behind Xia Tian, which meant there was no need for Xia Tian to be locked in a stalemate with him.

Xia Tian took a step back, and the tip of Flint's sword pulled away from his body. Blood gushed, but he paid it no heed. Instead, he drew a pocket knife from his waist and threw it at the head of the guy opposite him.

This move had no attack power, but even so, the guy still had to dodge. Flint sidestepped to evade it, but in the second that took, Xia Tian had already advanced two steps toward him.

Flint attempted to extract his sword again, but only managed to pull out about six centimeters. His longsword was stuck in the corpse, and his scimitar was locked in a stalemate with another. He was trapped.

He knew what he should do. He had to get the sword out at all costs—

But it was already too late. He saw Xia Tian raise his hand, holding a compact crossbow aimed at his head.

That was Luo Qingtian's crossbow, which had been hanging at his waist. He'd grabbed it from the resource point earlier and had never used it.

At the last moment, all he saw was Xia Tian's smile. A bright, dazzling smile, yet also spine-chillingly cold as ice.

Xia Tian pulled the trigger and shot an arrow through his head.

Bai Jing'an, who had been watching from above, finally leaped down to inspect the outcome of the battle.

The doctor also poked his head out from behind the tree. Seeing the horrific scene before him, he bent over and threw up.

Xia Tian handed the crossbow to Bai Jing'an. The tactician took it and weighed it in his hand before securing it at his waist. Then he passed through the corpses on the ground to tally the spoils of war.

Under the shadow of the hill, his still-as-water face bore a hint of madness.

Xia Tian glanced at him, remembering how his first reaction to seeing the corpse in Zhi Leng's suite was to stuff it into the suitcase. It suddenly occurred to him he would not object to this plunder-and-kill venture at all. He was that kind of person.

And this time, their near-suicidal risk-taking move had successfully netted them a handsome payoff.

Xia Tian went over to search the corpses, hoping to find a sword. When he saw a small bag of apples, he bent to pick one up. He wiped it clean on his clothing and started chomping on it.

He always felt hungry when he was injured; the same went for when he was in pain too. Any time there was a crisis, he would feel hungry. It was as if food could fill some void in him.

He stood among the corpses on the ground, munching on the apple in a blank daze as he watched his teammate collect loot.

He looked at Luo Qingtian's silver hair that had been soiled by blood and mud, then at the ground littered with corpses and gore. The seething burning in his heart subsided. After killing, he'd occasionally have such moments of calm and peace.

Throughout it all, the sky had remained gloomy, and now sunlight finally peeked through the layers of dark clouds to grace the ground. The whole world was shining.

Bright, dazzling light fell on him. There was blood all over him, and his face wasn't spared. His hair was also a tad messy. As he munched an apple standing among the corpses of the three people he'd just killed, he looked ruthless, unbridled, and kind of dazzlingly handsome.

Bai Jing'an stared at him coldly, and Xia Tian wondered, "What's wrong?"

The tactician averted his gaze. "Nothing."

The doctor gaped in disbelief at the corpses. "This...this is the SilverSquad! This is Luo Qingtian! Oh my god, and this is Flint, DeepWell..."

Xia Tian ruminated over these people's names before tossing them to the back of his head. There was already no point remembering them.

"But how is this possible?" The doctor continued. "They're the SilverSquad. They have their own production team. Do you know what that means?"

Xia Tian finished the apple, threw the core away, and went off looking for a second one.

On one hand, he relished the shocked reactions and admiration of others. He also liked fantasizing about future fame, wealth, and bright prospects. But at this moment, he only felt weary. The intense emotion in him that blazed everything in its path had dissipated. All he wanted was to clear his mind and leave it empty.

The doctor was still staring at him. "Do you know what it's probably like outside now?!"

Xia Tian didn't know what to say, so he stared back at him. The doctor averted his gaze, avoiding eye contact, as if there was something scary on Xia Tian's face.

"What's it like?" Latte asked excitedly.

The doctor answered that it must be wild out there. Everyone would be replaying this battle over and over, doing special features and video montages with background tracks, and calling their group rising stars of the battlefield.

Latte listened with a silly grin on his face. Bai Jing'an wasn't at all interested; he looked bored as he pulled the arrow from the corpse's head and stuffed it into the quiver. Xia Tian handed an apple to Bai Jing'an, who declined the offer, so he started on his second one. He wandered around the corpses, examining them for good stuff, which he took for himself. It was basically all food. He picked and chose between a few longswords before settling on one engraved with branch and leaf patterns that Flint had left behind. It was still quite sharp.

He wiped away the blood staining the sword on the corpse, and commented rather begrudgingly, "I'd take guns any day."

The doctor stood among the heap of corpses, all worked up as he looked around. It was as though he could see the pandemonium

beyond the arena through an invisible surveillance camera.

A crow perched on a tree branch, watching the scene before it. Bai Jing'an looked up at it. It stood innocently on the branch, like any other ordinary bird, lending an ominous atmosphere to the battlefield.

"Let's find somewhere out of sight to take a break," Bai Jing'an said.

Xia Tian nodded in agreement. Bai Jing'an turned and walked in the opposite direction, his expression grim. It was the look he always wore.

Following behind him, Xia Tian saw that lock of Bai Jing'an's hair sticking up again and reached out to press it down. Bai Jing'an sucked in a deep breath and told himself to stay calm. He wondered if he had overestimated his own patience before, when he thought he could put up with him.

Perched silently on the branch, the crow watched them leave.

An uproar broke out on the 199th Gilded Broadcasting Corporation Killing Show's text, video, and live-streaming posts.

Everyone was asking what had happened. The video in question was broadcast over and over again, and the click-through rate soared through the roof. Luo Qingtian's squad was the hot favorite to win the tournament. They had a dedicated production team. No way they'd die on the very first day of the pay-to-view match!

Meanwhile, everyone on Luo Qingtian's production team was completely dumbstruck after the death of the star under their charge. The assistant director called them all in for a last-minute meeting to discuss their next steps.

The conference room was in an uproar.

"Where'd that kid come from?!"

"He's too scary. It all went down in a matter of seconds. No warning at all…"

"How did his tactician ever agree to that kind of suicidal plan?!"

"I can't believe he successfully killed him!"

Everyone spoke fast, nervous to the core, but they didn't dare to ask the key question: *Now that Luo Qingtian was dead, what's gonna happen to them?* The incident could be painted as an unexpected mishap, or as a mistake. If it was the latter, they'd be booted out of the production team.

The conference room was bright and clean, but this group of people looked like they'd pulled countless all-nighters. With their disheveled hair and clothing stained with food scraps, they resembled a heap of garbage that was waiting to be cleared in the large, bright room.

They were senior producers—a title that sounded nice, but in fact, everyone was called that—and they each had a contract with GBC that was valid for over fifty years. Forget about jumping ship; the company could do whatever it wanted with them. And in these times, you couldn't lose your job. Everyone had a chunk of loans to repay, and if you couldn't, it wouldn't be just the house you'd lose.

"Will they kill him? Or punish him?" one of them asked.

"Maybe. You can't just kill a star, unless you're a star yourself," his colleague replied.

Silence fell around the conference table for three seconds, then a discussion erupted like a burst of sun rays on the horizon after the dark night.

"No, they won't kill him. He's quite good-looking—"

"Nah, you mean drop-dead gorgeous. He's also very popular—"

"He's from District N. Makes for quite the drama—"

"Luo Qingtian's already dead. We have to keep this one and see if he can be groomed!"

Within three minutes, everyone had reached a consensus: In their professional view, Xia Tian was extremely worth grooming, so they should place all their resources with him and set up a five-member production team.

Luo Qingtian? His death was regrettable, but on the other hand, it perfectly highlighted the outstanding qualities of this newbie. Only when there were losses could there be gains, and such was the nature of the Killing Show. They were certain that Xia Tian was a first-rate potential star in the making. Luo Qingtian would become a solid stepping stone for him.

Quick, quick, quick. They needed to work out a rough proposal before the assistant director arrived.

Discussion was in full swing online, but where Luo Qingtian was concerned, no one tried to salvage a thing.

In the Killing Show, dead stars had no value.

In the past, they'd still do a commemoration feature to see if they could sell the stockpiled merchandise. With the rapid advancement of 3D printing technology nowadays, there was no need for them to worry about inventory management; just throw them into the material preparation zone for reconstruction, and that'd do.

Everyone in the viewer section was discussing this unexpected attack and analyzing those few seconds of action. Xia Tian's name spread like the plague online.

Half an hour after the incident, a young producer who worked in the cyber department made a special column on Luo Qingtian's death on the main page, which came attached with a video along with a collection of relevant resources; he even started a small discussion corner. The number of clicks on the links grew rapidly, but hardly anyone was discussing the deceased; all of them were talking about Xia Tian.

They reveled in the plundering and killing, seeing it as not just a battle tactic but vengeance, glory, and justice. They bought virtual fireworks to celebrate, seeing Xia Tian as a hero figure and thinking he ought to kill more.

A peculiarly fanatical atmosphere rose. They repeatedly quoted Xia Tian's *"your lives aren't that valuable after all,"* making it rise to the top of the trending chart. They even started speculating who was next in line.

The gloating was in part due to Luo Qingtian's image. He was a true aficionado of killing, often unhesitatingly taking out other players who could have potentially co-existed with him. Some of these people—many of whom were popular stars—had even stayed their hands in advance as a show of amiability.

No one said a thing. These days, physical prowess was the truth; those not strong enough deserved to die. And to watch this kind of program, you had to be an adult who knew the impermanence of life. If you were afraid of death, then what the heck were you doing watching the Killing Show?

The fury had nowhere to go, but it'd never vanish. So when he died, countless people in the Upper City had already been waiting a long time to gloat about it.

Xia Tian's *"your lives aren't that valuable after all"* made it into the 199th Killing Show's famous quotes and sayings column. Every season had a similar column that compiled interesting phrases that had been popular for a while. The phrase *"I'd take guns any day"* also made it onto the list.

Folks suddenly started talking about Xia Tian, asking who he was and what resources were available for purchase. It was thanks to discussions on the internet that another rage-consumed rebel from the Lower City-cum-hero indistinctly took shape, emerging from the battlefield of bloodshed and carnage.

The producers of the Killing Show were familiar with this process. Attention and resources were now converging in one direction in the Upper World, where capital funds were a colossal behemoth always on the move.

A new hero was about to be born.

CHAPTER 04

BATTLE ENCOUNTER

The new stars of the Killing Show took a break downstream to regroup. Wildflowers they couldn't identify bloomed all around them, painting a picturesque scene. The art designers must have put a hell of a lot of effort into creating such a natural, untouched landscape.

The doctor applied medicine for Xia Tian and bandaged his wounds. To achieve the medieval times effect, there were no antibiotics at the resource point, only herbal powders. Their effects remained to be seen; all they could be sure of was that it wouldn't kill anyone.

In order to maintain viewability, however, the organizers put a large volume of anesthetic into the pharmaceutical supply, going out of their way to make them look like plant-based medicaments that fit the medieval setting. This was to ensure that players could keep fighting despite their injuries.

While their haul from the battle at the resource point was sizable, it left them with no doubt that Luo Qingtian and his team had not found a wardrobe there. There was not even a single piece of clothing, only a crudely made sewing kit. Xia

Tian took off his top without hesitation and let the doctor help him mend it.

For a moment, Bai Jing'an looked like he wanted to stop him, but eventually, he said nothing—after all, this was normal; he couldn't continue wearing it if it wasn't patched up.

Xia Tian tied his loose hair back. Old wounds were visible all over his body, and there was something tragic about them, but this was par for the course for those who lived hand to mouth in the Lower City. He sat there comfortably—it felt good to be basking in the sun.

The tactician cast a grim glance at his naked torso. It was an expression that Xia Tian was all too familiar with. He probably wanted to lecture him on *"one hundred and eight things you shouldn't do."* Xia Tian paid him no heed. It was just sewing a shirt, so what was his problem, man?

The doctor took the clothes away to wash and dry, getting everything completely wrong. What's more, his actions were beyond clumsy. Xia Tian was sure he wouldn't live for long.

He sat for a while, idly plucking some wildflowers in an attempt to make a flower crown. Latte scooted over, watching with anticipation before searching enthusiastically for various flowers for him to mix and match colors. The doctor watched with curiosity, probably wondering why the two hardened killers in their team would be interested in tiny plants and flowers.

In fact, it was quite normal. There were no flowers and plants in the Lower City; only mushrooms, mold, and pestilence everywhere. In addition, all the drama series from the Upper City liked to portray the former as a sight only found in paradise. It was why people like them always felt that sunlight, stars, and greenery were all important things, worth paying attention to. These were luxuries they could only earn by risking their lives, even though they actually did nothing to improve their lives at all.

From the first time they'd met, Xia Tian had sent out a clear *"get away from me"* signal to Latte, even throwing in a *"the sight of you annoys me"* to reinforce the message. But this man still kept coming to him, one-sidedly thinking that they would share a common language.

And now, as he watched Xia Tian weave a flower crown, he started talking to him on his own.

"I once stole a bag of cookies with a friend. We wanted to eat them so badly," he said, "and the shop owner sent a hellhound after us. He had a special fondness for watching that. You know hellhounds? They're the ones with several heads and spikes..."

"Of course, I know what a hellhound is," Xia Tian said.

Latte laughed, like he had also realized how silly the question was. The doctor tried to join the conversation.

"I've only seen hellhounds on TV. Are there really people in the Lower City that rear those kinds of thing? Furless, three heads, even eats people?"

"They're mainly for guarding the home," Latte said. "The ones you're talking about are a highly mutated breed that only the rich can afford to raise. The ones running around in the Lower City are actually scrawny, deformed mongrels. They're everywhere, hunted down by the dogfighting rings to the point they have nowhere to hide."

"Dogfighting rings?" the doctor parroted.

"Yup. When they capture the dogs, they'll inject them with mutagens, then let them loose in the arena to watch them kill each other for fun," Latte explained. "After taking the serum, they'll go berserk and grow as big as a calf."

Xia Tian listened to him in silence. He was familiar with the story. That kind of cheap, highly mutagenic serum was also called the "superstar serum." Grocery stores sold them for a

dollar apiece, or ten for a dozen. After being injected, the dogs' skin would become as hard as leather, and they would drool blood-red saliva. Sometimes, they'd even grow new, misshapen heads. Truly a macabre spectacle.

Dogs that had mutated could only live for a very short time. They rarely ate and were always compelled by the urge to kill something. Those people sought amusement by watching them kill one another. Sometimes, they'd bet on the outcome, although most just watched.

As a child, Xia Tian had also taken on work with disposing dog carcasses; a real nightmare of a job.

"It bit down on my leg and dragged me outside. It's got two heads, so it made it hard to decide how to hit it," Latte continued.

"Strike it in the heart," Xia Tian said.

"Or the spine," Bai Jing'an piped up from the side. Xia Tian glanced at him.

"I still have the scar on my leg!" Latte said cheerfully as he drew back the leg of his pants to show his wound.

Xia Tian looked. The wound was deep enough to see the bone, and half of the calf had been bitten off. It was simply too horrific to look at.

He noticed Bai Jing'an's right leg tremble a little. The man subconsciously pulled it back and put his hand with slightly quivering fingertips on it. His movement was covert, but Xia Tian knew it was the instinctive reaction of having formerly sustained a severe injury.

Some wounds, even when healed, would stay with you for life. In the middle of the night when you wake from a dream, or during a tense moment, or while engaging in conversations where everything was going just fine, something cold and dark would suddenly creep up on you and tell you that things would never ever get better in this life.

"I hid in the sewers for half a year," Latte continued, "surviving off garbage."

"Let me guess. In the end, you didn't even get to eat a cookie," Xia Tian said. "And that friend of yours was completely fine. He was surprised when you found him, saying he'd narrowly escaped the shop owner's pursuit, but thought you'd died. He was glad you were alive, but you'd better leave his house now, because you're now a wanted fugitive in the entire district, and he didn't want to get implicated. So you had no choice but to leave your hometown and turn to the underground battle arena."

"I know you think I'm an idiot," Latte said, "but Lars is a good man. The underground arena was terrible, but I survived and came here."

He even gestured like this was some kind of paradise. Xia Tian shifted to the side.

"Your desperation is too painful to look at," he said. "Stay away. What if you infect me?!"

Latte flashed him a goofy grin, not at all angry with the personal attack. He was Tragedy with a capital T, yet he still hung around every day, grating on Xia Tian's nerves.

Beside them, the doctor falteringly asked Latte about this cookie he was talking about. It couldn't be some sort of derogatory nickname for some valuable food he didn't know about, could it? Latte explained that it was just your average cookie. They were common in the Upper City but very rare in the Lower City. There were very few foods there that had received exposure to sunlight; crops only grew in the greenhouse, and because of the *Two Cities' Trade Agreement*, they even had to hand over half of their harvests to the Upper City.

"I'm sorry," the doctor said. "I've heard of that agreement, but...I didn't know..."

"Don't sweat it; it's not like you made the rules." Xia Tian

flashed him a smile.

Xu Peiwen looked down to avoid his gaze. Xia Tian's smile was always so brilliant, but there was an iciness lurking deep within that could give one frostbite.

Everything was relatively calm after that. On the third night, they bumped into a battered two-man team. Xia Tian killed one of them, and Latte fought with the other for a long time before letting him go, as the guy kept yelling his intent to surrender.

"He surrendered," Latte said, "and I don't kill those who surrender."

His tone was firm and steadfast, and he practically exuded the spirit of a true knight.

Xia Tian pulled a speechless, what-the-heck expression. "We need the points!" he exclaimed.

"He dropped his sword and kneeled on the ground crying. What was I supposed to do?!" Latte retorted.

Xia Tian considered it for a bit and found that he really had no answer, so he could only say indignantly, "Anyhow, your surrenderer won't last a few days!"

"He's not *'my'* surrenderer!"

At the time of speaking, they were taking a breather in a secluded area by the river. Many teams would quarrel over whether to let those who surrendered go, even to the extent of coming to blows over it. Any human life represented points, and points were essential. Aside from helping you advance through the ranks and being used as currency for bonuses, they could also prove that you were not slacking off on the field. After all, if the producers felt you weren't working hard enough, they would either find a way to create some unexpected incidents to help you get more points, or turn you into points for someone else.

Xia Tian cast a glance at Bai Jing'an. That guy was absent-mindedly surveying the terrain with the expression of one who had no worldly desires and had transcended the mundane world. Upon noticing Xia Tian's eyes on him, he looked back with a *"what-do-you-expect-me-to-do"* expression. Xia Tian indeed couldn't think of something.

Eventually, Bai Jing'an said, "At least we got ourselves a sword."

"All right, then," Xia Tian answered.

That was all their tactician had to say on the matter. What a peaceful and friendly team.

With the topic thus concluded, Xia Tian continued to idle his time away weaving flower crowns, while Latte assisted him. The doctor, apparently an expert on wildflowers, started to introduce the wildflowers around them, from the willow gentian to the bird's-eye primrose, and so on.

Just as he was grumbling that some of these flowers shouldn't be blooming in the same season nor located at the same altitude, Xia Tian suddenly looked up and gestured to Bai Jing'an. The faint sound of metal clanging drifted from where the wind was coming. Whoever was there had taken care to keep the noise down, but the tournament ran long and oversights were inevitable.

The surroundings immediately quieted down. Latte reached for the supplies. Only the doctor asked, "What?"

Bai Jing'an and Xia Tian quickly exchanged a few gestures. Five seconds later, the four soundlessly spread out to take up their respective battle posts. The flower crowns were tossed deep into the growth of grass, and silence instantly returned to the forest; it was as if no one had ever set foot in it.

Soon, he heard footsteps. It was more than the number of people he'd expected.

They all knew the plan for what came next. If the other

party was easy game, they would rob them; if they were tough nuts, everyone would just lie low in motionless silence and let them leave on their own.

The incoming party was trouble. It was a teamed-up squad of seven people.

The organizers didn't like players teaming up, because it'd inevitably culminate in a large-scale mass congregation that would deteriorate into a fight for supremacy, like that of the Three Kingdoms. All the fun of the Asajin's tournament system would go out the window. They'd tweaked the regulations multiple times, and the latest rule only allowed two teams to join forces temporarily at the cost of a considerable amount of points. As a result, most people didn't like to team up. If they did, then they must have a compelling reason.

These people looked to be in a terrible state as they passed through the forest, so they'd likely encountered a strong team three or four hours earlier and had temporarily joined forces in order to survive.

Xia Tian didn't know what happened to the team they ran into—hopefully, they all died—but he guessed that it'd probably been perilous. This team was down one person, and another three were injured, but their wounds had already been bandaged and would not impede them from fighting.

The group looked exhausted, but they advanced in strict adherence to a battle formation. Everyone was carrying dry rations with a longsword in hand, and they also had two crossbows. None of them seemed to be cyber support.

At the very moment Xia Tian saw them, he decided to keep quiet until they went away. Everyone would have an easier time that way.

Right at this moment, an owl in the clear, azure sky spread its wings out of the blue and swooped down onto the branch above Xia Tian's head. It looked at him with its cold, mechanical eyes, then let loose a shrill cry.

Everyone turned their head to look in the bird's direction. Xia Tian subconsciously tightened his grip on his longsword as his eyes locked onto the shocked eyes of another person.

He was completely exposed now.

This was exactly what the organizers wanted—a "harbinger of death."

They wanted battles.

More blood.

Deaths.

The person at the lead advanced towards Xia Tian, and the latter, gripping his sword in hand, met him head-on. The owl's shrill cry was a death knell that tolled for the two teams who bore neither grudge nor enmity against each other.

And only one would be the last standing.

The guy in the lead was dressed in red and had a wound on his waist. He also seemed to be a Killing Show celebrity. He charged at Xia Tian, who blocked the blow with his sword and delivered a kick to the guy's lower abdomen. The guy dodged, but Xia Tian backhandedly struck him in the temple with the hilt of his sword.

It was an unorthodox move, but effective. The guy went down, and everyone was too preoccupied to bother checking on him. Xia Tian turned around to see that the other two guys had already closed in on him.

The battle started in the twinkling of an eye.

Bai Jing'an was positioned at a Chinese parasol tree. Without a sniper on their team, he had to do double duty. When the events unfolded, he observed the enemy's formation and noticed their archers drawing back at the moment of attack.

He grabbed his crossbow and took a second to ready himself before pulling the trigger. A short arrow shot forth and struck one of them right in the forehead.

It had been years since he last killed someone, and he'd once wondered how it'd feel to do it again. Would it feel unfamiliar? Would his hands tremble? But there were no issues of the sort when it really happened. It was like picking up a blade he hadn't used in a long time and finding that he was still very proficient in using it. The memories from the past still existed in every cell of his body. Even if he couldn't recall some of them, they remained deeply ingrained within him.

He calmly raised his eyes to look for the second one. In that brief span of time, the second guy had already run five steps away to the periphery of the crowd.

When the guy saw Xia Tian striking his teammate's temple, he immediately raised his crossbow to shoot in his direction. Even if it didn't penetrate his head, it'd likely disrupt his rhythm.

Crossing the fine line between life and death only took a mere instant in times like these.

Bai Jing'an paid no attention to the battle situation below and fired the second arrow. The steady tip pierced that man's wrist, and the moment the man's wrist jerked, the arrow aiming for Xia Tian shot into the sky. Reacting quickly, the man ducked into the growth of grass.

Bai Jing'an remained motionless with the crossbow in hand and waited. He paid no heed to the chaotic battle. This was the medieval age; there were no encrypted channels, so tactics had to be shouted aloud. What's more, he was also doing double duty as a sniper. The message he wanted to convey to everyone was *"Look out for yourselves."*

For a brief moment, he felt like a carnivorous predator in

the midst of a hunt, waiting for his chance to strike. One slight breeze, and that might possibly be his opportunity to deal the killing blow.

On the chaotic battlefield, the two farthest pair of opponents went still, with the hunter and the hunted locked in a stalemate between life and death.

Moments later, the situation on the battlefield changed again.

The guy in red fell, and Xia Tian engaged in battle with the two other guys that followed right after. Both were experts proficient in swordsmanship and knowledgeable in the art of killing efficiently.

On the other side of the path, Latte was locked in a fight with a heavily-built man in armor, and it seemed like the battle would take a while.

As for the doctor, well, who knew where he was? Probably praying behind some tree. He really should have been a priest.

Amidst the chaos, a member of the enemy team discovered Bai Jing'an's location. In any given situation, the sniper always had to be eliminated first. Thus, this person didn't even give it a second thought as he dodged the glare of an incoming sword and headed for the Chinese parasol tree.

He was a man in linen coat, and his expression was cold and hard, but composed. Paying no attention to the chaos around him, he made his way through the battlefield and climbed the tree, holding his blade in his mouth.

Bai Jing'an didn't notice him, caught up as he was in another battle. The assassin thought his party's losses weren't all that bad, and the battle would be as good as won as long as he could leap up and get rid of the sniper.

He crouched low like an insect naturally born to hunt on tree trunks, his expression steadfast. Without even sweating, he focused all his attention, ready to deal the killing blow—

A longsword came hurtling toward him from behind. He was so focused on his prey that he didn't notice anything amiss, nor feel any premonition of doom. It all happened in an instant.

The force at which the sword was hurled was so immense that the sword completely pierced his back and heart and penetrated the tree trunk, nailing him to the Chinese parasol tree. He died instantly, never having stood a chance.

That was Xia Tian's sword.

After hurling the sword out, Xia Tian's situation immediately turned for the worse.

His situation was already bad before. Neither of his two opponents were pushovers. When it all went down, he'd already been thinking about whether he should simultaneously run and fight to separate these two, but then he glimpsed that man heading toward Bai Jing'an's hiding place.

In the heat of battle, he parried one of his opponent's swords, spun around, and hurled the longsword in his hand.

Later, some people said that he possessed a kind of reckless mania when he killed—the type that would compel him to gamble with his life at any time. Such a person was bound to lose it all sooner or later, and so he very quickly rose to become the one with the highest amount of money placed on him on the Killing Show's death betting tables. Some people even began to believe that he would never die—he'd survived so many times it was as though there was an invisible hand guiding him.

To Xia Tian, however, things weren't all that dramatic.

Everything happened so fast that even he himself couldn't say what he'd been thinking in that very instant. Sometimes, you had no choice but to follow your intuition.

This intuition didn't come from the training software, but was honed from spending countless moments on the brink of life and death. And to him, moments like these happened way too often. After all, he was always the one on the dark streets of District N who fought the most brawls, started the most feuds, and got into the most trouble.

In any case, Xia Tian never took another look in that direction after hurling the sword. After sidestepping a blow, he took two steps back and drew a dagger to ward off yet another attack.

Blood seeped from between his fingers. At the same time, the other guy's blade pierced his right shoulder. He felt the familiar harrowing pain, but at least it missed his heart.

Not bad. He was still alive, so he could still kill.

He still had a chance.

Bai Jing'an felt the shockwave rock the tree trunk and knew something must have happened, but he didn't have the time to care about it. He was staring at his own opponent, and crossing the fine line between life and death only took a mere instant in times like these..

A slight breeze blew, and the person in the grass stirred.

This man had been watching Xia Tian intently. He was moving now because he'd found an almost fail-proof opportunity to kill him.

It was also the opportunity Bai Jing'an had been waiting for.

The sniper raised the crossbow slightly and put his hand on the trigger, knowing that he could end the battle instantly. Their kind could always tackle the greatest threat in silence...

Right then, an arrow from the Chinese parasol tree shot forth soundlessly and pierced the assassin's carotid artery. He didn't realize it at first—not until he collapsed into the grass and reached up to cover his neck, only to find blood spurting between his fingers. He instantly understood what had happened, but he still struggled to grab the crossbow, thinking that he might still have a chance to do something; their situation was

extremely dire—

In the end, he didn't manage to lift his weapon. His hand drooped down again and went completely still.

It was mayhem all around. No one else other than Bai Jing'an had noticed him.

The tactician breathed a sigh of relief and looked down at the man nailed to the tree trunk. He must have been handsome when he was alive. Dressed in a linen coat, his eyes were wide open and glazed over, although they remained fixed and staring at him, as if he hadn't died in peace. Xia Tian's sword had nailed him to the tree, impaling him so deeply that the sword was completely embedded in his body and the tree trunk.

Bai Jing'an sucked in a breath and looked away to refocus on the battlefield.

In the few seconds following Bai Jing'an finishing off his opponent, the situation on the battlefield had taken yet another turn. Players often fought for ten minutes or so, but this had happened in a flash. Victory and defeat, life and death—all determined in the twinkling of an eye.

The man in red, who had been walking in front and was the first to cross swords with Xia Tian at the start of the battle, finally recovered from the blow. The impact of Xia Tian's sword hilt against his temple had been so heavy that it knocked him out for a while, but it didn't take him long to come to. He fumbled for his sword that had fallen into the growth of grass nearby, but he didn't stand up right away. He was a professional who knew that he was now hidden—a rare opportunity—and he had to first assess the situation before he made his appearance.

He immediately realized the gravity of their situation. In just a short period of time, several members of their party had already died; the one hanging from the tree in particular was terrifying. He glanced at the body. From the clothes, it looked like

Fuqing. Hopefully not; Fuqing was the calmest among them, and he was supposed to wait until the battle was well underway before he jumped out at the critical moment to help dispose of the other party.

Maybe it wasn't him. Maybe he'd still poke his head out among the grass in the next second and tell him his plan, then lecture him for not being calm enough, that it wouldn't do to be so emotional in this place, but their hope of victory was high... Or maybe he was dead as a dog, hanging from that tree with a sword pierced through him!

He was enraged. They'd just been through a brutal battle three hours ago in which they lost a teammate. The other party consisted of all experts, and they had a very high chance of winning the tournament. One of them was even his...former acquaintance.

Not a friend.

To enter the Killing Show was to be without friends, because this was a small world, and good friends would always cross paths as foes on a narrow path. It was a sight too tragic to behold, and the events that unfolded after would turn into cheap productions for the GBC... He'd never be the one dying in a trashy video! He'd always be the one who wouldn't get emotionally involved, right to the end. People would hate you, fear you, but they'd never talk about you like they were discussing a pitiful wretch, or treat your most anguished moments as another pathetic talking point!

So, he looked at that guy in the eye and killed him. He kept saying *sorry*, but he still went through with it, thrusting his sword in and pulling it out, looking at the guy's disbelieving eyes.

Then, he ran.

He deserved a moment of peace. Just think about how much fucking entertainment his killing had provided three hours ago...

Bloody hell, he killed his best friend and cried his heart out before the cameras. He was entitled to a moment of quietude!

A twisted smile materialized at the corners of his mouth. He climbed to his feet, knowing that he could get many things out of the Killing Show—fame, publicity, money, bed partners, an endless stream of attention and talking points... Everything except peace and quiet.

This was his second Killing Show. Even now, when his humanity had been so deeply twisted, he was still acutely aware that the situation was in his favor: no one had noticed he was still alive. Moreover, his position was excellent; he was right behind the long-haired guy, the one who was a downright pain to deal with. The guy was even injured. No way he could deal with attacks coming from two people.

If he killed this guy, he'd be able to survive this battle.

It didn't matter how warped everything was, or how many people he had to kill for it. All of them survived and lived like this—twisted and broken.

No one noticed him. They were too preoccupied to bother.

This assassination will be simple yet effective, he thought as he gripped his longsword tightly and thrust it viciously at the center of Xia Tian's back.

Latte saw him coming.

He wasn't the strongest one in the squad, and his performance in recent battles was so-so, which caused him some anxiety. But he was a natural-born warrior, and people needed him to fight. He just needed an opportunity.

And then, the opportunity presented itself.

He was locked in an intense battle with that guy in armor, and for a while, neither could kill the other. Both of them realized this after the initial flurry of blows, so they slowed down. It was at this point that Latte saw the other guy launching a sneak attack on Xia Tian.

He wasn't thinking about anything when he charged over.

Xia Tian was right; he wasn't smart enough. He didn't have the ability to think about self-preservation when he ran into trouble, and when he realized the danger, he could only use the most simple and violent way to deal with it.

He rushed up and intercepted the sword of the man in red.

The blade was approximately fifteen centimeters away from Xia Tian's back when he stopped it in its tracks. But going to Xia Tian's aid also simultaneously broke the stalemate between Latte and his earlier opponent. When he charged toward Xia Tian, he exposed his entire back to his opponent, who thrust his sword at him without hesitation.

The sword pierced right through him—an outcome he should have realized the moment he rushed over.

Actually, he didn't know if he'd realized it or not. He wasn't smart enough. But when he charged over, he was very sure that his decision was the right one.

Even now, as the blade embedded itself deep into his body, he still thought the same.

He knew death. Everyone knew death. It was the door to glory that awaited him ahead. But when it really happened, he still felt afraid.

It's time to put your nature and soul to the test, he thought.

That was what the advertising slogan of the Killing Show said.

He'd indeed passed the test. He was the perfect example of this category of players' function in the Killing Show—sacrificing their lives to save a star player with a promising future.

On the other side of the camera, the production unit watched with bated breath as the event unfolded on screen. A minute later, they would hug each other in ecstasy and cry tears of joy.

They'd kept their jobs. This battle encounter was a test for becoming a real star—it was to determine if Xia Tian had enough luck and capability to be allocated a slice of the company's resources.

And that guy passed the test. Their blunder was over and done with. The first rays of the dawn of a new star's era illuminated the dim workstations. They could still continue to repay their loans without being forced to join the Killing Show.

They didn't even look at the death scene playing out on the screen, so of course, they weren't the least bit upset. Securing a job in the Upper City sometimes required this many lives as stepping stones.

The moment it happened, Xia Tian felt the confusion of his opponents. He didn't know why yet, but to someone like him, a split second of distraction was enough. Seeing his opportunity, he thrust the short sword into the head of an opponent. The skull, however, was pretty thick, and Xia Tian couldn't pull the sword out, so he discarded it and drew his dagger to fight.

The guy fell to his knees, his eyes bloodshot. For all his attempts to stand up, he kept slipping down like an electric doll that had lost power. When all was said and done, death was never elegant.

Xia Tian turned his head just in time to see a long sword pierce through Latte. The guy was still stubbornly standing and intercepting the sword that was meant for Xia Tian.

In a hurry to break free, the enemy dragged the sword downward, almost splitting Latte in half—but still, Latte remained stubbornly in place. Had he been a smaller man, he'd have already been hacked in half, but Latte could keep being stubborn and refuse to back down.

Xia Tian was stunned. A sword came for him from his rear side; barely reacting in time, he turned aside to dodge it and nearly fell. The blade swept past his cheek, drawing blood.

He ignored the guy behind him and rushed forward to grab Latte's sword. His teammate had no more strength left in his hands, so Xia Tian got his hands on the sword easily. Latte glanced at him. Something that was almost a smile flashed in his eyes, and then he fell over. Xia Tian reached out to grab him, but didn't manage. Latte was so heavy, no one could catch him.

The same guy from earlier moved again to stab him from behind. Xia Tian jerked back, and the blade passed under his armpit. He nimbly spun around and broke the other guy's arm. At the same time, he brandished his sword and the guy's head flew off and tumbled into the grass.

Without a moment's pause, Xia Tian turned and strode toward the other guy who had slain his teammate, his eyes blazing with murderous intent. He parried a blow, ignoring the sword flying toward him, and thrust his sword into that guy's left eye, penetrating his skull.

He turned to look for the other assailant in red. He'd long known he wasn't dead, but there were so many of them, and he'd been too preoccupied to divert his attention—

But even if he hadn't slipped up, he didn't know what he could've done either.

The shrill cries of the harbinger of death had forced them onto the road of no return.

Xia Tian found the assailant collapsed among the grasses with a short sword piercing through him. Its blade had hit his liver dead on.

Xu Peiwen stood there with blood on his hands. He looked up at Xia Tian and stammered, "He tried to escape..."

He didn't finish his sentence and merely stood there blankly.

Words were meaningless in the face of death.

Bai Jing'an leaped off the Chinese parasol tree and cast another glance at the corpse nailed to the tree, making sure that it was really dead. It looked hideous. Its hands were still outstretched in its last moments, unable to even move an inch—a clear testament of the power of that one blow.

He quickly examined the dead bodies in the forest again to ensure no one was alive before walking over to Latte.

The guy lay among the grasses. His lungs had been pierced by the long sword, and kept coughing out blood. Xia Tian kneeled beside him, holding his head, at a loss for what to do.

The doctor looked at the injury and shook his head. The wound looked horrifying, but he didn't throw up this time.

Latte broke out in a violent burst of coughs, and blood splattered. His voice sounded weird, like he was drowning in his own blood. "I... passed the test..."

They listened in a daze as Latte continued, "I did what had to be done. The toughest victories are all borne out of tiny, incredulous hope..."

"The God of War title poem?" the doctor asked.

Latte continued, his voice breaking, "Having given myself in contribution, I shall be laid to rest on the battlefield, back into the embrace of the God of War..."

It was indeed GBC's God of War title poem.

The Killing Show had an official god named Ares, the God of War—a messy-haired god dressed in a punk outfit. Bearing a cigarette in his mouth and a heavy machine gun in his hands, he stood at the top of a skyscraper, stepping on the skeletons underfoot with a deranged smile on his face.

GBC had someone write a special prayer for it, along with various other kinds of inspirational Chicken Soup for the Soul. Most of these were about victory, sacrifice, hope, and the like—

they conveyed that if you felt trapped, desperate, helpless, and despised, the God of War would grant you a new, glorious life. Which, of course, was accompanied by the handsome photos of Killing Show stars who had made a name for themselves.

The massacre in District N back then was also often compared to a mass sacrifice to the God of War. It was also often inextricably associated with the leader, Bai Lin. People said that, *"He was so terrifying, he was almost the incarnation of the glorious God of War."* If Bai Lin were still alive, he'd definitely sue the Glided Group for infringing on his reputation. But he was dead, so they could cook up whatever they liked.

It was an advertisement and a trademark, with the production team and sales data behind it. But legends of its miraculous effectiveness circulated all over the internet, and people kept praying, so much that it sank deeper into their souls as the marketing efforts kept up.

Even as Latte was coughing up blood without letup, he was still stubbornly going on and on about honor, embraces, and victory. He looked at his unscathed battle buddy in front of him—well, not exactly all that unscathed—and his eyes shone bright, as if he'd accomplished a sacred goal of the highest order.

Xia Tian had once derided his pride and honor; even as he was dying now, he was surprisingly still reciting this stuff. All Xia Tian could do was to listen solemnly. At a time like this, no one could bring themselves to mock someone.

"In the trial of blood and death, I shall strive...to contribute...to victory..." Latte murmured, like a valiant warrior martyred in a movie.

It wasn't until the light in his eyes had faded into a dull grayness that Xia Tian realized he was gone.

They stood before Latte's corpse, not knowing what to do.

After a while, the doctor said, "He said...he wanted to be

buried in the arena. Is that in compliance with the rules? Is it allowed by the organizers?"

"Nope, not allowed," Bai Jing'an answered. He paused for a moment, then started the gears of a tactician's intelligence turning. "But there are special circumstances. If we hold a ceremony and they broadcast it, maybe they'll agree to leave the body here."

"I know the argument," the doctor said. "Death will add to the history of a place. Maybe they'll use the corpse as a landmark to fluff out the season's plot or something. The official website could start a poll to let everyone decide whether they're interested..."

He suddenly started laughing, on edge. "Sorry, it's just kind of hilarious... Our friend died saving us, and he spouted their advertising slogan before he died. And to fulfill his last wish, we have to hold a funeral and earn sympathy points so that we can score a victory in online voting!"

No one responded. He was the only one laughing. Some things seemed solemn yet worthless, so much that no one knew how to react.

Bai Jing'an thought for a while before squeezing out a comment, "It does make one sympathize."

"I feel like throwing up," Xia Tian said.

He turned, walked over to the trees, and braced himself with one hand against the trunk. He didn't retch, but he didn't want to look back, so he just stared at the pitch-black forest.

If only he could never look back and just forge on ahead. There'd be no need to face this absurd and tragic scenario.

But life had to go on, and after standing for a long time, he finally looked back and said, "All right then, we'll hold a funeral."

They were going to dig a pit and put Latte in.

Latte was always the one who did this kind of labor before,

but since he was dead and Xia Tian was still injured, the doctor had no choice but to do the job. He only had himself to blame for having the lowest kill count.

Xia Tian stood for a moment before turning to examine the corpse. His battle vision had always been top-notch, and it took only a sweep of the surroundings to realize what had happened.

"Thanks," he said to Bai Jing'an.

Bai Jing'an nodded. "Thanks, too."

They said nothing further. Xia Tian walked into the growth of grass and picked up the discarded flower crown. It was still fresh and undamaged.

He took the flower crown and carefully sat on the ground. Bai Jing'an gave him a hand. As a tactician, he had to be on the alert at all times, but if there was one thing he understood about the Killing Show, it was that it was absolutely safe now. You see, the organizers wouldn't dream of letting them die before they were done holding this theatrical funeral.

Bai Jing'an took the medical kit and said to Xia Tian, "Take off your shirt."

Xia Tian did as he was told, and Bai Jing'an went over to check on him. The bleeding had already stopped in most places, but the old wound on his lower abdomen had torn open and blood was oozing out non-stop.

"It needs to be stitched," he said.

Xia Tian picked up the sewing kit and handed it to him with a nonchalant expression.

"We still have some anesthetic left," Bai Jing'an said.

Xia Tian fiddled with the flower crown in his hands. "When I came to the Upper City, my situation looked terrible. I once told others I'd made a name for myself, but no one believed me except for my youngest sister. She wasn't even six years old then, and she believed everything I said. I said I'd make a flower crown for her to wear when that happened, and she was so happy that it was all she talked about every day."

His voice was very soft because he didn't want it to be picked up by a recording device; this was a private conversation. So, Bai Jing'an tried his best to look like he wasn't talking. He picked up a stone and bent a needle while tossing Xia Tian half a bottle of liquor from the backpack.

"We don't have enough anesthetic."

Xia Tian drank a mouthful. It was a strong liquor that didn't exist in the medieval ages. From how he took that swig, he seemed already accustomed to this sort of surgery.

"The day before the lot drawing ceremony, I got a call from her," he said. "She said momma was dead; beaten to death by a john. We all told her he'd beat her to death sooner or later, but she didn't believe us."

His breathing didn't even hitch when Bai Jing'an's needle pierced his skin.

"My sister said poppa was gonna sell her. She overheard him discussing the price. I told her to look for a friend...like most friends, they're unreliable, but they might take her in for a few days if she helped them out enough. At least they should have enough conscience for that, right? It's hard for me to imagine what'd happen to her if I died. I promised her I'd survive, come back for her, and bring her up here," he continued.

Bai Jing'an suddenly realized that he'd seen Xia Tian answer that call. It was in between training sessions, and it was an audio-only. Xia Tian had sat in the corner of the training room with his head leaning against the wall, as if trying to draw warmth and security from it. He'd looked exhausted. His voice was gentle but serious, full of soothing reassurance, but he was fiddling with a pocket knife, and the blade had cut his fingertip.

He stared at the crimson blood, his expression dark and cold.

Bai Jing'an had never seen him like that. Even in the worst situations, he could quickly decide what to do next. He was a maniac, and he definitely wouldn't mind going a little wilder and crazier.

Now he knew why Xia Tian was the way he was. He was making a promise he couldn't fulfill. He bluffed, promising a child he could fix everything, but he didn't have a single trump card in his hand.

But still, he confidently reassured the panicked little girl, as if he had never doubted for a second that he would escape death and everyone would live happily ever after.

Bai Jing'an felt a suffocating sensation in his chest. How in the world could there be such a torturous conversation, such an unbearable predicament?

"She really believed it all—the flower crown and the sunshine, a big house in the Upper City, and that things will take a turn for the better," Xia Tian said. "I always thought there was something wrong with her brain. That kind of hope...is too terrifying, too preposterous. You can't be like that, or you'll die a horrible death."

Xia Tian lowered his head, and some of his hair cascaded down. Meanwhile, the sky grew dimmer. Bai Jing'an couldn't get a clear look at his expression.

"In this world, you can't pin your hopes on anything," he said in a subdued voice.

Seeing the way he looked, Bai Jing'an felt like giving him some words of comfort—to tell him that things weren't that bad and it'd all get better. But he couldn't bring himself to voice any of it.

Because Xia Tian was right—this world was just that sad and cruel. Sometimes, you had to grab onto something to anchor yourself in place so that you wouldn't slip into the abyss, but everything within sight was so fragile.

In the end, Bai Jing'an merely cut the stitches and secured the bandage. After some thought, he patted Xia Tian on the shoulder.

Once the doctor was done digging the pit, they put the body in and stood there, wondering if they had to say a word or two. On television, they always had to give a eulogy during a funeral.

The doctor glanced at Bai Jing'an, but the tactician didn't seem inclined to say a word, and they were usually the ones who presided over the funeral. He stared at his toes, as if there was something notable to see there.

The suffocating silence lasted for over ten seconds. The doctor decided to stand in for the eulogy portion, so he stammered, "I...I guess I'll sing then."

And then he started singing. It was a song from *Son of Darkness*, a TV drama series he'd been following. The song was about the time the male protagonist went to save one of his friends; the guy eventually only recovered the body. The rescue had no hope of success from start to end, and he'd long known that, but he still went anyway.

This song wasn't all that famous, but he was moved by the tender despair the first time he heard it. It was the first song that came to his mind whenever someone died.

The doctor sang, "One warm spring morning, she kissed him and took him away. He lay in the bosom of the earth, where the trees rustle, like a child who has returned home. One clear summer night, she kissed him and took him away..."

The lyrics cycled through all the four seasons. The melody had a sort of singsong, folksy vibe. He wasn't sure if Latte would like it, though he thought Latte ought to be more than satisfied with the solemn scene of them standing and singing before his grave.

He was a little worried about being ridiculed before he sang, but it was apparent now that no one was in the mood to laugh at him.

They filled in the soil, and the doctor asked Xia Tian, "Do you want to say something? He was quite fond of you."

"He was fond of everyone," Xia Tian answered.

"Maybe say something," the doctor said. "Like...anything. We can't have no one saying a word."

Xia Tian threw him a gloomy glance and turned to look at this lonely grave—which had to depend on online votes to determine if it could remain intact.

"All right, then," Xia Tian answered. "Here lies Latte, buried in death. He was born in District T15 in the Lower City. I don't know who his parents are or if he ever loved anyone, and I guess no one knows or cares. This kind of person is just an appetizer on the Killing Show. His life was mediocre and worthless."

The doctor coughed once. He found Xia Tian's words inappropriate, but he couldn't muster up the courage to interrupt. Bai Jing'an just stared at the newly filled-in soil and said nothing.

"I didn't like him. I guess nobody did," Xia Tian continued. "He was destroyed. All his life, he was used and hurt by others, but he still wouldn't give up. He kept longing for something important or meaningful... Fools usually die that way.

"To be precise, he died to save me, even though I didn't deserve it. There are many things in this world worth dying for; a full meal more or less counts. But not me, for sure. Not the God of War prayer, either."

Xia Tian bent down and put the recovered and still-fresh flower crown that was now a wreath on Latte's grave. There was some blood on it, but Latte was dead; he wouldn't mind.

"Hopefully, they will allow him to be buried here after listening to your eulogy," the doctor said.

"He's dead. He's not going to be picky," Xia Tian replied.

The doctor swallowed back the words on the tip of his tongue and looked at Bai Jing'an, hoping he could say a word too. But their tactician was staring intently at the fresh soil on the grave. On noticing his gaze, he looked up and asked, "Are we done?"

"Yeah," the doctor replied wryly.

Bai Jing'an stood up, indicating that this matter was over and done with. He had a knack for making everything dull and boring.

"Then...are we going to find another place to hide?" the doctor asked.

"That's admittedly tough to do now," Bai Jing'an replied.

He looked up at the owl. Even after causing such a tragedy, it still hadn't flown away and was perched on the tree watching what was left of this squad and their silent funeral.

"What's wrong?" Xia Tian asked.

"They like you," Bai Jing'an answered.

Xia Tian froze for a moment.

Bai Jing'an turned to leave, thinking, *They want to see him, and they keep drawing the fight to him. I've got to tweak my plan.*

Xia Tian glanced at the owl, his face turning cold as he turned and left. After he took two steps, he suddenly looked back to blow a flying kiss choked with murderous intent at the owl.

Bai Jing'an really wanted to lunge over to grab his hand, yank it down, and drag him away from the robotic bird's line of sight. He could practically hear the cheers of the production team on the other side of the camera.

The chief director of the 199th Killing Show was called Yakovsky. That wasn't his original name, but he wanted to have something with more exotic vibe. Hair dyed yellow, he always carried the neurotic air of an artist and drank a lot of booze every day. Most of the time, he found the job to be mentally exhausting to the point of a mental breakdown, but booze made everything better. His occasional bouts of sobriety made his blood run cold, and he dealt with it with even more booze.

He was rich, but the GBC had his lifetime contract in their hands. This was no longer the era where you could flee somewhere far away after making enough money. You see, the company had to protect its own investments.

The largest of the screens before him cut over to the Flower Crown Cemetery—that was the name they'd just come up with for it. Latte's body was buried in the soil, covered in blood. An iron sword had almost cleaved him in half.

Yet another desperate man driven to the end of his tether, chasing the wrong light to make his way here—to money, promise, and comfort. And then he died in this huge, bloody, sticky web of corpses.

Xia Tian's three-man team was in the midst of passing through a sparse wood, and he could clearly see their expressions in several windows—especially Xia Tian's.

Their golden boy had already changed his clothes, but he didn't look particularly anguished. Yakovsky decisively switched to a background perspective with sad music as accompaniment—a slow version of the song *She Kissed Him*. It ought to be a little sorrowful just after a funeral, and they also needed to slow down the pace after the recent string of battles.

CHAPTER 05

MARKETING OF A STAR

The largest secondary screen before Yakovsky remained locked on Xia Tian's face.

He stared at it pensively. Compared to how cold-blooded, decisive, and mercurial Xia Tian was while killing people, the contours of his facial features were pretty soft; sometimes even appearing harmless.

And now, he was about to decide on the direction in which this new star would be molded.

He recalled the way Xia Tian spoke about his younger sister. Yakovsky knew he didn't want to be overheard, but technology was evolving, and when it came to the Killing Show, it would increasingly progress toward stripping you of your privacy. Discussions and sales of that particular video had hit a new, astounding high, and surely that said something about it.

Yakovsky drank another mouthful of booze. It was not until he forgot the feeling of sobriety that the gears in the chief director's mind began to turn as he considered who to make or break.

How to make, and *how* to break.

He looked at Xia Tian's handsome face on the screen and thought just how much he'd looked like he'd lost all hope. He'd stop at nothing to break free of this, and the desire burned in him like fire. It'd destroy him.

But before it destroyed him, Yakovsky had to make him.

He looked like he was going places, and he had good looks and a top-notch figure to boot... To someone like Yakovsky, the main thing was that he had a certain power in him, reminiscent of an excessively sharp, unstoppable blade.

People like this might very well be killed early, but they would never be overlooked.

If stripped of that thick layer of despair, sorrow, and rage, he'd probably be a gentle person, one who could protect something and would be at peace cooking for others in his pajamas, turning a house into a home... Although this was mostly wishful thinking on his part, a song named *Homecoming* had been lingering in Yakovsky's mind for these two days, and he couldn't shake it off. But this felt like a good idea. Iyashikei—or healing—was all the rage nowadays. Everyone in the Upper City had a lot of psychological trauma that needed to be soothed.

He brought up the communication interface and was about to issue instructions to Xia Tian's production team when Xia Tian whipped his head around in the synchronized video and threw a flying kiss at the owl.

His expression in that very instant gave Yakovsky goosebumps.

He wouldn't describe it as "extremely beautiful," although it was. The moment was dazzling. It teemed with murderous intent, and it was so brazen and powerfully impactful that it made one feel as if their personal space had been violated.

It took him a while to realize that he had subconsciously moved his chair back a few inches.

Feeling a little chagrined, he pulled his chair back and looked at the guy on the screen. This kind of person was essentially a criminal used for amusement and entertainment, but they always believed that they were special enough, that they could truly possess something...so it was really quite intimidating when they went all out to resist and fight to the death.

At that moment, his hatred and fury were like the glaring glint of a blade that was all too lethal.

How very splendid, this one star.

But he still wanted him to be a *healer*, and a decision that had commercial value was not an easy one to change.

Yakovsky noticed his hands shaking a little. He was used to it—that was the double effect of excitement and alcohol.

"Xiaoluo!" he yelled. He quickly searched for Xia Tian's data on the screen. Without even looking up, he continued, "Take *She Kissed Him* and add some kind of magnificent interlude to it. Come out with a video clip before prime time. I want it tender, sorrowful, and heroic—you don't need me to tell you who the protagonist is, do you?"

He didn't ask if they had the copyright to that song; no doubt they did. His chief editor said nothing and made an "OK" gesture before leaving with her orders.

Her name was Tian Xiaoluo. It wasn't her original name, which was so banal that the viewership ratings would drop if they were to voice it. Her black hair was charmingly braided over her chest, and she had a doll-like face, tweaked with a bit of help from non-surgical cosmetic surgery. Her dressing style even matched her name.

However, incongruous with her cutesy style, Tian Xiaoluo was extremely reticent. She also had a serious issue with substance abuse; she always kept some brightly-colored pills in her pockets, popping one into her mouth like they were candies whenever she felt vexed or troubled. It allowed her to forever work tirelessly without complaint. There would be no emotional issues, no nervous breakdown, and she wouldn't think about her ex-boyfriend who'd met a gruesome death on screen—hung by his opponent on the city wall for ten days. That was back in the 197th season, and GBC would occasionally broadcast it; it was one of the signature shots of that particular season.

Yakovsky knew she often threw up in the bathroom. She would also curl up in a corner and keep calling the guy she knew was dead. She was highly intelligent, but she acted as though the call would one day connect if she kept calling and calling.

But she never told anyone about this, and she had always done a good job on her work.

Yakovsky was glad she didn't say anything, because he certainly didn't want to talk about it. They handed out loads of hallucinogens at department parties precisely because they hoped the staff would say nothing and just keep their heads down and do their jobs.

It wouldn't solve anything, anyway.

If the doctor was worried that the Killing Show wouldn't like Xia Tian, it meant that he didn't know the first thing about the show. The Killing Show was not a program with a sense of shame. They only cared about one thing with their whole soul: viewership ratings.

Ratings determined everything. You could cuss all you wanted in front of the cameras. The fact that many people cussed and swore was a testament to the fact that these words reflected the voices of the masses, so it was welcomed. People would click to watch, comment, and spend money, and that was a good thing.

The Battle of the Flower Crown Cemetery was personally produced and approved by the chief director, Yakovsky, who also directed the broadcast.

At the time of Luo Qingtian's death, he was so dead drunk in the bathroom that he couldn't stand. Fortunately, the assistant director was an old hand and didn't screw things up. The bosses, however, didn't like that, so he psyched himself up for the new battle campaign and gave full play to his talents.

First, he held an all-nighter meeting with the staff from the division. Everyone agreed that Xia Tian was a promising talent, and that they had to immediately arrange a big event for him. Then, the group selected an opposing team and arranged for a battle encounter. It all happened within an hour.

The Killing Show had evolved from a small-scale work studio that provided rich people with entertainment into its present, highly commercialized status, and so it had its own set of rules. The rise and fall of its criminal stars happened swiftly, and you had to move fast in order to capitalize on their value in the shortest time possible.

As a professional, multiple award-winning director with a cabinet full of trophies, Yakovsky personally took charge of broadcasting the entire battle campaign. Under his direction, the battle was both magnificent and brutal, yet full of tenderness and sadness. It'd only just aired, and already it was considered a definite classic of the season.

Yakovsky closed his eyes. His effort was worthwhile, and he'd reaped the brilliant yet bloody fruit of his labor.

The images of the battle were still very vivid. It was like someone suddenly turning on a light in the darkness. Even if it was turned off immediately, the image would remain seared on the retinas.

What remained was those people's rage and sorrow, which gave this battle soul and depth. What's more, people liked things that were real—those were the things that held power. That was why it'd have appeal, and that meant it'd be popular, which in turn translated to high purchase rates and subsequently, financial gain.

This was the true essence of the Killing Show. Everything was merchandise on the shelves, dolls in the dollhouse. He couldn't think of any way out; just like it was with his own life, or the life of his chief editor. All you could do was borrow all sorts of things to piece your broken soul together as best as you could and keep working, hoping those specters would disappear on their own.

At that time, Yakovsky didn't know that his decision on Xia Tian in his drunken stupor would trigger a frenzy, nor did he know that this would be the most successful decision he'd ever make in this life. It rapidly took root in the Upper City and propagated like crazy to build a colossal, terrifying idol.

Although a creator of celebrities and god of destiny, Yakovsky was so drunk most of the time that he didn't know where he was and had to rely on alcohol to think things through. He couldn't stand the feeling of sobriety. All was now still on the battlefield for the time being, so he poured himself a glass of booze and got ready to drink himself dead drunk. In this line of work, you couldn't do without alcohol.

In a place unknown to Xia Tian's team, the purchase count for the Battle of the Flower Crown Cemetery video had already broken the seventy million mark, and it was still rising rapidly. In the world outside, countless people clicked to watch the battles unfold, and to post in the comment section and various discussion forums. Some even created derivative products—especially for Xia Tian, whose registered fans and relevant email subscriptions were growing at an exponential rate.

In reality, the stars were battered and scarred as they walked through the bloody woodlands, dispirited and sad. The

possibility of losing their lives any time hung over their heads like a dark cloud.

The trio took a while to find a large caved-in boulder with some climbing plants obstructing the view, making it an excellent hiding place for a short break.

Xia Tian sat in the moss-covered shade. The scenery here reminded him of the Lower City somehow—it was completely different, aside from the humidity, but he still thought of the Lower City. It was in his head, and he couldn't break free of it.

He picked a small cerise flower next to him and started to weave another flower crown. Now that he had experience, it looked a little better than the previous one. Bai Jing'an silently plucked a blue flower for him.

"The man I killed," the doctor started in a hushed tone, "was called Lan Qi. They were saying out there that he was getting married. I don't understand why anyone would want to marry someone in this line of work; maybe she just loves him very much. He also had a close buddy. You guys might have heard of him before; he's pretty famous... In the last season, they collaborated on quite a number of classic scenes, but this time he didn't get onto the same team as him. Three lot-drawing rounds, and not even once... I wonder how that guy is now. Maybe he's dead, but if not, he'll definitely come to seek revenge on us."

His voice was hushed, but he kept blabbering on and on without end.

"Players of the Killing Show shouldn't make friends, but there are always people who can't remember that. They think that life is only meaningful if you let yourself loose a little. And Lan Qi was exactly the type. He was even in a relationship... She must have seen it; saw how I killed the man she loves, as well as the expression in his eyes in his last moments. That was so... I had no choice...but I always think there must be something more than just this simple explanation, don't you think? 'I have no choice' sounds so stupid. There must be a more significant reason..."

He kept going on and on, but the other two were so exhausted that they didn't have the energy to tell him to shut up. He even pushed his luck and started crying. Even so, they didn't stop him. It reminded them that Latte was the one who used to do that.

Xia Tian stood up and went out. After a while, Bai Jing'an followed suit. Rummaging through his pockets, Xia Tian found a small apple and handed it to Bai Jing'an. The latter glanced at him and took it.

And so, they stood in silence outside. It was a tad more dangerous here, but Xia Tian knew that they didn't come out to talk. They just didn't want to stay under the boulder and listen to that guy cry.

CHAPTER 06

EASTER EGG

The next few days were uneventful.

Xia Tian and his team came across a few battles from afar, but did not join the fray. From time to time, they'd also come across some fallen corpses on the side of the road. The organizers wouldn't clear these away; those people wanted all too much for this to be a warzone of carnage and bloodshed. Imagine how exciting it would be to come across a corpse while walking!

One time, they ran into a guy who was on his own, and he shrieked his surrender and handed over everything he had. They let him go.

Another time they came across the ruins of a battlefield. One of the guys was surprisingly still alive, and he just curled up there and kept coughing up blood, making weird moaning and wheezing sounds. Rarely, there were players who would inflict this level of damage on a target and not kill them off. In all likelihood, it was the handiwork of some sadist—there were a lot of sadists in this place.

They gathered around and watched him for a moment.

"My god, just kill him already," the doctor said.

Xia Tian slashed his neck and asked Bai Jing'an, "Does this get us points?"

The doctor moaned, and Bai Jing'an answered, "Yeah."

Nothing else was worthy of mention.

According to Bai Jing'an, however, it was the calm before the storm. The production team was most likely in the midst of preparing something big for them.

This came ten days later.

By then, it was already the fourteenth day of the third round of the tournament. The doctor kept count every day, rejoicing and saying how much income he could bring to his family if he successfully survived the first round of the Pay-to-View match. He even said that going by the death count so far, the match should end smoothly, so there'd be no need for an extension.

They were crossing a grassy flatland when it happened. It was a good place for battle encounters; someone hiding in the grass would leave no visible traces, so the group proceeded with great caution.

If this was real life, they might've gotten a little lucky, but the Killing Show was like being in hell. Here, good luck didn't exist.

They passed through wave after wave of grass and came to an uninhabited village. It was empty, and there were a few still-fresh corpses lying in the corner. They looked in every room, but there was nothing they could use; obviously, looters had been here.

Not willing to give up just yet, the doctor continued his search. Xia Tian found a few antiquated coins under the kitchen counter. Although he knew these were reality show props, he still subconsciously stuffed them into his pocket.

At this point, he froze for a moment. "Did you hear that?"

"What?" Bai Jing'an asked.

"It sounds a little like..."

Xia Tian suddenly stopped and pressed his ear against the

ground to listen.

"...A lot of people heading this way."

They exchanged glances, then jolted to their feet and prepared for retreat. Xia Tian looked around.

"Where's the doctor?"

Xu Peiwen wasn't here. He'd wandered too far. Perhaps in the world outside, it wasn't all that far, but here, it was the distance between life and death.

As soon as Xia Tian and Bai Jing'an stepped out of the door, they saw two people. Both stood beside a house ahead of them. Dressed in red outfits with a style that resembled a uniform, they were easy to spot.

At the same time, those people also saw them.

Bai Jing'an quickly drew an arrow and nocked it, but it was too far for the crossbow to aim accurately. Xia Tian was surprised he knew how to operate such an ancient contraption.

The other party was also making a grab for his arrows, but he was a step too slow and Bai Jing'an's arrow hit him right in the chest.

Meanwhile, Xia Tian sped over to the other person and sidestepped to dodge their blade. Capitalizing on the force of the charge, he gripped the man's neck with both hands, threw him down to the ground, and severed his artery with one slash.

He turned his head and saw another body—the doctor's.

He was dead, curled into a small ball, looking increasingly frail and thin. He was still holding the sword he never got to use. His blood was still spreading on the ground, turning black. His limbs were contorted—it had taken him a while to die after being stabbed.

They hadn't heard a sound. It'd been too far away, and the Killing Show experts always knew how to keep their victims quiet before they died.

It was then he suddenly remembered that the doctor's name was Xu Peiwen. He hadn't gone to the particular effort of thinking about his name, since remembering it would be a waste of time—he'd die quickly, anyway. But when he did, Xia Tian suddenly realized that he remembered it clearly. He was a doctor who was in debt because he'd lost his job. He had a wife and a daughter. He once thought he could survive; after all, only two rounds were left.

Xia Tian also remembered what he'd said to his wife on the phone, quoting lines like, *"Sometimes, death brings hope. I'll never give up hope, so I'd rather die."* He even said that if his death could save his family, then he'd be happy to die.

But regardless of who he once was—what he said, what TV drama series he was a fan of—he was ultimately just an ornament on the field, one who provided a little bit of bloody thrill in areas where it didn't matter, just as the Killing Show hoped. This was all that people like him were good for on the field.

Bai Jing'an walked over and looked at the corpse for a few seconds, but it was only for a few seconds. Both of them simultaneously turned their heads—someone else was coming.

Another two soldiers.

This shouldn't happen in a survival match, yet they were appearing in droves now. It was definitely no coincidence.

Xia Tian swiftly hid behind the door, while Bai Jing'an kneeled behind the table on one knee, raised his crossbow, and fired an arrow at the person at the forefront. It struck him right in the lower abdomen.

His companion charged over, ready to tackle the sniper. When he rushed in, Xia Tian grabbed the door and smashed it into the other guy's head. When the other guy went down, Xia Tian grabbed his hair and slammed his head twice against the wall until he went still.

Xia Tian put the corpse down, his expression not letting up at all. He traded a quick glance with Bai Jing'an.

Outside, the wind picked up. Unexpected and intensifying, it was like an invisible army of thousands upon thousands of soldiers and horses thundering across the grassland. No doubt it was an army of phantoms; evil, cold, and malicious.

Bai Jing'an hurried out. The guy who had been shot was still alive, so Bai Jing'an pulled out his dagger and dealt a blow to the man's head. The man collapsed to the ground, dead. Without even a pause in his steps, Bai Jing'an continued onward. Xia Tian followed after him. They had to evacuate immediately.

But they had only just stepped out when *those* people showed up.

The wind was so strong that it was hard to hear their approach, so it looked like the army had simply materialized out of the grass. They wore soldiers' uniforms in a style similar to the earlier guys, with a somewhat oriental design. There were about thirty of them. The guy in the lead was riding a tall, white horse—yes, they had horses, but they were mechanical and, therefore, not edible.

Xia Tian reached for his sword, but Bai Jing'an grabbed his wrist. Xia Tian stopped mid-motion and stared at this group of people, his body taut with tension as he considered the odds of survival.

The guy in the lead looked down at them from above. His black hair lay loose over his shoulders. He was a handsome man, well-suited for his uniform, although god only knew if that was why he was the leader.

"This is the territory of the Grand Duke of Skymoat," the handsome dude said with a jaded look. "Given the..."

He paused for a moment, as though he'd forgotten his lines. Then he continued.

"...Given the various circumstances, soldiers in this territory have the right to arrest all trespassers and throw them into the dungeon to face trial. Do not resist. We would like to avoid unnecessary casualties."

He pointed behind him. There were four or five guys who looked to be captives for demonstrative purposes. Some looked fed up, while others tried enthusiastically to chat with the soldiers at the side. One even warmly raised a hand in greeting when he saw Xia Tian looking over at them.

Two soldiers with indifferent expressions and shackles in their hands stepped forth. Behind them, the troops stood ready with daggers drawn.

Xia Tian cast a glance at Bai Jing'an, who was still grabbing his wrist. He knew what he meant, but he wasn't sure why.

The other guy's expression was certain, however, so Xia Tian slowly let go of the hilt of his sword and let the two soldiers take away the weapon and put shackles on him. They shoved them to join the sparse group of captives.

"It's an Easter egg," Bai Jing'an whispered to him.

"What?" Xia Tian asked.

"Easter egg."

"I know the word, but..."

"The Asaijin Tournament System does this sometimes," Bai Jing'an explained. "They call it a survival match; you'll encounter a storyline if you enter a specific territory."

"Oh, so that's why it's called an 'Easter egg,'" Xia Tian said. "What a...fucking surprise."

He looked at the soldiers around them. These were probably players who'd drawn the lot to be NPCs in this Easter egg. He wondered if they'd also been surprised when they got their lots.

"This is a film studio, so it wouldn't be windy for no reason," Bai Jing'an went on to say.

Xia Tian nodded. Since it wouldn't be windy for no reason, then it meant there was a purpose. This bizarre weather was meant to mask the sound of the army—these people wouldn't take the initiative to kill on their own accord, since their job was to lead them to a specific location to partake in a storyline match.

Not making a move was the right decision.

Xia Tian glanced at Bai Jing'an. His only remaining teammate's eyes were downcast, looking meek and harmless, dull and unperturbed, as if he wasn't taking a gamble on the people that had just killed their doctor. Xia Tian remembered the way Bai Jing'an had looked when he killed earlier, when he thrust a blade into another guy's head and kept on walking without even so much as a pause.

Bai Jing'an was not at all the pacifist he was pretending to be. He was a venomous viper hiding deep in the mud, Xia Tian thought gleefully, ruminating over whom to kill first for a higher chance of a successful escape if someone among the troops were to change their mind.

The soldiers didn't find and take away the old coins in his pocket. Xia Tian coolly took one out. The edge had already been worn down until it was very thin, and it looked shabby as heck— a clear testament to the prop team's dedicated efforts. But often, you had to rely on shabby weapons to save your life.

When he noticed Bai Jing'an looking at him, he flashed him a dazzling grin. His teammate too, tugged at the corners of his mouth to wear an expression that looked like a smile.

A soldier with light yellow hair the color of straw walked over from the village. Scrunching his brows into a frown, he said to the leader, "They killed four of us!"

"Jesus, I really need a smoke," the leader said, but made no other comment. He tugged the reins, and the horse obediently turned around.

"They killed our people!" the guy with straw-yellow hair hollered.

"Not *my* people, anyway," the leader said. "I know you want revenge, but we have orders to bring them back alive. If there aren't enough of them alive, then we have to make up the numbers ourselves, so don't go around looking for trouble, okay?"

The man cast a hateful glare at Xia Tian and said nothing further, while the others kept up with the leading troops and headed in the other direction in a mighty display of force.

The wind gradually died down, and the sun set in the west, where the fake firmament of tournament grounds looked as beautiful as a dream.

To stand among so many people taking in the beautiful scenery without having to fight to the bitter end—now that was truly a novel experience in the Killing Show.

The group passed through the village and the large expanse of grassland. When the plot didn't call for fighting, the players' interactions were weary but amicable.

They soon entered an area that had never been marked on the map the organizers gave them. Xia Tian glanced at Bai Jing'an to signal the need to find someone to ask about the situation. The other guy looked back at him and signaled for him to be careful.

Xia Tian took two quick steps over to a captive at the side with a stalk of grass in his mouth and raised his chin at him in what could be considered a greeting. They'd nodded to each other before, and at a time like this, they could be considered acquaintances.

Xia Tian extended a hand to him. "Xia Tian."

"Saijo," the other guy responded and shook his hand.

"Know what's going on?"

"Can't say for sure," Saijo replied and glanced at a soldier next to him. "They said they've been serving as soldiers in the castle. Every day, the Grand Duke ordered them to grab people as sacrifices, and if they failed, they'd have to use their own people as substitutes."

"Sacrifices?"

"New show producer, new hobby."

"Bloody hell. We've only had to grab and fight for resources in the past, and now we need to act," another captive groused.

"Just our luck for encountering an Easter egg with a sacrificial plot," his teammate said.

"Who doesn't know how the game works?! Anyone they fancy will always run into it somehow!"

They all started complaining at once about how horrible it had been so far, with so many people dead—and such gruesome deaths at that—and how much effort they had to expend to barely escape with their lives. Then a guy acting as a soldier also butted in and joined the chat, talking about the celebrity squad he'd encountered in the second round, how he had to think on his feet, and how a certain someone had excellent marksmanship... Other than the end-of-tournament dinner part, the storyline match was probably the only other time the players of the Killing Show got along this well.

According to this guy, they were acting as "soldiers under the command of the crazy Grand Duke." Because life hadn't gone as this Grand Duke wished, he offered himself to a maleficent god and let evil contaminate the entire land. To obtain power, he had to sacrifice living people. This flavor of evil was like a vortex, with a gravitational force that drew outlaws from different eras to the area. The plot was pretty self-explanatory.

As the Killing Show's players, they were already darn unlucky. Now, they had even been drawn into a contrived space-time travel vortex to the medieval times. They really had the worst luck ever.

"So," Xia Tian said, "do we get to see a palace later?"

"Gothic-style. Super huge," another soldier said. "We've been 'slaves of the maleficent god' since our arrival. We go around capturing people, and if we fail, we have to remain there forever and receive the maleficent god's freaking eternal punishment."

"Eternal punishment?"

The man gave him a heavy-hearted look. "You don't want to know the details, I assure you."

That said, this Easter egg was extremely impressive. They saw the castle from afar. It overwhelmed their vision like a dark cloud crushing down on them. It was a work of architecture so colossal, it was as if all the roads in the world led to and ended here.

The building had been produced within the current year, yet the air hung heavy with a sinister, pervasive sense of foreboding and menace, as if primeval monsters lurked within.

Upon their arrival at the castle, the guy at the lead whom they called Doug abandoned his horse and ran off somewhere that was probably a tavern or similar. He'd been looking hungover and despondent the entire way here.

The soldiers took the captives to the dungeon. Given how magnificent the castle was, it was conceivable that the dungeon was equally luxurious. After all, this was the area where the story would mainly unfold.

The captives followed the soldiers through a long corridor with torches lit on both sides of the wall, each with an exquisitely carved devil-head pattern at the pedestal. The firelight lent a ghostly, eerie atmosphere to the surroundings.

After walking the entirety of the long corridor, the group

walked down a steep flight of steps, where the entire building seemed to veer farther and farther away from the regular world. The corridor and stairs were designed in a style that made it feel as if they were walking into hell, giving one a despairing sense of hopelessness.

Xia Tian caught the smell from afar: the smell of blood and decay.

Every one of his cells felt a miniscule shiver rock through it. He knew this smell—it wasn't the kind that was just for show.. Although it hadn't been around for long, it was definitely real.

People had died there.

Lots of them.

Soon, the soldiers led them to a circular underground hall. The ceiling of this place was almost twenty meters high. Not a single ray of light penetrated, making it clear they were deep underground. A huge chandelier hung overhead, with candles that blazed menacingly, casting flickering light.

Compared to the naturally-formed hall, the surrounding prison cells seemed much more manmade. There was already a dense collection of captured mercenaries locked within. Faint traces of blood could be seen on the bars, and there were instruments of torture hung up on the walls. The whole space felt very oppressive, like a place with an ancient, cruel history.

Xia Tian immediately spotted the rectangular sacrificial altar in the middle of the hall, inscribed with runic characters that looked like some kind of mysterious, evil curse from some foreign lands—probably the work of art direction. Blood had stained the stone black; clearly, far more than just one or two people had died here.

It was not so much a dungeon as it was an execution ground.

Nearly a hundred people were imprisoned in the surrounding cells, all unlucky enough to encounter the Easter egg segment.

The soldiers found a cell at random and shoved them in.

"What's this situation?" Xia Tian asked one of the soldiers who they'd gotten on familiar terms with on the way here.

"The kind the organizers like," the other guy answered as he locked the door to the cell. He sighed. "You'll get to watch a live show later."

"Live show?"

"You won't like it," another person in the prison said.

Xia Tian turned to look at the speaker. The handsome man leaned against the cell's wall, carrying an air of frivolous self-confidence like a cloak around him. Even though he was wearing old, worn-out clothes in a dungeon that reeked of blood, he still looked like he was at a high-end cocktail party.

There were four or five people in the cell, as well as an injured guy obscured in the darkness. His shoulder had been crudely bandaged twice over, yet blood was still seeping through. Someone seemed to have died earlier, as there was a large blackish-red bloodstain on the ground. Craved patterns and runic characters could be seen on the floor with a little help from the firelight. The blood extended a short distance along the grooves of the characters, as if they were written on the grounds of hell itself.

What happened next was the same old routine; everyone introduced themselves. The one who was putting on airs like a rich young master was called Vosen, and his profession was Warrior. The guy with silver streaks in his hair was a sniper named Grassblade, and so on and so forth. Had this been modeled after the modern world, they would probably also trade cigarettes, mobile phone numbers, and whatnot, but all that was being exchanged right now were complaints.

"Just why the fuck do the organizers have to do an Easter egg? Wouldn't it be better to just fight it out?"

"The hell; why'd they have to make such a big show of it? Too much money to spend?"

And so on.

"The rule of the entertainment industry is to keep innovating and bringing in fresh ideas," the one named Vosen suddenly piped up. "This looks pretty good so far."

No one paid him any heed. This topic would be welcomed at a dinner party, but it was annoying when the parties involved were going through it first-hand.

All this while, Bai Jing'an had not spoken; instead, he'd been surveying the cell. But he suddenly asked, "Any leads on how to get out of here?"

Everyone around them fell silent for a moment, probably not expecting him to ask such a question. Eventually, the sniper named Grassblade answered, "A few."

Bai Jing'an nodded and turned his head to indicate he was listening.

Later, it occurred to Xia Tian that since the Easter egg was in plot mode, the organizers naturally wouldn't let the group of players wait for death in their cells; there would be no viewability to speak of. There'd definitely be an escape route.

This suspicion was correct. For the next three minutes, those in the cell explained the escape plan to them.

The dungeon here was made of stone. Not long ago, they found a crack in a stone slab under the straw, and it went quite deep. Someone had put their ear to it to listen, and they could make out the sound of flowing water below.

"In other words," Vosen explained, "it's either an underground river or a sewer."

He had a smile on his face as he said it with clear articulation, knowing that he was saying an important line.

An oblivious young man beside him continued, "We tried

to pry the slab off, but it wasn't easy. It's heavy as hell, and we have nothing to use—"

He paused, and the sounds of the soldiers' footsteps rang from outside their cell. Orderly and imposing, it didn't sound like they were just taking a casual stroll.

The young man flinched, and the entire cell fell silent.

Guess this is the live show they were talking about, Xia Tian thought.

The grand appearance of the Grand Duke of Skymoat was pretty terrifying. First, a heavy rumble rang out from the main entrance. Light from the flames fell upon the ground, making his shadow extraordinarily huge. It was clear that he was wearing a thick fur coat. He ambled toward them, like a wild beast with a hunger and thirst for blood.

Those in the cell quickly covered up the floor with the straw and stood in front of the crack, acting like nothing had happened.

The Grand Duke walked into the hall, entering everyone's vision. Xia Tian realized he wasn't tall, and he was bundled entirely in fur. His complexion was pale, and his facial features were elegant, but there was something fanatical in his demeanor.

"As is customary, I have to say a few words to the subjects who step into my territory," he said in a hoarse voice that seemed to have been injured before. "Welcome. You're all going to become my eternal residents, a part of my land. Your blood and flesh will feed my castle and my power. You will be the subjects under my eternal youth and rule."

"Does anyone find him a little familiar?" Saijo asked from the back.

"It's Wei Ling," Vosen replied.

"Who?" Saijo asked again.

"Wei Ling, guys," the other guy replied again.

"That star?" the young man asked. He'd introduced himself earlier as Fang Youtian, a sixteen-year-old sniper.

"A clone, or maybe a cyborg, who knows?" Vosen said. "GBC has all of Wei Ling's extended rights of publicity. They can do whatever they want with him... You guys know about extended rights of publicity, right?"

"The comprehensive extended rights that cover everything related to one's appearance?" Fang Youtian said weakly.

"I don't think there's anyone who doesn't know."

Grassblade stared at the Grand Duke as the latter walked in. "I think he's mad. Normal people don't act like that."

"The Killing Show likes it a little insane. There are always a few crazies in classic scenes," Vosen said.

Xia Tian listened to this explanation of "comprehensive extended rights" with great displeasure, because all his rights were also being held by GBC. Back then, those people had dragged him out of jail, injected him with a stimulant, then shoved a pile of papers before him and stuffed a pen into his hand.

Xia Tian signed it without even reading. It wasn't like he had a choice.

He didn't have a single clue about the extension of personal rights and whatnot; he only knew that celebrities, or at least their faces, would often appear in the Killing Show. The show would also feature real monsters. He didn't expect the two things could be fused into a new product.

Of course, he'd still have signed even if he'd known, since he would never go back to jail. But that didn't mean he wouldn't have been extremely peeved about it.

The creature of unknown circumstances sauntered across the cell and said softly, "Now, I need someone to grace my sacrificial blood altar with their presence."

Everyone fell silent. Regardless of whether this product was a robot, a clone, a cyborg, or some other genetically modified monster, it held the lives of everyone else in its hands right this very moment. It stopped for a while in Xia Tian's cell, ecstasy written all over its face, its eyes glowing dark red in the shadows. Who knew what genes had been added?

Xia Tian was suddenly curious what this one-off creature was thinking. Was it really desperate for power and immortality regardless of the cost? Did it know it'd incinerate its entire soul, only to be a mere commodity for purchase?

Xia Tian clutched the thin piece of metal in his hand. Its edges were so sharp that they dug into his palm.

But then the creature walked away and strolled toward another cell.

It was in this way it unhurriedly walked past all the cells, looking into each one for a moment, inducing an atmosphere of terror and looking like it was enjoying the process.

Eventually, it stopped once again by Xia Tian's cell. It reached out and pointed at a person.

Everyone in the cell froze, then cautiously looked around to determine who it was pointing at.

Three seconds later, everyone swiftly moved away from the area, revealing the person at the back.

Xia Tian hadn't even noticed him before. He was dressed in clothes so filthy that it was impossible to make out their original color. He hadn't spoken a word or introduced himself to them before. Instead, he'd curled up in the corner of the cell like a large heap of garbage.

Seeing the Grand Duke of Skymoat's action, he shook his head desperately and ducked to the side to avoid that lethal finger. The Grand Duke wore a smile of enjoyment—what exactly did they add to his genes?—as it cackled and continued to point at him with a slender fingertip.

After a brief spell of silence, a soldier called out to the guy, "You, come here."

The guy curled up in the corner and refused to cooperate, remaining still as he kept his eyes closed and muttered something. The soldiers were apparently very familiar with this lack of cooperation. One tall soldier instructed the prisoners in the cell to put their hands out, which he cuffed to the bars before entering to grab the guy.

While everyone in the cell was now a player and a star, most of them had been in prison before. They knew the procedures, so they cooperated and let the wardens lock them up. Then they watched as two soldiers entered the cell and forcibly dragged the guy out.

He struggled desperately and screamed frantically, completely falling apart as he kept yelling that he would surrender and do anything they asked of him. He looked like one who'd been grabbed from the animals-for-consumption cage to be slaughtered.

Those around watched the scene unfold with cool detachment. From their brief conversations and exchanges of glances, Xia Tian knew the guy was not on familiar terms with them and did not belong to any team. Besides, this situation was so common it wasn't worth kicking up a fuss.

Vosen, who was handcuffed next to Xia Tian, watched the unfolding scene with calm and composure. Fang Youtian, the sixteen-year-old sniper, was staring at his toes, looking like he was about to cry.

"He's on the blacklist," Saijo comforted him.

"What?" Fang Youtian said.

"He surrendered before," Saijo explained.

Momentarily taken aback, Fang Youtian nodded, although he didn't look all that much reassured.

Every Killing Show player knew this unspoken rule, which they must never violate no matter what. The organizers hated it when someone surrendered in the Killing Show, but they couldn't ban it, so they tried every means possible to retaliate and make it a truly impossible option.

That was the deadly blacklist.

Once you got on the list, the organizers would very quickly send you to your doom. You could be used to liven up the show, or to garner more capital for the more popular stars. Sometimes, they'd even make an effort to employ clever editing techniques and make you look like a cowardly villain who eventually met his end at the hands of the hero, thus creating a small climax where evil gets its just desserts.

But even though you'd most likely end up dying tragically and getting spurned by millions of people when blacklisted, there were still countless people screaming to surrender when it came to the crunch.

And now, they were seeing "retribution" carried out live.

The soldiers dragged the surrenderer out of the cell and threw him onto the sacrificial altar, where they got a clear look at him losing control of his bladder.

A guy in the cell next door yelled, "Pissing altar!"

Several people laughed, but the fear saturating the air did not dissipate.

With practiced moves, a guy in a black, cult-like robe handcuffed the other guy to the altar. The latter struggled desperately, but to no avail. The guy in the black robe was very proficient at his job.

A soldier walked over and uncuffed Xia Tian and the others, but they didn't notice. Everyone was staring at the altar.

The field of vision here was excellent. For a moment, silence reigned all around.

"They keep screaming so horribly," Vosen said in an intrigued tone. "You know, there's a quote from *Origins of the Killing Show* that says screams like these were helpful for ratings—they come from the heart and create an authentic atmosphere of savagery and cruelty that can't be mimicked by acting. And, of course, the most appealing part of the Killing Show is its authenticity."

Xia Tian glanced at him. Noticing his gaze, Vosen turned to look at him too and gave him a haughty smile.

"Xia Tian... You're from the Lower City, right?" he asked. "It's quite an imaginative name."

Xia Tian flashed him a dazzling smile. "I think so too."

Saijo grabbed a soldier who had yet to leave through the bars. "What's this about?"

Xia Tian glanced at him. The sacrifice on the altar screamed desperately, so much that his voice became hoarse in no time.

"Let me go," he cried. "I have information! They're thinking of escaping—"

The guy in the black robe deftly picked up a piece of coal from the stove beside him, forced the sacrifice's jaw open, and shoved it into his mouth. The sight of this silenced even the battle-hardened players in the hall. The sacrifice opened his mouth wide, but could no longer scream.

Eerie silence enveloped the dungeon. After a while, the sacrifice started making intermittent noises which sounded extremely odd—like those of an animal, and not at all like a human.

Perhaps the live coal was not quite fully scalding; the organizers still hoped he could scream.

The Grand Duke of Skymoat, with his celebrity looks, walked over to the sacrifice with a fanatical and cruel smile.

Then came the prolonged sadistic torture and killing. The

process was highly gory and bloody. Xia Tian knew there'd be some...restricted content on the Killing Show, but he'd never seen anything like this.

The dungeon was like VIP seats for the sacrifices, and what they'd witnessed had far exceeded the acceptance level of the average person. It reached a level of inhumanity.

Someone in the cell threw up. It was impossible for such a scene to be broadcast on TV, but...Xia Tian suddenly realized that there must be someone watching.

The torture process was too meticulous, awfully long, and professional to be required by the plot. It was definitely geared toward a specific viewer group.

The Grand Duke of Skymoat was a professional, and the guy in the black robe—also a talent in the industry—worked in tandem with him. Both of them were adept at controlling their rhythm to ensure that the prisoner being tortured wouldn't die.

On the sacrificial altar, the Grand Duke moved with precision, and his expression was one of madness and enjoyment. This bloody act was extremely detailed, and it came with its own set of standards.

On the other hand, the guy in the black robe looked more like a skilled practitioner. His timing in stuffing the coal piece had been exact. Even though he knew this wasn't a real dungeon, he still wouldn't allow the one being tortured to betray the others and beg for mercy. This was a show—no matter how hard you tried, your role was already predetermined. You were the fellow who was meant to suffer a fate worse than death on the altar, sacrificing yourself to entertain the public.

Watching the sadistic torture play out, Xia Tian felt like there was a saw grating on his nerves, stretching something in his brain tauter and thinner to the point it was about to snap.

This kind of thing would destroy a part of your brain. It

wasn't a matter of drinking a few glasses of booze or taking hallucinogens; you'd never be the same again.

Everyone hoped the torture would end quickly, but there was no end in sight.

Someplace out of sight, eyes watched with concentration and relish.

Maybe they're top-tier members with unique fetishes, Xia Tian thought. They'd be someone with enough power, and with enough money to pay to see and hear all of this—from the flaying of skin and flesh to the screams that didn't sound human...every single detail.

Deep down in his heart, Xia Tian knew the darkness of human nature. It was what he'd done his utmost to escape from in the Lower City. But when he came to the Upper City, where the sun shone bright upon an idyllic scene of springlike charm, he realized that this place was just as much as a nightmare. He'd only exposed more of himself to such desires, putting himself at their mercy like a fish on the chopping board.

He stood behind the prison bars and looked at the red, bloody thing on the sacrificial altar, thinking it was more of a stage than a torture platform. Carrying out the act *there* had been to ensure everyone could see it.

This was the kind of place they were in.

Someone in one of the cells started to jeer and hoot, although there was nothing to raise a din for. They probably wanted to occupy themselves and drown out the screams with laughter, but it didn't work.

The guy being tortured was no longer screaming, but even so, it was hard to overlook.

Blood flowed down the thin grooves on the sacrificial altar through layers of runic symbols and patterns, resembling a slowly blossoming flower in the firelight. This thing had been meticulously designed with colors so bewitching it could suck one's soul in.

Eventually, even the last breaths and moans of the human figure on the altar vanished. Silence descended.

Someone in the dungeon said, "This is what you get for dragging down the ratings!"

Someone laughed, but most didn't. The one who'd spoken must have wanted to make a joke, but his voice was so dry and hoarse it didn't sound like a joke in the slightest.

Someone in the dungeon threw up. Xia Tian had almost puked his guts out when he first made his appearance, but now, there was no such urge. He simply stared fixedly at the sacrificial altar, clenching the piece of metal in his hand. Its sharp edges left fine bloodstains on his fingers.

All this time, Bai Jing'an had been watching soundlessly. Xia Tian could barely even hear his breathing. Then he suddenly reached out a hand and patted Xia Tian on his shoulder before turning away to the inside of the cell to look at that underground passage.

Xia Tian stepped away from the bars. He knew what Bai Jing'an meant: *it won't be us.*

Not long ago, they had just been through a brutal battle and caught the production team's attention. They had viewership value, so they wouldn't die in such a way.

With his draping furs and celebrity looks, the Grand Duke made a stately exit, looking very much satiated. Meanwhile, the guy in the black robe and a few other soldiers cleaned up the scene.

Whispers resumed in the cell again. Someone in the cell next to them said that no one knew who the next sacrifice would be. At times like this, you could only hope that there were still people in the dungeon who had been blacklisted. If not, anyone—other than the celebrities—could be next.

It was at this moment Xia Tian suddenly realized the significance of being stars in the Killing Show. The players had to climb to the top at all cost. Just like your own skills and abilities, it was concrete life insurance. If you weren't popular or cool enough, you'd be treated as a sacrifice, a sacrificial lamb to the twisted desires behind the scenes. Someone to be killed before the cameras in the most brutal way possible.

The organizers kept saying that this was the time to test your courage and wisdom, but no one could ever escape from these sacrifices.

This was no battle.

It was merely entertainment.

CHAPTER 07

ART OF FABRICATION

The clean-up of the sacrificial altar was completed. Under the firelight, the bloodstains on it looked almost black, while the stench of excrement—which viewers couldn't smell through their screens—hung in the air.

"It's my first time coming to the live scene. The stench's really horrible. It's better using the virtual terminals," Vosen said. "This is definitely going on *Plunge into Hell*... They say the spots where the players are positioned are the VIP seats, but the air quality here is just too terrible. After this is over, I have to tell those fellas that it's better to stay on the boat and watch the 3D models instead of letting their curiosity get the better of them."

Fang Youtian looked at him with an expression of awe. Vosen didn't belong here; he could leave any time. He had that air about him, which they could make out at a glance.

"Wow, you have a boat," Xia Tian said.

"That's right, I have a boat," Vosen said. "A Barque. I guess you don't know what the heck that is, but the members of your family are all very imaginative, anyway."

"Bones," Bai Jing'an piped up.

Everyone turned to look at him. He stood before the crack on the floor and continued speaking without looking up.

"Bones are hard enough to wrench this open."

Someone at the back queried weakly, "Tactician?"

"Great." Vosen turned to look at the injured man. "Who shall have the honor of putting an end to this guy's suffering?"

The man's eyes widened in horror. "Wait a minute, I'm just mildly injured—"

No one paid him any heed. The injured had no say in such discussions.

Xia Tian didn't even glance at him. Instead, he stared at Vosen and asked, "Do you think you're the boss here or what?"

Arching his eyebrows, Vosen straightened up and took a threatening step toward Xia Tian. Everyone around them took a step back. They all knew how this would play out. It was a classic fight for control in prison.

"If you want to change it up, your tactician's not a bad choice," Vosen said.

He glanced at Bai Jing'an. The tactician was filthy; the cuffs and hems of his clothes were stained with blood. It'd gotten on him earlier when Latte died.

Xia Tian was still staring at him. Vosen glanced at the injured guy again, wanting to snap back with a few words to show that he wasn't someone to be taken lightly. Players did that all the time. In places like this, you couldn't show weakness.

Xia Tian took a sudden step forward and walked over to Vosen. His expression was quite relaxed, not unlike the expression of any young man looking for a little trouble.

Vosen subconsciously reached out to block his advance. This looked to be the start of a typical prison brawl. There were many such fights in the Killing Show, and he was confident he'd be pretty good at them.

Xia Tian parried his hand away and used the momentum to wrap an arm around his neck. Something in his hand slashed across his neck.

His movements were swift and stealthy. Following right after, he released his hand and took two steps back. Vosen stood bewildered as everyone looked at him. He touched his neck and looked at his hand. It was covered in blood.

Standing two steps away, Xia Tian looked at him coldly. Blood dripped from the edge of the metal in his hand. The coin was a little blunt, but it was enough to kill a person if enough force was used.

Blood spurted wildly from his artery. Vosen finally realized he'd been attacked, but he didn't quite understand why this was happening... He charged at Xia Tian, and the latter deftly took a step back and smiled at him.

That smile reminded Vosen of some wild animal he'd killed before. Exceedingly beautiful, but its expression had been one of pure hostility. The animal had looked at him with terrifying malice, watching him as he panicked and frantically tried to do something about it.

But Vosen didn't know what he could do. He staggered forward, trailing splotches of blood on the stone slabs. Everyone stepped away from him, most of them looking like this was all too common.

No. They stood in a circle, watching his death play out.

Vosen still couldn't be sure what had happened. He was already in the final moments of the third round. He was sure he had made a small name for himself out there, given his performance. Everyone knew the stars of the Killing Show were the coolest of all celebrities these days; they could throw their weight around whereever they went, spend money however they pleased, bed anyone they wanted... Everyone would make way

for you, because you were a real villain.

He was also familiar with the Killing Show, and he even interned at GBC as a producer for a time. He knew all the rules, and his immersive simulation training scores were always very high. He knew the wonders and dangers of this world. He didn't understand...

He stumbled around the cell for two more rounds before he finally couldn't walk anymore. He dropped to his knees and slowly fell to the ground. In the end, he never figured out what'd happened.

Everyone gathered around and watched as the blood gushed out of his body. The life in his eyes faded away, and then he died.

The injured guy who had thought he was a goner watched this scene, looking like he couldn't wrap his mind around it.

Xia Tian looked at the others. Tossing the coin in his hand, he quipped, "These are our bones right here, yes?"

Yakovsky gaped at the latest developments on the screen, dumbstruck. He guessed there were stunned faces out there too, flummoxed over the situation.

Several thoughts collided chaotically in his alcohol-abused brain, one of which stood out particularly: *You little punk; I knew you were a psychopath and would give us huge spike in viewership ratings. Can't believe you really had the fucking gall to do it!*

The call icon at the bottom of the screen kept flashing. The Vosen family was a shareholder of GBC's Channel 7, so they must be calling in to demand that he take out that little bastard in the most miserable way as soon as possible, but GBC had so many shareholders that this sort of call was completely meaningless.

Xia Tian was already on the Killing Show. How much more miserable could it get?

A little hallucinogenic in their drinks would help them deal with the problem, Yakovsky thought, *What's one dead son to them, anyway?*

He threw his head back and downed all the booze in the bottle, then stared at the screen and let his mind go blank for a few seconds before switching the broadcast rights over to his terminal.

This segment was going to be broadcast in ten minutes, and he had already found a starting point for the killing. He switched the camera over to Bai Jing'an.

Bai Jing'an had no reaction whatsoever to this sudden attack. His attention was on the stone floor. But that was okay; give him a close-up, and the shot itself would represent a reaction. The viewers would interpret it in their own ways. And besides, in scenes like these, you can always capture something if you put the shot in slow-motion.

Yakovsky sized up Bai Jing'an. He was quite good-looking, but there was apparently no chemistry between him and the camera. At the very least, he was making sure of that himself.

Smart guy. A pity there's no escaping the cameras when you're here.

He slowed down the shot and saw a flash of an expression on Bai Jing'an's face when Xia Tian killed Vosen in slow motion—one that said, *"Good grief, here we go again."*

Yakovsky continued to stare at the screen. When the severely injured Vosen charged at Bai Jing'an, Xia Tian lifted a hand to grab and steer him out of Vosen's path.

He smiled. This was what he wanted. You had to have a reason; the viewers needed to know your motivations.

Yakovsky didn't know why Xia Tian killed Vosen. Maybe he was a quintessential fucking crazy kid; there were too many crazies these days. But that was okay, he would find a reason for him.

After a moment of awkward silence, Saijo said, "Uh, which bone would be better to use? I recommend the ribs. Bones from the arms or legs are too...hard to handle."

The others voiced their agreement. Even if Vosen's teammates were among them, no one expressed their views or objections. No one looked Xia Tian in the eyes, either.

Five minutes later, things got a little bloody—the kind where you had to pay more to watch the full version.

The criminals supplied weapons they had privately concealed, and Grassblade actually brought out a pair of pliers and half a blade. The group cut open the corpse's skin and extracted the bones. Two of them threw up in the middle of it, but at least it was finally done.

Xia Tian looked at the corpse's handsome face. A satisfied smile spread on his face; almost gentle, but also malicious and cold-blooded.

This smile later became one of Xia Tian's most renowned expressions.

The moment Yakovsky saw this scene, he knew that this was what he wanted. It was the face of one who had been suppressing great fury and hiding boundless darkness, yet it was also so dazzling and bright that it felt unsettling. And this downright psychopathic expression was particularly suited for his motivation: to protect a person.

Of course, Yakovsky didn't know if Xia Tian wanted to protect Bai Jing'an. Maybe he did, or maybe he didn't give a damn at all. He didn't know what Bai Jing'an was thinking, either. Even in slow-motion, that guy's expression was still tough to decipher.

But he didn't care.

This was the Killing Show, and its true essence—the core of its core—was the art of fabrication.

In the cell, Saijo asked Xia Tian, "Do you know his background?"

"A rich guy," Xia Tian replied. "How's his sailing game; do you know?"

Saijo glanced at him. Grassblade replied, "Probably not bad. He said he belonged to the Skymirror Lake Sailing Club, and he was only three hulls behind Georg in the last season's race."

"He can't go boating on the lake anymore. What a pity," Xia Tian said.

"Can the conversation not be so morbid?" someone at the side said.

They completed their work in an almost light-hearted atmosphere, and no one spoke of Vosen, as if they'd come to a sort of tacit understanding; it was as if his death was only to be expected.

The outlaws very quickly finished their work. Shoving the bones into the crack, they worked together to pry open the stone slab.

A burst of water vapor assailed them from the darkness below. Xia Tian jumped down first. He landed in a body of water with icy-cold currents that didn't go higher than his ankles. The area felt wide and spacious.

He looked up and gave Bai Jing'an a hand when the latter jumped down too. Next up was Saijo, who looked around.

"A sewer?"

It was indeed a sewer, although a particularly crudely made one that seemed to be temporarily built, based on the terrain.

It wasn't all dark around them, either. Moss climbed on the stone walls on both sides, emitting cold, green light. It made the entire space look grim and spooky, as if they were in an alien world.

Xia Tian moved closer to examine the walls. Strange

patterns were faintly visible, part of the same system as the sacrificial altar. It seemed like the castle had been built on top of an older and weirder structure, and they were standing in its subterranean area.

The sixteen-year-old sniper threw the bone into the water as soon as he hit the ground and anxiously attempted to wash his hands clean.

Saijo glanced at him. "You'd better pick it up."

Fang Youtian looked up at him uncertainly, and Saijo explained, "We don't have any weapons, and we don't know what we might encounter."

The boy stood in place for two seconds before he silently fished out the bone from the water. In this line of work, you didn't have the right to feel disgusted.

The injured guy jumped down last. His mobility seemed to still be okay.

After discussing for a whole, the group determined the direction of the main gate. Hopefully, going that way would allow them to leave the area through the sewer system. But it seemed rather unlikely—they were prey who had entered the maze, and it was impossible for them to leave without being put through some intense stimulation. However, there was no other way.

The power of choice had never been in their hands, after all.

CHAPTER 08

UNDERGROUND PALACE

The group walked in the direction of the main gate, but a couple steps later, Xia Tian abruptly came to a stop.

If they still had their weapons with them, the sound of swords being drawn—or even better yet, the sound bullets being loaded or energy weapons being activated—would be audible right this moment. But now, there was only a silence that underscored just how unarmed and defenseless they were.

A hideous and mutilated face loomed in the darkness, its neck greedily stretching forward, its tongue sticking out.

"Fuck!" Xia Tian swore.

The others followed suit and swore too. Only when they got a closer look did they realize it was an ancient statue with a human-like face and an avaricious, malicious expression. Realistically modeled and engulfed in darkness, it was a scene right out of a horror movie.

They carefully walked around it. Even though they knew it was a statue, they still felt ill at ease.

There were such statues at regular intervals along the way, and some were still perfectly intact and lifelike. Xia Tian didn't want to know what the organizers had in mind for these things, but the answer would probably still be shoved into his face when the time came.

"Let's introduce our professions," Bai Jing'an said.

"Sniper," someone said.

"Cyber support," another said in a self-deprecating voice.

"Another sniper here."

All in all, there were two warriors, four snipers, one cyber support, one mechanic, and one tactician—who was Bai Jing'an.

"Not too shabby," Saijo remarked sarcastically.

They continued onward. Not long later, they left the watery underground area and the sewer space widened.

It no longer looked much like a sewer; the rocks were no longer as rugged, having clearly been retouched and finished. The ceiling was higher, resembling an ancient underground corridor that had never seen the light before. Green and red moss emitting a cold, gloomy glow still grew on damp places.

All of these were props which GBC had commissioned Gene Studio to create in the early years of development of the underground plot. Where there was a lot of glowing red moss, the horror level of the entire area would kick up a notch, and the place would become truly dangerous. Props could always accurately reflect the direction in which the plot developed.

The scene grew more and more bizarre as they continued onward. By now, they had completely entered the ancient architecture beneath the castle.

Xia Tian looked up at the statues in front of him. They were grotesque figures five to six meters tall, with thin arms holding up the ceiling, looking much like an archway. The tongues of both statues stretched out long in the air. Red moss grew all around the tongues, making it look like the statues had yet to wipe their mouths clean after consuming raw human flesh.

Dark red sewage water kept running down from the tips of their tongues, giving the statues a particularly gross appearance.

The group simultaneously stopped in their tracks and stared.

"Maybe we're on the wrong track," Fang Youtian said pleadingly. "Can we not go in?"

"I get what you mean. This doesn't seem like a route that'll get us out alive," Xia Tian said.

"Let's put it this way," Bai Jing'an chimed in. "This gate was built exactly for us to enter."

They lamented in silence in front of this terrifying landscape for a moment before they resigned themselves to their fates and walked in.

In no time, they walked into an underground palace.

The space around them grew increasingly spacious, and even more statues and decorations appeared. This place had been abandoned for a long time, and the castle had temporarily converted a tiny part of it into a sewer. But the architecture itself was even more sprawling, reaching even deeper and wider into the deepest recesses of the darkness where god knows what lurked within.

The only good news was that they'd found several ancient skeletons in the corner—although they certainly weren't actually old. A few long spears made of bones were scattered beside them. No one wanted to know exactly where those bones came from, but at least they could replace the bloodstained, poor-quality ones in their hands. They were in dire need of weapons.

As they continued on, everyone sensed the stench of rotting flesh and wild creatures hanging in the air. It was so thick that it was impossible to ignore when they passed through certain areas.

Saijo scratched the plantain herb tattooed on his arm. Supposedly, he'd gotten it tattooed when he first arrived in the

Upper City. He'd found it trendy when he first saw the plant, but later, he regretted not tattooing something rarer.

"There must be something else here."

"And it's by no means small," Xia Tian remarked.

The scattering of people sparingly expressed their agreement. Anyone who lived in the Lower City could tell from the smell that it was the scent of predatory creatures in the darkness.

They proceeded cautiously, getting into squad formation almost naturally. Xia Tian walked at the forefront, with Bai Jing'an behind him. This action also came naturally. Similar scenarios would quickly develop in team-based Killing Shows. You'd naturally start to walk beside a particular person and grow accustomed to seeing him with every turn of your head.

Their surroundings had already taken on the shape of some ancient pagan god's palace. Spacious and massive, it'd been eroded by the humidity, and the faint glow of the mosses lent a dreamlike quality to the underground architecture.

The only thing worth mentioning was that they found two other bodies that weren't too badly decomposed in a corner. From the looks of their outfits, they seemed to be soldiers of the castle who had already been dead for some time. They didn't know if it had to do with the "eternal punishment" thing, but they finally got to upgrade their weapons, as there were two rusty swords next to the corpses.

Given that they had two warriors in the squad, the swords went to Xia Tian and Saijo. Xia Tian privately thought this thing would break if it struck something more solid, but he didn't have the luxury of being choosy at this point; the rest were still in the age of spears forged from bones.

They badly needed weapons. The illumination here was weird—the scattering of light from the moss made the darkness even darker and disparities in visual perception more likely to occur. It was a good place for ambushes.

As Xia Tian saw it, they were stepping into a huge trap, a prime hunting ground for creatures of the dark.

And they were the feast.

It really lived up to its name as a mega Easter egg.

They were passing through a walkway when it happened. The walkway, nearly six meters wide, was flanked by beautifully carved stone columns on both sides. The style did not resemble that of underground architecture, and some installations were clearly used for lighting.

Xia Tian sized up the stone statues around them. Their clothes, though elegant, were incongruous with their avaricious and twisted faces. Occasionally, exquisite earrings could be seen on their monster-like pointed ears. It was as if the statues were originally something brighter and more refined, but one day, they suddenly turned malevolent and monsters grew from their bodies and deformed their slender limbs into something more grisly.

This must be some kind of profound setup, Xia Tian thought. *The art designers of the Upper City sure are professionals.*

He wanted to say something, but then, he decided to drop it. All he could think of was the bloody scene on the sacrificial altar earlier. The omnipresent yet invisible cameras made him nervous. It was like he was naked and being studied by a group of people bearing knives and forks in their hands.

If the previous two rounds were free-for-all melees, then it became clear to Xia Tian by the third round just what kind of ingenious and extreme method those behind the scenes would employ to kill off the players one by one.

The ones really killing people here were not their opponents or the cyborgs—it was the cameras.

It was at this time they ran into that *thing*.

They were walking across a hall where statues of the

maleficent god were visible everywhere. The statues looked like they would crawl off their pedestals in the darkness and pounce to devour them.

The creature had obviously been hiding in the darkness observing them for quite a while, and as they approached, it sprang out suddenly from behind the remains of a wall. Fast as lightning, its target was evident as it charged towards Grassblade, who had deviated slightly to the left from the formation.

Reacting swiftly, Grassblade jumped to the side, but it was too late. It missed his throat, but bit hard through his right shoulder at the same time it slammed into his body. Grassblade fell to the ground, screaming as blood spurted and his shoulder dislocated. The creature dragged him toward the darkness.

Xia Tian was right beside Grassblade, but didn't get a clear look at what the creature was. He cleaved his sword down at its head. In the ensuing chaos, he felt the blade strike bone. Xia Tian heaved down diagonally, and the blunt sword cut through with difficulty. But then, he felt a change in sensation at the edge of the blade—

Xia Tian jerked the sword back and thrust hard into that spot. The unidentified creature let loose a blood-curdling scream and twisted its body fanatically, but in the next second, the sword broke.

Xia Tian fell to the ground, still clutching the broken sword in one hand. The creature loosened its grip on Grassblade and let out a baby-like wail as it receded into the darkness.

Grabbing Grassblade by the back of his collar, Xia Tian dragged him back, but the moment he saw him, he knew the guy was a goner.

Xia Tian let go. There was a long trail of blood in front of him. Someone ran over to check on Grassblade's injuries. In the span of a few seconds, the sniper's right arm had almost been yanked entirely off.

It seemed like the surprise attack had come to an end, but something was definitely wrong. There was some sort of smell in the air...

Everyone froze in place, staring at a specific spot in the darkness.

The monster had not fled. Instead, it was crouching on the side of the hallway.

They finally got a good look at it. It was a ghastly white behemoth with wrinkled skin, covered in sparse fur and filth. It was about two meters tall, and one of its dirty dark red eyes had a broken sword stuck in it. It crouched there like a human.

Most in the squad recognized the creature at a glance. A mutated, furless rat...and three times bigger than the ones in the Lower City.

Xia Tian had seen its kind during the massacre in District N—some of the things were still scurrying around in the sewers. It truly was the case that scourges lasted for a thousand years— and he'd thought he'd seen the last of them. But apparently, there was a market for ugly, crazy, and deadly stuff everywhere.

The group stared at the creature. Their weapons were so inadequate that pathetic couldn't even describe them. Grass-blade was still screaming. The stench of blood pervaded the air, and although the air was warm and damp, everyone was chilled to the bone.

The creature crouched there like a deformed human figure, twisted thanks to this game from hell. The next second, it charged over again at a speed so fast it seemed at odds with its huge body.

This time, it went for Saijo. Xia Tian tightened his grip on his sword, ready to rush over, when he heard Bai Jing'an's voice.

"Xia Tian," he said, his voice a little tight.

Xia Tian turned his head.

The mutated rat swept past him, bringing a gust of fetid wind in its wake. At the same time, Saijo's long sword stabbed fully into the mutated rat's nose and broke into two, just like Xia Tian's sword—*just what the fuck is this quality?!*

It let out a wail, did a partial roll, and retreated back into the darkness. But Xia Tian was too preoccupied to bother with it. With eyes wide, he looked at the thing poking its head down from the ceiling.

Crawling silently out of the darkness, it had countless legs, and there was no telling how long it was. It looked like a variant of a centipede, and it was really...fucking...long...

"Uh, Saijo?" Xia Tian called out.

Saijo finally chased off the mutated rat, which could be considered a major victory of sorts—after all, it was impossible to take it out with a sword like this.

Then he turned his head and saw the creature crawling toward them overhead.

Dead silence reigned all around for a few seconds.

When something like this happened, the entire area would take on a different atmosphere. You could sense it in the air— the certain kind of sound that came infinitely close to the breath of death approaching.

Everyone fell silent as they stood there and stared at the gargantuan creature above.

A long spell later, someone swore, "Fucking deranged..."

None of them doubted he was cussing the organizers.

"Try to spread out," Bai Jing'an said drily.

Someone took a few steps back. Right at this time, the creature probed the air with its antenna and charged right at Xia Tian without warning. The monsters in the Killing Show innately knew how to kill.

Xia Tian scrambled to dodge. It grazed past the ends of his hair and suddenly changed direction midway, hitting someone behind him. The guy didn't move away in time, and the pincers of the giant insect severed his carotid artery and half of his neck. Xia Tian didn't know his name, only that he was a mechanic. He'd been quiet along the way, looking rather pessimistic, and now his predictions had come true.

The mechanic toppled to the ground. Everyone was too preoccupied to worry about him. The insect had turned back and continued its assault. Everyone was on their own, unable to even fend for themselves. Fang Youtian grabbed a rock and flung it, hitting it squarely on the head. As expected of a sniper.

In the chaos, Xia Tian heard Bai Jing'an's voice. It was still quite composed, giving others a sense of security amidst the mayhem.

"It's not venomous," Bai Jing'an said. "Try to strike it in the head as much as possible."

This was no easy feat, but at least it was a direction, and that was what they needed the most now.

But the monster was extremely agile. It stopped for a moment, then suddenly changed direction and charged at Saijo. The guy dodged the attack, but in the chaos, the other part of the mega insect's body coiled over, and its long, arthropod legs sliced his calf. Saijo cussed and fell to the ground.

Once again, it charged at Saijo. Xia Tian shoved whatever was left of the sword in his hand into its mouth. Unable to crush the sword to pieces with its fangs, it writhed madly. Every part of its body was as sharp as a blade.

Xia Tian did not see exactly who it slashed next, but the cyber support specialist grabbed the rock that had just bounced off and slammed it hard into one of its eyes. He smashed its carapace to pieces, and the bug let loose a hiss of

pain from the injury—now, that was something, coming from a cyber support specialist.

Saijo stepped back and readied himself for the next attack. Meanwhile, Bai Jing'an grabbed a discarded spear made of bone and mercilessly nailed a part of its body deep into the stone crevice.

Xia Tian gripped the rusty hilt hard to control the position of its head as he waited for Saijo to attack again.

But the attack never came.

No one had noticed the rat quietly creeping out of the darkness once more.

It must have had some sort of nefarious intelligence to guide it as it lurked around the battlefield, keeping itself out of sight as it watched them fight the giant centipede. Saijo retreated, ready to outflank the centipede—well, that was probably his plan; no one but him knew for sure—but when he stepped into the darkness at a particular spot, the rat sprang out and bit down on his head.Its sharp fangs crunched through his skull like it was munching on cookie. It was at this time that Fang Youtian picked up the rock again and smashed it on the giant centipede's head, flattening half of it. It struggled in desperation as Xia Tian gripped the hilt of the sword and plunged it deeper.

All he heard was a muffled curse and the bloodcurdling sound of bones shattering. Xia Tian turned his head and saw that giant, mutated rat—the same one, no doubt about it; it still had half a sword stuck in its eyes and a big gaping hole in its nose—biting down on Saijo's head like he was a toy figure and dragging him into the darkness.

Xia Tian loosened his grip on his sword and rushed toward them. Saijo's legs were still kicking, but... he was a goner. That much was clear.

In that instant, Xia Tian saw the monster's eyes. It was

staring at him. The eyes were intelligent, full of hunger and raging pain.

Behind him, the others swarmed in and smashed the giant insect's head to a pulp. Its body was still writhing, but it didn't take long to go completely still.

Xia Tian was still staring at the darkness, although he eventually stopped in his tracks and did not pursue any farther. The sound of dragging and what seemed to be the sound of chewing wafted out from the depths of the darkness. It lingered in the air for a long time, reverberating through the architecture.

He felt a pang of resigned powerlessness. The feeling was not unfamiliar; it was like a chunk of crude iron sinking in his stomach, stirring up a burst of frigid rage. His fists clenched tightly; he didn't even have a sword anymore.

Everyone looked in that direction, and no one recklessly chased after it. It all happened too fast. They didn't stand a chance...maybe they never had a chance to begin with.

Xia Tian looked back at the battlefield, only to realize that there was another body. It was the injured guy whose name he couldn't remember. The insect's long, sharp carapace had sliced his abdomen open, almost cutting him in half. He'd struggled for a while before he died.

In front of the giant bug's corpse, it felt like they were the ones who had gotten smaller.

They were toy figures trapped in the underground palace. Few in number and weak in strength, they only had primitive plastic sticks while enormous rats and centipedes lay ahead on the path before them. They ran in all directions, but there was no way out, and all that awaited them was to get chewed to pieces one by one by the creatures underground.

Meanwhile, the owners of the toys were waiting with great relish before the cameras.

"Aren't we...going after them?" Fang Youtian's voice rang out uncertainly, sounding so puerile and fearful that it felt vexing to hear.

"There's no point," Bai Jing'an replied. His voice was so flat and bland, it was as if the catastrophe they were facing was no big deal; that it was all quantifiable data.

Xia Tian turned to look at him. Bai Jing'an always looked calm and unruffled, but he was far from being as unfathomable as he had been when they first met. He'd practically become a source of comfort.

He was doing his job. As a tactician, he not only had to assess the situation and devise tactics, he also had to be the most cool-headed one on the team, providing rational suggestions in the worst of situations and maintaining his ruthlessness.

The darkness was too deep; they needed a person like him.

Fang Youtian still wanted to say something, but in the end, he didn't say a word. Xia Tian turned around to check the cut on Bai Jing'an's arm. The centipede had grazed it earlier, drawing blood.

"I'm fine," Bai Jing'an said.

Xia Tian nodded and turned to inspect the battlefield. Grassblade had fallen into a coma due to excessive blood loss. Those around looked at Bai Jing'an, who said, "We can't take him with us. The smell of blood will draw monsters."

No one said a word. They were all in agreement with what he'd said. It wasn't the first time they'd participated in the Killing Show, and they knew just what kind of world it was.

They gathered the weapons scattered on the ground and left the area. The sound of fighting could have attracted something else. As Grassblade lay there, Fang Youtian placed a bone spear in his hand, but everyone knew it wouldn't be any help.

The makeshift team continued onward. With the fighting and constant detours, they could no longer make out their current position. The underground palace was a world of its own, trying to hold everyone who'd been trapped here captive for eternity.

For a while, Xia Tian felt like they were straying farther and farther away from the exit, and this was very likely not a misperception on his part.

Time was their only guarantee of leaving.

It was already the fourteenth day. In about thirty hours, the game would end. The sky would brighten, the music would play, and the host would tell them in a sweet voice that their ordeal was over, that everyone had passed the test, and that the third fucking round had ended.

Xia Tian once found the fireworks and the host's affected voice at the end amidst a battlefield of bloodshed and carnage to be very ironic, but now, he missed them. Unlucky encounters had a way of changing one's perspective.

Along the way, they took out several smaller mutant creatures, and lost another of their number to death—a sniper. A monster had appeared out of nowhere as they passed an underground river and dragged the sniper into the water. Before the others could react, fresh blood and bubbles rose to the water surface, and then it was over.

Xia Tian held the bone spear in hand and carefully shielded Bai Jing'an behind him. The guy's expression had been calm the whole way. Such composure wasn't feigned, nor was it just indifference thanks to losing hope in their situation—instead, it was more like the placidness of a warrior.

Bai Jing'an was very familiar with the mutant creatures, and he was also familiar with this kind of treacherous and despairingly hopeless scenario. It was hard for Xia Tian to explain it, but it was more like a vague recognition between those of the

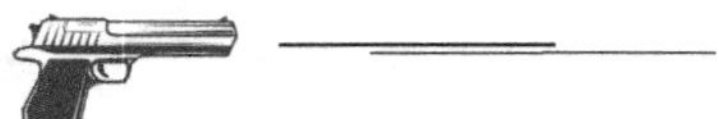

same kind. This thought came to him without reason.

After becoming teammates, Xia Tian asked around about Bai Jing'an, but almost no one knew him. All he knew was the information on the official website.

Bai Jing'an had ended up in this predicament because of a GBC contract. But unlike Xu Peiwen, his contract was under the parent-child joint liability clause. In other words, the contract had been signed by one of his parents and was probably already in existence before he was born. Ever since then, it'd controlled his entire life. Even by the standards of the Upper City, it was also the most deranged contract Xia Tian had ever seen.

At that time, Xia Tian wondered what it'd feel like to be born knowing that you had to go on the Killing Show for others' amusement. Probably not too good; it was already a feat of sorts that he didn't drink himself to death every day.

He looked at Bai Jing'an again, trying to imagine what the guy had been through. On the surface, he always looked so bored and dull, but when Xia Tian attempted to look closely, he couldn't see beneath the veneer.

As they passed through a corner, Bai Jing'an stopped and looked back at the darkness behind him.

"Still following us?" Xia Tian asked.

"What?" Fang Youtian said.

"Something's following us," Xia Tian replied.

"I knew it. There *was* a sound!" the cyber support named Johan said.

"Wait a minute, what are you guys talking about?" Fang Youtian asked.

"That rat," Xia Tian answered, "has been following us all this time."

Silence fell, and everyone felt a little chill run down their spines.

"We have to get rid of it," Xia Tian said.

"How?" Johan asked. "We only have two primitive spears made of bone. That creature is shrewd; it's been waiting for us to run into trouble, just like what happened with Saijo..."

"Fortunately, we're human beings and have an advantage," Bai Jing'an said. "We have brains."

Xia Tian turned to look at him, and Bai Jing'an continued, "We have to make a trap."

The final plan was very simple. The group put on a show, acting like they were arguing. The reason didn't have to be logical; in any case, the rat wouldn't understand...probably. If genetic engineering technology in the floating cities continued developing at this rate, a highly intelligent BOSS rat that could play everyone for fools would appear sooner or later.

One of two popular themes in the film and television industry lately was world domination by mutant creatures. This was much more credible than the other theme, which was the Lower City residents rising in revolt and destroying the world.

Anyway, Xia Tian broke off from the team and set off alone. Pretending to have lost his way, he led the rat to the designated spot.

The group didn't even have a sword, and being bait like that was so dangerous it propelled him right to the top of trending topics for death. That was also the reason it had to be Xia Tian—of the four people left, he was the one and only remaining warrior. And besides, they had no other advantage other than human intelligence. There was no room for even the slightest error.

Human intelligence also told them that the mutant rat chiefly held a grudge against Xia Tian. Just like how it had remembered Saijo for hurting its nose, it would never forget that Xia Tian had blinded one of its eyes.

Before the plan kicked off, Bai Jing'an drew a map for Xia Tian, telling him how to make the turns and to be sure to return to the marked location. They'd be lying in ambush there, waiting for it to arrive before launching a surprise assault.

He couldn't draw on the ground, as the rat would see it, so he drew on Xia Tian's palm with his finger. This felt very intimate, and also itchy to boot. Xia Tian had to hold himself back from laughing out loud.

He could sense Bai Jing'an's discomfort. It must have been a long time since this guy last engaged in a serious conversation with someone so up close, and he was distracted and vexed.

Xia Tian really, *really* felt like teasing him. He reached out to touch the lock of Bai Jing'an's hair that was sticking up again. It must have stuck up because he was nervous; when he was calm, his hair would be relatively smooth.

Bai Jing'an waved his hand away and gave him an annoyed look as he continued to explain the plan. Xia Tian listened to him with the patience of one looking after a restless child. When the guy repeated it a third time, Xia Tian finally couldn't help but blurt, "You know I grew up in the Lower City, right? And that I'm not directionally challenged."

"You'd at least have a fruit knife in the Lower City," Bai Jing'an countered.

"It's fine, I can handle it," Xia Tian flashed an undaunted smile at him. Of course, he wasn't dauntless, but he was pretty adept at pretending all was peaceful in the world—even though Bai Jing'an wasn't his younger sister, nor was he someone who could be easily fooled; he knew what they were facing.

The tactician stared fixedly at his palm, which still bore a bloodstain from the earlier battle. Xia Tian couldn't see his expression, but Bai Jing'an didn't say anything more. He merely sucked in a breath, stood up, and prepared to put the plan into action.

Time was running out.

Xia Tian walked alone through the underground area. The more he continued, the more this place looked like a different world.

Stacks of statues crowded around him, each meticulously crafted with a slightly different expression—although the stones' facial features similarly exuded the same greed to see blood and death, the desire to see the sacrifices' tragic fates, and the desire to be pleased.

Xia Tian subconsciously touched his nape. He knew that once he left the group, the mutant rat would follow him, searching for the opportunity to drag him into the darkness. He had to lure it all the way to the designated spot without losing his way, and he couldn't show any vulnerability en route either, lest it get the idea that it could attack before the trap they'd planned.

In that short period of time, the remaining people would attempt to make a simple, makeshift trap in said spot...although there was hardly anything in this godforsaken place that could make a trap. They couldn't make too many changes to the architecture, either, even if they had the capability. The rat had the home advantage here, familiar as it was with all the passageways and terrain.

Out there, all it took was just one bullet to deal with a mutant rat. But in a place like this, danger abounded everywhere, and their impotence and helplessness made them realize just how vulnerable they were.

Xia Tian continued in the darkness. His stomach was twisted into a knot, but you couldn't tell from how he moved. He was no stranger to desperate situations.

He could hear the footsteps of the giant rat behind him.

When he came to the Upper City, he felt his life undergo a major change. He still had a chain around his neck as he killed left and right for the wealthy to watch, but this was the Upper City. It had the sky and sunlight, lush vegetation, cocktail parties, and an endless supply of food.

But as the mutant rat seemed to emerge from a long-running nightmare, he realized they were the same. They came from the same place, and they had never ever left.

Being born in District N, Xia Tian had seen—and killed—his fair share of giant mutant creatures. When the insurrection broke out in District N Upper City that year, the Upper City dealt with it with no scruples whatsoever. The disaster spread far and wide and many people were massacred, so much so that the population count had yet to recover to where it was before. Predators roamed in the darkness even now, and no one knew if those creatures had once been a dog, a rat, or a person.

Of course, the Upper City could carry out a massacre using a small vial of poison gas, a plague, or whatever else that could kill people. Instead, they used the meticulously crafted latest variant of a mutant gene virus. The stuff would quickly cause mammals to mutate into deformed, bloodthirsty monsters that only wanted to devour everything that moved—sometimes, they'd even eat cars.

The elites then sealed off a large area of the Lower City. At the same time, they stuffed as many cameras as they could into the energy field. In this hell, the drooling flesh-eating creatures crawling toward you could be rats, dogs, weasels, or even your loved ones and friends.

What happened beneath the bustling Upper City was a real-life version of a monster movie; a game with real deaths. The higher the death count, despair, and gore, the higher the viewership ratings.

It was too exciting; countless people fleeing and screaming in the dark city down there beneath the round-the-clock opulence and debauchery of the Upper City... Perhaps this was inappropriate to note, but they didn't turn off the lights so they could see even more details.

The massacre was mass televised by GBC, and viewership ratings were sky-high. It was a legend and the apex of the entertainment industry, and there was no recreating it—because no one had started another insurrection.

Nearly a decade after the massacre, it still had a strong presence in their lives. The Upper World continued using this as a blueprint for producing movies, games, and reality shows. They sealed away brewing insurrections, resistance forces, liberty movements, and other such things in the Lower City, then crushed them to pieces before packaging them separately to put up for sale.

It was during this time the tradition of creature mutation in the Killing Show originated.

Xia Tian walked the dark passageway, feeling like he was walking on the same path he had as a child—but this path stretched too far, all the way to this distant future.

And there was no end in sight.

Regardless of the outcome of this matter—whether he lived or died—he hoped it would be over soon.

Things didn't really go that well.

Xia Tian arrived at the ambush site without a hitch. There were quite a few pointless steps here. Previously, they'd found a cracked slab at the end of the passageway, and it'd been on the verge of completely falling off. His teammates were going to try to loosen it further and ensure that it'd tip over and tumble off the stone stairs as soon as it was stepped on. Maybe they wouldn't be able to pry it loose, or maybe that particular stone

step wouldn't collapse. Even if the rat fell, Xia Tian still had to confront it on his own for at least half a minute. The others—just three, actually—couldn't get too close for fear that it'd discover them. Thank goodness its nose was toast, or it'd have been able to sniff out the trap right away.

If everything went well, everyone would rush over as soon as they could and kill it together. In any case, this was a step he had to take, no matter how dangerous.

Xia Tian carefully stepped over the trap and listened intently to the movements behind him. Once the mutant rat stepped on the stone step and slipped, he'd turn back immediately and attack.

But there was no sound at all, even though it was getting closer and closer; he could smell its pungent, rotting stench. Too close. It was already past the safe distance, and now it was poised to act—

It didn't step on the trap, but strode right over it.

The thought of running away flashed through Xia Tian's mind, but then he realized it was impossible. This was a hopeless case, and he was familiar with such situations. Sometimes you'd end up like this, face to face with death in the darkness.

He absolutely could not turn around and run away, because there was no escape.

Xia Tian sucked in a breath and halted in his steps, then he spun around. The bone spear in his hand struck the hideous face behind him hard. This time, it hit the creature's injured nose right on target. Not anticipating his move, it let out a whine that sounded like a sob and took a step back. It tried to steady itself before pouncing again, but this time, it stepped on the trap stone and tumbled down the stairs. Xia Tian chased after it, and his second blow landed right in its remaining eye. It let loose a human-like cry and rolled, hitting the wall, but it didn't hesitate to lunge at him again.

His companions, lying in ambush on the other side of the passageway, finally rushed over. Bai Jing'an glanced over at the creature, his eyes cold as he raised his hand and thrust the bone spear into its carotid artery with his first blow. He moved with such practiced ease that it seemed like he'd been doing this all day long.

He jerked the weapon out, and blood spurted.

It took them about five minutes to finish it off, but it still wasn't dead yet; just incapacitated. Everyone was a little hysterical, and the wounds on the rat's body were definitely crossing the standard threshold for overkill. Its belly was riddled with wounds, and its entrails were spilling out, but its claws were still slashing in an attempt to grab and rip something apart.

Something sticky peeked out of its belly. Staring intently at it, Fang Youtian picked up a bone spear to probe it, and the contents within spilled out: human limbs, chewed flesh, and internal organs, most of which had been swallowed whole. Clearly visible in the nightmarish tableau was an arm with a plantain herb tattoo that had been corroded by gastric acid. It suddenly dawned on them it was Saijo's arm.

Fang Youtian threw up, and Xia Tian thought that if he didn't die this time, he could very well be considered to have undergone a baptism of fire, Killing Show style.

In Xia Tian's opinion, this was when everyone should shut up, stay silent, and look sad and indignant, but some people clearly didn't think so.

Walking at the back of the squad, Fang Youtian began, "He told me he brought his parents up to the Upper City, and they were watching his game on the terminal. Do you guys think that after they see this—"

"Can we change the subject?!" Johan interrupted.

Bai Jing'an walked on the periphery of the squad, his expression pale.

Xia Tian glanced at him. "You okay?"

Bai Jing'an didn't speak and merely nodded in response. He never spoke much unless it was necessary. Most of the time, Xia Tian was sure he wasn't doing too well...he didn't know why he hadn't noticed before.

He patted Bai Jing'an on the shoulder and walked to the front of the squad without saying another word. He was the only remaining warrior, so it was only right and proper for him to do so.

While passing through the doorway of a hall, Xia Tian suddenly stopped. Stepping back, he made a "silence" gesture. Bai Jing'an gestured to ask him what it was, but Xia Tian couldn't answer, so he motioned for him to see for himself.

The tactician cautiously craned his neck to look, then he drew back and said nothing, no doubt already getting the intended sentiment—"*You have to see this for yourself.*"

This was the Killing Show. It never gave you time to be disheartened, because the show was on fire and never lost steam.

"Are those zombies?!" Fang Youtian exclaimed.

"How could there be zombies? Isn't this the medieval age?!" Johan added.

"This isn't medieval times; it's a reality show," Bai Jing'an said.

Behind the stone wall, two creatures in soldier uniforms were dragging their feet as they wandered about. With their ashen complexions, swollen skin, and vacant expressions, they were the very picture of typical zombies seen on television. The group watched for a while, marveling at the guts of the Killing Show to shove such a highly contagious virus into the program.

Xia Tian stared at the long sword on one zombie. It was

severely rusty, but a sword was a sword.

"Looks like this is that 'eternal punishment,'" Johan said. "Turning into a zombie. Creative."

They retreated quietly. Although the people infected by the zombie virus looked stiff, they were actually faster than portrayed in movies. What's more, they were teeming with the virus. If you got even the tiniest injury while fighting them, you'd be condemned to "eternal punishment" too.

They quietly passed through the passageway, trying to get as far away from them as possible. Along the way, they bumped into another giant centipede-like creature, except that the way it crawled looked more like a snake, and it wasn't as big as the previous one. Xia Tian deftly smashed it to death.

Fang Youtian didn't speak for a long while, but then he suddenly said, "Did you guys notice that rat's mouth? I just thought back. A rat's mouth can't open that wide; it must have some snake-like genes. They mixed a lot of other stuff in. If it had swallowed Saijo like a snake would, then Saijo could've still been saved if we'd cut its stomach open earlier."

His face was pale. That tragic death still haunted him.

"Hybrid genes," Xia Tian muttered. "Great. I'm already looking forward to the Grand Duke Wei Ling plays."

"Before that, we need to find a sword with a blade," Bai Jing'an said.

"Oh my god, I miss my .45 caliber pistol from the last round," Johan remarked.

"You don't say. I miss my 100mm caliber rocket launcher too," Xia Tian replied.

"Fried drumsticks. I miss those the most," Johan added.

"I miss having screenwriters who are a little more normal," Bai Jing'an quipped.

The group burst out laughing. At this time, you couldn't do

anything other than have a little fun under adverse circumstances.

"If only they'd mixed in a little more snake genes," Fang Youtian continued. "We might've still saved Saijo. They say snakes swallow their prey whole, and the prey is just unconscious for a while before it's digested..."

Xia Tian glanced at him. "It'd strangle him to death first before devouring him."

"But it's possible that he would just pass out," Fang Youtian said.

"It wouldn't have been any better," Xia Tian said. "The production team would've been only too glad to have him go through the whole digestion process."

"But we might've been able to save him!" Fang Youtian persisted.

No one answered, and an awkward silence hung in the air. Xia Tian felt like Johan still had something else to say, but in the end, the latter dropped it. Sometimes you wished someone would just come to their senses, but decide that it's better to let them be. Let him hope if that's what he wants—why make everyone unhappy? That'd probably be the more despairing outcome.

The group continued onward, and their surroundings grew even more chilly and bizarre. They navigated several stairways leading downward, as if they were setting off toward the center of the earth.

Xia Tian knew the physical stats of this city suspended in the air, but its enormous size still shocked him when he really set foot in it. It was clearly a floating city, but it also looked like hell.

No matter how far they descended, there was no end in sight.

CHAPTER 09

HOW IS HIS SAILING GAME?

Outside the arena, *"I miss having screenwriters who are a little more normal"* sparked a mini craze. On the chatboards, some would even remark *"I miss having chefs who are a little more normal"* when discussing changes of restaurants to try out, much to the exasperation of several screenwriters.

Yakovsky followed the squad's broadcast the entire journey. They were still newbies in the arena, but he could smell a superstar aura on them, so he paid close attention.

When Fang Youtian said, *"He brought his parents up to the Upper City, and they were watching his game at the terminal,"* he made a special point of giving Bai Jing'an a close-up shot. The tactician's face was a little pale, although it was impossible to say what was up with him—no one looked too good after that incident. However, it was a different story with a close-up.

He'd been avoiding the cameras all this time, but the squad's popularity had been soaring over the past few days. As a professional, top-notch tactician, he could no longer hide, no matter how he attempted to do so.

And once he grew popular, his past would be unearthed.

Even as Bai Jing'an was starting to gain a little attention from the public, his profile was already on Yakovsky's terminal. He knew Bai Jing'an's father was Bai Xiaoqi, a pretty well-known player of the Killing Show who had died in the final battle of the 182nd tournament. It hadn't been a pleasant death. What's more, his wife and son had been watching on TV at that time.

Because of the contract he signed, his son was now beholden to the Killing Show too. It was really dramatic. The producers were joyfully working on a special feature, and Bai Jing'an was upgraded from being "that perpetually bored-looking tactician" to a man with a tragic past. Once again, his popularity skyrocketed.

The third round of the Killing Show was coming to an end, and the plot in the castle was more or less wrapping up—the Grand Duke was finally done sacrificing his wife and children in an attempt to summon the maleficent god, and a great battle was about to break out.

Whether it'd be a hero show or a horror show would depend on the players' final performances.

Numerous lit screens spread out before Yakovsky, resembling a gaping wound in space.

He was a tad too drunk. His eyes were vacant as he looked at the screen in the corner, where Xia Tian was walking alone in the darkness. His expression was calm and composed, as if he was no stranger to entering the depths of the battlefield alone. In actuality, it was hard to read anything from a person's face when something significant happened, for they wouldn't make a big show of delight or sorrow. Still, Yakovsky found Xia Tian's quiet calm particularly special.

He'd always been restless, and fans said he was brimming with desire and vitality, sending even hearts numbed by alcohol aflutter. But his heart's temperature was below sub-zero. Xia Tian himself must have known vivaciousness to be meaningless, for he was in a world without hope.

Yakovsky drained the alcohol from his glass and poured himself more. Fine, fine. So this was a game of creation. Some paid, and some had fun. He'd have to do more work while he was still clear-headed. At the rate he was drinking, he would soon be in a tranquil state of unconsciousness.

In his drunken stupor, the tune *Homecoming* haunted his mind like a lurking villain who refused to leave. The villain kept singing about how someone was his destined refuge, letting him know where his home was, and telling him he wouldn't get lost no matter how heavy the snowstorm—so on and so forth.

Xia Tian's and Bai Jing'an's lives had nothing to do with that love song, but Yakovsky *had* to piece them together.

He switched the camera to Bai Jing'an. That was the unruffled face of someone unflappable. Imagining what he felt when he watched his father being burned to death alive on television, Yakovsky felt his own hair stand on end, so he decided not to think about it.

At least in his camera shots, the darkness would pass. Bai Jing'an was once a person who had tasted the pain of loss; disillusioned, he isolated himself, but this fucking reality show would heal his wounds.

When Bai Jing'an spoke to Xia Tian before the latter went to act as bait, a vexed expression had flashed across his face. That was how micro-expressions always worked. Yakovsky decisively applied slow-motion—to be precise, he added close-ups and slow-motion to all of their physical contact, dishing those effects out like nobody's business.

Because, truth be told, their interactions were pretty much normal. The content of their conversations and the nature of

their physical contact was typical for battle buddies—like a touch to convey tactical intent, a friendly reminder, or comfort.

To Yakovsky's professional eye, it was both casual and common, nothing extraordinary. Sure, Xia Tian was a tad touchy-feely, but he was like that to everyone. Yakovsky had seen him imitate the way Latte and Xu Peiwen spoke and walked several times, which made him wonder how exactly he had lived past the age of eighteen without being slaughtered by annoyed adults.

While the two of them didn't have much contact, they had a certain rhythm that needed slow-motion shots to emphasize.

They had little physical contact before the third round began, but were getting acquainted now. This was perfectly normal; they were teammates, so they had to talk somehow. But that acquaintanceship could be easily upgraded into a visible process where antagonistic battle buddies warmed up to each other. Throw in some music and gorgeous edits to the mix, and they could even turn into sworn friends who'd go through life and death together. It would be loaded with tenderness and yearning; they would be the one and only person who could soothe the other's pain. Top it off with a *homecoming* metaphor, and the viewers would love it.

People liked real things. They liked the healing of wounds, and they liked things taking a turn for the better. And when it came to this sort of thing, you couldn't fool your way through.

However, you could exaggerate. Exaggerate all you can.

Xia Tian's fanbase had already grown quite substantial. They called themselves the "Summer Flames" and discussed his combat style, and even dug into his past—which had an exciting story full of twists and turns.

He was born in District N21, one of the areas that had been most affected by the District N insurrection. In the imagination of the people in the Upper City, that place was the most classic of the Lower City areas—highly terrifying, cruel, and twisted...and so, very cool.

In the history books, if someone had a harsh living environment or was suspected of rebelling against the government, people would feel bad for them or have them arrested. But now, everyone was putting a crown of thorns on him and merrily tossing him onto a parade float for consumption.

The unremarkable phrase "*how's his sailing game?*" was a big hit with Xia Tian's fanbase, making its way into the trending chart purely based on the sheer number of searches and quotes. Actually, nothing was surprising about the sentence on its own in the list of top memorable quotes. What made it remarkable was the person saying it, and the circumstances around which it had been said.

The Vosen family had been a snack supplier at the foot of GBC Channel 3 since the last generation, and they'd gone on to make a respectable name for themselves from it. Being the son of a wealthy family, Vosen was also a member of the preposterously expensive Skymirror Lake Sailing Association. It was a picturesque lake that was never open to non-members.

Vosen himself had a bad reputation—he'd killed vagrants in a cruel manner, and there had been several lawsuits against him for killing his bed partners during intercourse. Someone in the replies said that he was also a member of an elite hunting club for the bigwigs, and even as a child he'd often boasted of his interest in killing, as if driven by some supernatural fervor.

This fanaticism was obviously already impossible to suppress, which was why he joined the Killing Show—he thought it would be a free-for-all where he could kill in an assortment of ways to his heart's content. And now a chorus of mocking voices in the posts was saying that even Xu Peiwen lasted longer resisting his opponents than this "god of war-inspired killer."

In the vast cyber world, the term "sailboat" quickly deviated from its original meaning of a large luxury product. What came up in searches for this term suddenly turned malevolent.

This was how the term was now used:

Say, for example, that the rich guy next door was holding yet another nude party at home—the kind where the guests had no choice but to participate because he had their contracts in his hand—and the death toll hit three or more. Before long, you'd see professional cleanup crews coming and going, hauling out a dozen large garbage bags. Apparently, the party was very "upscale." At this point, if you wanted to express your displeasure, you could say, *"I wonder, how's his sailing game?"*

People had said similar things before; like stating someone "ought to be taught a lesson," or that "death is too good for the likes of so-and-so." But those words had always felt distant, and there was a risk of sounding like an embarrassed victim. On the other hand, "how's his sailing game" was like opening a door to describe and define a phenomenon and attitude that many people found themselves desiring.

Xia Tian was the spokesperson for that desire. Now, the video of him killing Vosen was spreading like an epidemic.

Yakovsky's main screen had the image of that particular killing on it. The cameraman had found the perfect angle, where Xia Tian was holding Vosen's neck in a chokehold from behind, the broken piece of metal in his hand cutting into his artery. In that moment, their movements were almost intimate, and Xia Tian's expression was gentle—almost affectionate—even as blood oozed.

What a psychopath, Yakovsky thought. *He was completely enjoying it.*

Going by the latest engagement distribution report, most

of Xia Tian's fans had no idea of who he was at all. They had merely followed him because of "sailboat." These days, everyone had a bit of the blues, and an anger in their hearts that needed to be vented. But they soon came to understand him, and approved of all that he represented.

That's a good direction, the chief director thought to himself.

A communication signal flashed on the main screen. Yakovsky opened it to find that it was the official clip that Tian Xiaoluo had just turned in.

This was a new round of promotional clips, and Yakovsky was pleased to find that she'd rendered the killing in a way that'd both terrify and send the adrenaline pumping. It was exactly as he'd ambiguously asked for at the meeting. And she'd actually found a clip of Xia Tian watching from the side with a grim expression as Luo Qingtian tortured and killed a newcomer during the second round. Coupled with the scream of the sixteen-year-old lad, it was very impactful. In this age, video material was everywhere. Tian Xiaoluo's querying skills were truly incredible.

Tian Xiaoluo's real specialization was nano-interactive viruses. She'd joined the Ministry of Defense back in the day and had signed a lifetime contract. She was a top-notch programmer, however, her flair for video editing was clearly more in demand than her expertise in cutting-edge programs. And so, the Gilded Group transferred her contract. In fact, contracts were easily transferred back and forth like this.

What's more, she wasn't your average outstanding editor; she had a real talent, a power that could touch people's hearts. Sometimes, Yakovsky found it to be a painful power blazing and moaning amongst the musical notes. Even to viewers who had grown increasingly numb to commercialized tragedies and comedies, survival and death, she could still rouse whatever bit of emotions they had left.

And she was uncannily skilled at grasping Xia Tian's tenderness; completely conjuring it out of thin air. Under her hands, the terrorist appeared gentle and sad, hoping to protect an infinitesimal happiness in a dark and cruel world. He killed because he had no other choice. The world was pitch-dark and terrifying, which made his smile appear all the more naïve and innocent in contrast.

And just like that, under the guidance of the chief director of the team tournament, Xia Tian was an enraged and brazen avenger, a terrorist who killed without blinking, a rebel with a hatred for the powerful in the Upper City who would fight against them at all cost. He was also a great man; a gentle, considerate battle buddy with a younger sister complex, and a master chef to boot.

The last one had been added by Yakovsky himself—after all, how could a protective, family-oriented man not know how to cook a meal?

In any case, this guy was both gentle and deranged, a killer and a protector, a grim reaper and a good man...but it didn't matter. As Yakovsky looked at Xia Tian laughing heartily on the main screen, he thought that there was something about him that could bridge this gap.

Most people thought viewers only wanted to have a blast when they watched the Killing Show, but that was just scratching the surface. All violence had to have a reason, and he'd give him one. He didn't care if Xia Tian was that kind of person—he didn't look like it, but it didn't matter. He'd have a reason, one way or another. If he was going to die, it would be for this.

And the reason he gave him would be exactly what the viewers from the Upper City needed.

Making a star—Wasn't that what it was all about?

Xia Tian was the theme of today's cover image on the official website of the GBC's Killing Show. In the picture, the tall young man wore a dazzling but cold-blooded smile while the massive God of War statue in the Upper City towered behind him—like the prelude to a grand hero epic.

CHAPTER 10

SUSPENSION BRIDGE EFFECT

In the arena, the stars were unaware that they were attracting widespread attention or that they already had a hand in various industries from gaming to pornography.

They came to an unfamiliar underground area that no longer bore any resemblance to the sewers. Instead, it was full of heterogeneous subterranean architecture. The damaged parts of the stone had been repaired, and there were signs of human activity around, which showed that they were getting close to the disaster site.

On the way, they ran into a snake...well, it was probably a snake, as it was hard to get a clear look in the darkness. It slithered out of a pitch-dark pool at the foot of the stairs, coiled around Johan, and dragged him into the water. The cyber support specialist only managed half a scream before he was gone without a trace.

It even tried to take Bai Jing'an with it, but fortunately, he reacted quickly and dodged. Xia Tian thrust his bone spear at it, and it reluctantly shrank back into the water; however, its tail still dragged Bai Jing'an along briefly. It caused him to hit his head, making him dizzy for quite a while. He even threw up once; he was likely suffering from a concussion.

The group chased a few steps in the direction it had disappeared, but soon gave up the pursuit. In the face of death, their judgment was cold-hearted and efficient. The chance of saving Johan was zero. The underground river was unfathomably deep, and only the production team knew what lurked within. There was no luck to be had here; everything was planned. If you met with danger, you were sure to meet your doom. Heck, you might even die a creative death.

Looking back now, they didn't really know much about Johan. All they remembered was that he'd joined in place of his father, who had been disabled in an accident and couldn't afford treatment. No doubt his father would've died if he'd entered the Killing Show.

This was Johan's first time participating. The only thing he'd been well-acquainted with was the internet, so he registered as a cyber support specialist.

Xia Tian wondered if his family was watching. If they did, what went through their minds when they saw that scene?

He thought of Dee Dee, his younger sister. Fortunately, she didn't have the money to watch. He tried not to think about how she'd feel when she learned of his death, or what fate might await her in the dark Lower City. Just the thought of it could send a chill down his spine.

Xia Tian tightened his grip on his bone spear—still no new weapons—and continued onward with his remaining two companions.

After leaving a corridor, he realized that the place they were in looked a bit familiar.

They looked around, and it took them a moment to realize that the setup of this place was similar to the previous dungeon.

Both had high, circular ceilings, but the bars on both sides here had decayed, and the inside reeked of rotting matter and blood.

This place was another dungeon, another sacrificial altar; it had just been abandoned.

Bai Jing'an touched his arm. Xia Tian followed his gaze and saw the creature lurking in a dark, decrepit cell.

He wagered that the plot stated it had been here for thousands of years because there was nowhere else for it to go. As it crouched, it looked more human-like than the one before. Its complexion was frightfully white, with fold after fold of wrinkled skin. It had the pointed mouth of a rat, but its ears resembled a human being's. Its hands...almost resembled a human's, with five fingers that were a tad too long. They looked very dexterous.

It was over two meters tall when it stood erect, and at first glance, it looked...more like a person, who looked very much like a rat.

A genetic disaster.

A nightmare creature.

There was a moment of dead silence all around before Fang Youtian stammered, "Is...is this legal?"

"They...must have amended the details of the *Genetic Act* again," Bai Jing'an said.

The trio stared at it. For a moment, they were unsure of how to react. It looked so much like a human that it made them wonder what was going on in its mind. What was it thinking when it was eating humans? And how did it feel to have one's mind permanently trapped alongside a rat's?

These thoughts flashed through their brains, while the creature looked at them from the darkness with a creepy chill in its eyes. Its form was beyond human comprehension.

Bai Jing'an found this scene extremely familiar. For a fleeting moment, he felt as if he'd been standing before such a monster for decades and had never left. He didn't know if this was because of the concussion or a cerebral injury from a long time ago, but a distant pain rose deep in his skull, and he realized it was about to launch an assault—

The rat charged without warning. It moved extremely fast, like an apparition.

Bai Jing'an got a clear look in its eyes—eyes corrupted by agony and killing intent. All it wanted was to torture and destroy every living thing in sight!

The creature instantly seized him, and he seemed to return to that dark place again—the place where it had existed for eternity, and all that was left in the world were eyes clouded by hunger and hatred and nothing else.

It took just that instant for the mutant rat's face to be right in front of him. At the same time, a bone spear rammed hard into the creature's eye socket from the side with a force so great that it pierced its head.

It didn't make a sound, but its body twisted violently, veering off-track and stumbling past Bai Jing'an with a foul-smelling wind in its wake.

Bai Jing'an felt a tremendous vile force brush past the tip of his nose. All it would've taken was a few more centimeters, and his face would've be gone.

In the chaos, he felt someone at the side yanking him. He fell to the ground just as a whip-like tail swept over his head.

Xia Tian's chin hit the top of his head. The monster crashed into the bars behind with a heavy *thud*, but it wasn't affected in the least as it pounced again. It was like it didn't know what pain was.

Even though its eyes were both blinded and blood kept gushing, it still had its memory and nose. It'd use the last of its strength to kill anything alive. That was how it was designed.

Bai Jing'an watched Xia Tian strike it with the bone spear again, and once again, it crashed into the wall ahead. This time, it finally stopped. The injury to its eyes had affected it significantly, after all.

It reached out with its human-like claws to grab the bone spear in its eye and attempted to pull it out—bloody hell, it didn't look like it was going to die at all, and that spear had pierced through half of its head—but it didn't succeed, and it *still* didn't make a sound.

It took a few steps back, and they could only stare at it as it scuttled back into the darkness to the sound of rustling footsteps.

Dead silence still reigned all around them for quite a while. When you encountered this sort of creature and traded blows with it, it'd linger in your mind for a long, long time.

Bai Jing'an lowered his head. Fang Youtian was dead.

The young, naïve sniper they couldn't put to use had died without so much as a sound. It was upon seeing the corpse that Bai Jing'an realized the monster had penetrated Fang Youtian's temple with its tail when it'd charged earlier, moving so fast that no one noticed.

He'd barely bled at all. By the time they saw him, he was dead, through and through.

He looked particularly young and boyish in death. He'd hardly spoken about himself, only that he had a lot of friends out there and was running some kind of website. That was about it.

Bai Jing'an felt that he should kneel and check Fang Youtian's injuries, but he didn't move. He knew it himself. Fang Youtian was gone.

He also knew that if Xia Tian hadn't yanked him just now, he would also be lying on the ground like Fang Youtian. Death would've claimed him, swiftly and without warning.

They stood there without saying a word. In just a few hours, all the cellmates who had come down with them together were gone, leaving only the two of them standing alone in the underground palace.

Bai Jing'an's dizziness had yet to subside. A part of his soul was still trapped in the darkness, and it didn't seem like it was because he'd hit his head. That darkness seemed to be the real deal, and leaving was just an illusion.

The guy beside him bent down and picked up Fang Youtian's bone spear, a move that struck Bai Jing'an as familiar—it was typical of the way folks of the Lower City acted. Even their grief was cold and efficient.

Xia Tian turned to look at him. "Are you okay?"

"A little better," Bai Jing'an answered.

Xia Tian flashed him a smile, a dazzling, handsome, all-is-well-in-the-world smile.

"I'll take care of you," he said.

"That's an unrealistic, overblown statement," Bai Jing'an said.

Xia Tian laughed, then raised his hand to smooth down Bai Jing'an's hair—that cursed lock was probably sticking up again. Bai Jing'an didn't move, thinking how scary it was that he actually didn't feel vexed; he even felt a little reassured.

Xia Tian looked down at the corpse. Fang Youtian's head was still oozing brain matter. The darkness stretched around them, thick and treacherous.

"I need a sword," he said.

Bai Jing'an turned to look at him, and their eyes met for two seconds. He realized what Xia Tian was talking about. His first reaction was that this was absolutely insane, but it was the best idea they had.

So he nodded. "We need to come up with a plan."

Xia Tian flashed him another smile.

How are we a killer and a tactician? Bai Jing'an thought. *More like two madmen making plans.*

They retracted their steps along the route and looked for the zombies they had seen earlier.

That's right. The creatures were dangerous, and they were carriers of the virus; what's more, they often appeared in groups. But the duo had no other choice.

The zombie virus was originally a drug that caused users to develop symptoms that put them in a daze and made them act on instinct. They'd be just like a corpse—albeit one with intense hunger, and a craving for bloody meat and the like. These symptoms had been highly trendy for a time, and young people fell all over themselves to experience what it was like to be a zombie, even going as far as to *actually* eat a few people for real.

And now, GBC had developed it into a specific virus for use in their programs.

Only GBC would research this sort of technology. They'd immobilize and extract the nefarious parts of something, then turn it into contagious diseases to be used as props for entertainment.

"Their hearing and vision would be compromised, but they move fast; not much slower than they were while alive," Bai Jing'an said to Xia Tian. "Attacking their heads is most effective, but the real danger is the virus they carry. You can't get scratched or bitten, not even a little..."

"I've dealt with these things before," Xia Tian said.

Bai Jing'an nodded. This virus had broken out in several districts in the Lower City, and District N21 had been one of them.

"My elder brother died because he was infected with this virus," Xia Tian continued, speaking of his tragic past nonchalantly—as if these facts were meaningless and all too commonplace.

Bai Jing'an knew that tone. He truly felt those deaths and the accompanying anguish to be meaningless. There were people and pain like that everywhere, and you could only turn a blind eye—you wouldn't be able to keep on living otherwise.

"These creatures were all over the city at the time; I was the one who killed him and burned him. I know what a zombie can do," Xia Tian said.

Bai Jing'an knew it all too well too, which was why he wasn't in the least reassured.

But at this point, they could only steel themselves and tough it out.

Xia Tian and Bai Jing'an quickly found the two zombies. They were kneeling on the ground, eating a person.

Apparently, someone else had come down here during this short interlude of time, where he met his end. From this angle, he looked like a pretty handsome young man, and his face was still well-preserved, except that he had been disemboweled and was being slowly devoured by two zombies. The production team would definitely never let such a splendid shot go.

The zombie virus was actually an infectious disease, so while these people looked very much like they were dead, they might still have minds of their own. But everyone tacitly agreed that they were dead corpses, an anomaly. God knew what they were thinking as they ate people. That was a desire that had been crafted to precision in a laboratory.

The duo quickly reviewed the plan they'd made earlier. Bai Jing'an made some minor corrections to ensure this crazy stunt would be feasible and tried not to think about what would happen if either of them was scratched or bitten.

They needed swords, and that was non-debatable.

The plan was simple. All he had to do was to rush over and make it look like he was on his own to lure the zombies into chasing him.

Even among zombies, there were fast and slow ones. Everyone who'd fought them before knew that tackling them one at a time was much easier than taking down a pair.

In the end, Bai Jing'an finally gave the nod, and the plan commenced. Xia Tian stood up, took a breath, and walked toward the zombies.

They lured the zombies into a T-shaped corridor.

Xia Tian sprinted around the corner and braked to a standing stop to wait for the first zombie to come charging before he stretched his leg out and tripped it, sending it falling to the ground. He grabbed its hair from behind and slammed its head hard into the floor.

Its skull shattered. At the same time, Xia Tian grabbed its sword.

Bai Jing'an cleared a few glowing mosses nearby and hid in the darkness a short distance away. When Xia Tian made his move, he was to use his bone spear to deal with the one following behind.

The second one moved quickly as well, just two or three steps slower than the first. Bai Jing'an walked out of the darkness and stabbed his bone spear into its right eye socket, since it was softer, and through its head.

Its forward momentum stalled briefly, but it didn't stop. Instead, it picked up speed as it charged toward him, as if the sight of a living person excited it. Its mouth opened unnaturally wide, revealing sharp canine teeth. Had it been a human, its jaws would have already dislocated, but it must have undergone some sort of genetic modification.

Bai Jing'an quickly let go and retreated, but the zombie

charged so fast that, in the blink of an eye, it was close enough for him to see the color of its irises.

He waited, and the next second, Xia Tian's sword plunged straight into its head from the left side, stabbing right through the zombie and nailing it to the wall opposite.

Bai Jing'an stood there and watched as that decaying face right before his eyes slid past him, nailed to the wall, where it went motionless. Xia Tian pulled out his sword and flashed Bai Jing'an a smug smile.

Anything could've gone wrong at any stage of their plan, but both of them were now fine and unscathed. It made it seem like there was nothing safer in the world than standing beside two zombie corpses.

Bai Jing'an smiled back at Xia Tian and bent over to search for their loot. They found another sword and a dagger, which could be considered quite a haul.

Xia Tian reached out a hand, and Bai Jing'an grabbed it to haul himself to his feet. He weighed the other sword in his hand and tucked it away at his waist. "I can't believe I'd wind up calling this a 'bountiful harvest,'" he said.

"It's a bad year for the harvest, Your Majesty. Just make do," Xia Tian quipped.

"This Majesty likes a little optimism. There must still be more around here..."

Bai Jing'an stopped abruptly, realizing he'd made a joke. Cold sweat broke out on his body, because it'd dawned on him what this was.

The Suspension Bridge Effect.

When you secreted too much adrenaline, everything that happened would be imprinted into your memory like a mark from a branding iron. It'd become something you would never forget, something that would truly change you.

The Killing Show claimed to be just a stage that tested strength and courage. They went on and on about naked and un-disguised human nature, but this was their game: they'd create the stage and the events to stir up human emotions, using these as materials to clash and distort at will. They intensified and dramatized the relationships between people, so that you'd throw caution to the wind, compelled as you were to trust someone and relax your guard around them...and then they'd destroy you for all to see.

You couldn't like *anyone*. They'd make use of that to toy with you and destroy you. That was what people wanted to see... Your emotions and feelings were the light that drew in monsters.

Xia Tian glanced curiously at Bai Jing'an, not understanding why he'd halted in the middle of speaking. He came from afar, and he had no qualms doing as he so inclined in everything he did. He didn't know what it meant.

But Bai Jing'an knew.

He couldn't see Xia Tian as a friend. It'd be a catastrophe, not only for tactical strategizing but also for his entire existence.

Just then, he suddenly looked up into the distance.

"What's wrong?" Xia Tian asked.

"There's wind," Bai Jing'an replied.

He took two steps in that direction, and Xia Tian probed, "Exit?"

"The finale," Bai Jing'an answered.

They didn't speak again. There was nothing else to say. All they could do was grab their weapons and head in that direction.

Not long after they continued onward, the finale began.

In the official words of the Killing Show, the final period when deaths mounted was when *"the meat grinder was in motion."*

First, the whole space shook slightly, and a fresh, cloying smell permeated the air while gravel fell noisily overhead.

They grasped their rusty longswords tight and looked up. The engravings on the architecture above had a weather-worn and rustic effect, but now it appeared as if tumor-like objects were growing from the elegant decorative patterns. Spread messily over a long stretch, they looked extremely repulsive.

At the same time, they heard a shrill and bizarre voice from far away on the footpath. They only made out a few words, like "maleficent god" and "kill"...

It occurred to them what that voice was. Above them, a brown bird burrowed out from the tumor-like stone sculpture, exuding the stench of rotting flesh and blood and oozing red mucus that dried in the blink of an eye.

It had a human-like face, and its eyes possessed none of the ignorance that came with being an animal—instead, there was only malice.

They stared agape as countless strange birds emerged from the wall. The power of the maleficent god or whatever was spreading all over the underground palace, allowing malformed birds to hatch from the stone wall.

Bai Jing'an didn't know the principle behind it, but...it must have taken a lot of work and effort to create such an effect. There was simply no knowing how much money GBC could spend and what kind of technology they could come up with, all for the sake of visual effects.

In any case, countless strange birds dug their way out of the wall with creepy visual effects. The moment they emerged, their shrill voices kept repeating the same passage of words:

—*The maleficent god has descended upon this world, and this castle is its starved vessel. His Majesty demands more sacrifices, blood, and death... Every one-third of a quarter of an hour, the blood of a person must taint the earth; otherwise, It shall personally summon the individual to become its servant in eternal servitude…*

It also hopes everyone will be more proactive and conscientious about slaughtering one another. Perish the thought of gaining a reprieve with stalling tactics. The real gods are dead, and bloodshed and carnage are the true intent of evil in the new world—

In other words, the organizers' intent.

"'Servants'?" Xia Tian parroted.

"Zombies, I guess," Bai Jing'an said.

It spread its wings and flew away, joining countless other human-faced birds in the underground palace to deliver messages of death that described the organizers' chilling orders:

Players should kill each other as soon as possible. The command of God is not to be defied.

"Now I understand why you miss normal screenwriters," Xia Tian quipped.

The stench of decay and blood in the air grew increasingly stronger. Both of them continued onward, gripping the hilts of their swords tightly. They both knew that this place had become extremely treacherous. A bloody massacre was about to begin.

It was hard for Bai Jing'an to imagine that he would one day be heading for the most troublesome place on his own accord, but he was already in the Killing Show, and there was no safe place to go.

The maleficent god wanted everyone to die here, and the only way out was to find it and kill it. Anyone who did not advance following this route would end up in the production team's sights.

And in the Killing Show, you didn't want to be on the production team's radar.

Sure enough, they hadn't gone far when they saw two corpses lying up ahead. They'd just died, and their blood was still warm.

They were two guys dressed in mercenary clothing, although they didn't have any decent weapons on them—or maybe their weapons had been looted. Their killer had used a sword, doing a clean and efficient job of disposing of them.

"On the plus side, we've got ten minutes now," Xia Tian said.

"On the downside, we definitely got *more* than just those ten minutes to worry about," Bai Jing'an said.

They continued, and their surroundings grew more and more sinister. Some malformed plants were hanging from overhead. Although they knew these had been deliberately planted, it felt like the entire underground palace was becoming more bizarre with the maleficent god's arrival.

"This place reminds me of the Lower City," Xia Tian said.

"What's it like there?" Bai Jing'an asked.

"The lights are always on, but it feels very dark."

"Yeah, there are clearly lights, but it seems like it won't ever be bright," Bai Jing'an murmured.

Xia Tian glanced at him. "You're pretty familiar with that place, aren't you?"

"Not really."

"It feels like you..."

Xia Tian suddenly stopped and turned to look at Bai Jing'an. They quickly exchanged hand gestures, taking no more than three seconds.

Xia Tian walked on ahead, while Bai Jing'an stayed put.

A mercenary suddenly sprang out behind Xia Tian from the shadows of the numerous overlapping stone sculptures in front, but it was as if Xia Tian had eyes at the back of his head as he backhandedly blocked the short sword coming at him. As he turned aside, the sword hilt struck the guy's head. The sneak attacker fell to the ground. Xia Tian dealt a blow to the back of his head, and the guy went still.

At the same time, Bai Jing'an dealt with the other guy who'd lunged at him. That dude was a little hesitant when he saw his partner dead, and for a moment, he turned his back to Bai Jing'an. This was way too easy. Bai Jing'an's sword pierced his neck from behind, and he collapsed to the ground, instantly dead.

Xia Tian and Bai Jing'an searched them, but there was nothing decent on the attackers except for a short sword and a crudely made longbow with a bowstring that looked like it could snap at any time. It looked like the organizers had the minds to go with a style reminiscent of the era of cold weapons. Xia Tian tossed the bow to Bai Jing'an, but in this kind of terrain, there was basically no use for it.

"Now we have twenty minutes *more*," Xia Tian quipped.

Twenty minutes later, they teamed up with others.

This was significant to Xia Tian, because he'd finally found someone to extort and, for once, replace his weapon with an upgraded one.

At that time, they were going down the stone steps. All the pathways seemed to converge in the same direction. Two guys were lying in ambush behind the shadow of the stone wall. They were both pros; prior to that, Xia Tian hadn't noticed anyone here at all.

He suddenly stopped in his tracks and cast a glance at Bai Jing'an, wanting to say something, but he wasn't sure what exactly. It was vaguely along the lines of "*Something's off.*" The smell of death wasn't always distinct.

Right then, a sword stabbed toward him swiftly and soundlessly.

Xia Tian raised a hand to intercept the blade. This was the result of intuition honed through life-or-death fights in the Lower City; it'd be impossible to survive otherwise.

They traded blows. Behind him, Bai Jing'an swiftly nocked an arrow on the bow and aimed it at another person hiding in the darkness, facing the other guy in a confrontation.

The guy who attacked Xia Tian was wearing a soldier's uniform. His blade slashed Xia Tian's arm at an angle, while the hilt of Xia Tian's sword struck him in the chest and even left a bloody mark on his neck. Just a wee bit deeper and the battle would've been over, but that was fine. Next time, he would get it right.

Just then, the guy suddenly took a step back. "Wait a minute!"

Xia Tian didn't stop, and swung his sword. The other guy, being sharp-eyed, deftly parried the blow and continued, "How about teaming up? There are only two of us on each side—"

Xia Tian kept up with his attack, and the guy added, "The Easter egg is a plot-based match. Points won't be deducted for team-ups!"

Reluctantly, Xia Tian stopped. The tip of his sword was pointing at the other guy's throat. He only had to send it forward a little to finish him off, but he also realized that they did indeed need to team up. Their chance of winning would be higher. Bai Jing'an must have thought so, too.

It was then he realized he'd seen this guy before—this guy was called Doug, and he was the captain who had taken them captive in the grasslands at the beginning of the plot-based match. Tall and handsome, he had the kind of classic looks favored by the Killing Show.

During the trip earlier, he'd looked like he was wool-gathering, but this was the Killing Show. No one could be out of it all the time, no matter how handsome you were.

His sword was polished and shiny with no traces of rust. Only those who drew a soldier's lot would have that kind of benefit.

"There's an underground battle arena ahead. You need

someone who knows the way," he added.

Xia Tian looked at him for a while before he said, "I like your sword."

Doug stared at him for two seconds, then pulled back his sword and tossed it over. Xia Tian reached out to catch and inspect it. He handed his own rusty sword to Doug, and the guy took it with a grim expression.

Bai Jing'an put down his arrow too, and the person in the shadows walked out. He was also wearing a soldier's uniform, and there was a long scar across his face that extended to his throat. His expression was so gloomy it was indistinguishable from the shadows from which he walked.

"So," Xia Tian said as he checked over his new sword, "you guys are joining the fun even though you drew NPC lots?"

"No one can say no to fun," Doug answered. "Doug."

Xia Tian reached out to shake his hand. "Xia Tian. And this is Bai Jing'an."

They quickly introduced themselves. Doug was a warrior, and his companion was called Feng Dan, a fellow warrior who didn't really like talking, claiming to have some issue with his throat.

And then Xia Tian said, "My teammate needs a sword too."

"Why in the world would a tactician need such a good sword?" Doug said.

"Just because."

Doug glared at him, then grabbed Feng Dan's sword and handed it over. Feng Dan opened his mouth, but eventually acquiesced and took the rusty sword that was handed back.

They made their way over to the location where the maleficent god had awakened.

Xia Tian asked Doug if he had anything to eat, and Doug said no. Then Xia Tian groused that the sword, which looked like some mass-produced bargain buy, was only *marginally* better than the zombie's sword. In retort, Doug asked him to please understand the position of a junior soldier short-changed by his commanding officer. He looked at the rusty sword with disdain and said that he'd definitely be able to find a few sharper ones later. He had more or less a hundred "colleagues" down there, and there'd surely be more than enough swords to go around.

In a nonchalant tone, he went on to say he was an old hand at the Killing Show. He had already survived two seasons, and hoped to make it through a third. Although Doug had quick wit, Xia Tian suspected it was predominately because of his good looks that he'd been able to survive this long by the skin of his teeth. These days, you couldn't commit a crime if you weren't handsome; otherwise, you wouldn't even be qualified enough to be a seasoned soldier in the Killing Show.

All this while, Feng Dan didn't say a word. He simply walked on the fringes of their group, his expression dark.

According to Doug, the Grand Duke of Skymoat was once a young and promising man, but he was poisoned in an assassination attempt while fighting for power and position. Although he was saved, he was confined to his sickbed for years, and because of the toxins, his body began to decay from the inside. Oh yeah, and the looks he was so proud of corroded too. After all, Wei Ling was so handsome, how could he not mention this?

At his most desperate moment, he heard the call of the maleficent god and found this forgotten underground architecture. The suffering and the thirst for the blood of the people aboveground had awakened it... Anyway, that was how the plot went.

The Grand Duke was fascinated with the strength of the maleficent god and obsessed with immortality and power. He sacrificed his wife, his three children, and the residents of the en-

tire stretch of land. Meanwhile, some sort of evil being invaded his mind and body.

He often recruited mercenary groups to patrol his territory, saying that they were there to kill monsters—but in truth, they were to be offered as sacrifices.

Soon after Xia Tian and the others' arrival underground, the Grand Duke announced that he'd start summoning the maleficent god again.

"Isn't the plot a tad too simple and crude?" Xia Tian said.

"This is a reality show. The plot is supposed to be simple and crude," Doug said. "It's not like anyone wants to see our marvelous acting.

"Anyway, the maleficent god's awakening began three hours ago. Supposedly, it'd resurrect in the Grand Duke's body and rule the world going forward. Honestly though, I have no desire whatsoever to find out just how fascinating his genetic profile is.

"The Grand Duke drove everyone underground, saying that it was to kill the mercenaries who had fled there, but it was actually a mass sacrifice."

"...So all the exits are sealed," Xia Tian said.

"That's right. No one can get out until we kill to the organizers' satisfaction," Doug said.

They encountered another four-person team on the way, and both sides immediately crossed swords.

Four against four.

The match-up was a piece of cake. Bai Jing'an, who had an arrow in his hand, immediately killed the other party's sniper. Meanwhile, Xia Tian stepped forward and traded blows with the other party's warrior who was at the head. Doug, on the other hand, intercepted a sword that came for him and drew the guy away.

Their two new companions were pretty skilled.

Feng Dan was responsible for the last guy. Xia Tian could tell at a glance that this guy came from the battle arena in the Lower City; his fighting style was all too familiar.

Xia Tian's opponent was no expert. He had decent swordsmanship, but it was clear at first glance that he'd learned it from instructional software. He didn't know how to consider the whole picture and make use of geography.

Xia Tian turned aside and stepped behind the statue, and his opponent thrust his sword. The blade went under the arm of the stone statue, and Xia Tian stabbed his sword in from an angle so precise that it wedged his opponent's weapon in place.

The other guy looked at him with murderous intent, as if he was ready to engage in a war of attrition with him, but the next second, Bai Jing'an's arrow pierced his head. *Geez*, just how optimistic did he have to be to forget that the other side had a sniper?

Xia Tian happily pulled his sword back and turned his head to see how the battle was going.

Doug's fight was already drawing to a close. Meanwhile, Feng Dan had just taken down his opponent and sustained a minor injury to his shoulder. However, as a trade-off, he also managed to stab his blade into his opponent's heart at that very instant. People of his ilk fought like this all the time.

But when he extracted his sword and stepped back, another sword suddenly came at him from behind the stone wall.

This person had obviously been lying in ambush there all along, and it was only when he saw the situation did not bode well that he had the idea to launch a sneak attack. Feng Dan couldn't pull his sword back in time on such short notice, so he grabbed the blade of the incoming sword and kicked out at the attacker's lower body.

This one blow was enough to make the guy scream. As he bent over, Feng Dan kicked him in the jaw and the guy collapsed to the ground. Throughout it all, Feng Dan was held onto the blade as if he didn't feel pain. Xia Tian thought Feng Dan was just the kind of person who fought with no regard for his life, but then again, no one who got involved in the Killing Show was ever sane.

Perhaps he'd moved too hastily, or perhaps he'd choked on something, but Feng Dan suddenly bent over and began to cough violently. Xia Tian could tell at a glance that it was an old injury. Medical science might be advanced these days, but if you had no money, then a lifelong disability would still be a lifelong disability. That wouldn't change just because human technology had advanced. Xia Tian's own right knee was always in bad shape on cloudy days. He hoped he could make enough money this round to get treatment for it again.

Feng Dan kneeled on the ground for quite a long while, supporting his weight with his sword as he broke out in hacking coughs. The blood on his sword was dripping in a never-ending stream while the corpse by his feet slowly went cold.

Doug looked at him coldly. He'd taken down his own opponent earlier, but he didn't seem inclined to help Feng Dan at all.

"I bet it hurts a lot—like there's countless insects crawling in your throat," he said to Feng Dan.

Feng Dan was still coughing non-stop. He couldn't stand up straight, but he still threw Doug a sullen look.

"Too bad that was a blunt blade, or I'd be freed of you already," Doug said.

Xia Tian looked at him, then at the other guy. As the only surviving members of their team, the two of them worked decently well together, but the mood between them was obviously not quite right.

Feng Dan finally stopped coughing and said in a hoarse, choppy voice, "Well, I'd rather take a sharp blade any day than to be stuck with you."

Then they ignored each other and went their respective way to check on the loot. Xia Tian sized them up for a moment.

"Were you...on familiar terms with each other before?"

Doug said nothing. Instead, it was Feng Dan who spoke up. He pointed to his throat. "Courtesy of him."

"We met in the last tournament," Doug clarified.

Both of them fell silent, but even if they didn't say a thing, it was clear what had happened.

The four of them continued on in the oppressive atmosphere. There was a deep and unfathomable animosity between Doug and Feng Dan, but they were both professionals who knew their priorities, so it seemed like they wouldn't suddenly start strangling each other.

And that was indeed the case. They soon encountered another squad and crossed swords again, and the four of them worked in perfect tandem to finish the fight in three minutes.

They still didn't come across a much better sword, but they got a decent bow, and Xia Tian outright gave it to Bai Jing'an.

CHAPTER 11

FINALE STAGE

Xia Tian never found a better sword despite his attempts, and he was out of time too.

Even though they were going slow, they still encountered more and more other players or traces of fierce battles as they continued onward.

As Bai Jing'an said, everyone was converging in a single place.

Xia Tian's squad moved at an overly cautious pace. There were always heroes rising to the occasion even in the toughest of challenges, and it'd be much better to encounter a maleficent god that was already exhausted from continuous fighting when they arrived, rather than a spirited, energetic one.

Xia Tian felt that Bai Jing'an really was a first-rate tactician.

They saw the remains of a great battle near an underground lake. Seven or eight people lay dead on the ground, along with the corpses of some unidentifiable monsters strewn around them.

Looking at the state of the battlefield, these people had been ambushed; the mutant creatures had hidden behind the statues, waiting for them to show up. The Killing Show grew more and more bloody season after season, and these monsters were getting smarter and deadlier year after year.

A young man sat on his heels among the dead bodies. One of his shoulders was badly wounded, but he didn't notice. He held a teammate's body tightly in his arms, trying to staunch the man's bleeding—even though the guy's blood had long ceased to flow. From the looks of it, the guy had been dead for a while.

The young man didn't even look up when Xia Tian and his team walked past him. Stubbornly, he grasped his comrade-in-arms' body, trying in vain to stop the bleeding.

Bai Jing'an glanced at him. He didn't attempt to talk to him; neither did Xia Tian. They'd seen this kind of breakdown before, and they knew that sometimes, all you could do was sit there holding your battle buddy's corpse in your arms. Crisis, logic, and warnings—all of it were meaningless.

Doug stared at this scene for a while before he turned and left. Feng Dan silently followed after him. Although they probably wouldn't, it felt like they were always on the verge of a verbal clash, or crossing swords until one of them died. The one left standing could then heave a long, long sigh of relief.

Xia Tian found it too oppressive. He needed to liven up the atmosphere. Thus, he asked Doug, "So, he killed your friend?"

The others turned to look at him. Xia Tian's smile remained in place. He was used to being the one who asked questions, even if it was a topic everyone deliberately avoided. And besides, even if Doug didn't like it, he couldn't win against him in a fight.

Doug stared at him for a moment, as though he might be calculating the price he'd have to pay for killing him off. Then he answered.

"No big deal. This sort of thing happens every day in the show," he said softly. "His name was Sang Ning... We'd known

each other for a long time. He was the best sniper I knew."

"You killed two of my teammates, too," Feng Dan countered in a hoarse voice.

"That's what I told myself, but that's scant comfort," Doug said, his expression frosty.

When they first met, Doug seemed to be a person who liked to joke around. The corners of his eyes still had the laugh lines of days bygone. But when his face took on a severe expression, not smiling seemed to suit him more. Deep down, he no longer felt like laughing anymore.

"We are both alive," he said, "and we have no choice but to be fucking teammates. But until the day we perish, there's no way we can ever forget that battle and those who died."

"So dramatic," Xia Tian remarked.

"They did it on purpose," Feng Dan said.

"The Killing Show lives for drama," Doug said.

Xia Tian froze for a moment, wondering how he hadn't thought of such a simple thing himself. Of course, the Killing Show could form teams without resorting to "random encounters." They could simply group whoever they wanted together, as long as it was exciting enough.

Doug glared viciously at Feng Dan.

"We were teammates. No matter how natural his death was, I had to go to court," he said. "Who told me to bawl my fucking eyes out last season and provide so much fodder for the production team's amusement and entertainment?!"

His expression reminded Xia Tian of the young man in the pool of blood from before, desperately trying to hug the corpse tighter. At that moment, he was no longer an adult Killing Show player, but a lost little boy who could no longer exit his nightmare.

"The production team will get their bonuses regardless of

who dies," Doug continued, "and then they get to go out and go wild partying. Nope. I'm not fucking going to provide any more entertainment for anyone."

He turned around with a frosty expression and left. The others followed silently. Feng Dan trailed the furthest back, clearly not wanting to walk among the group. Xia Tian didn't want to call him over to rejoin the team and keep up pace with everyone else; everyone had the right to stay in a dark corner if they so wished.

As they continued forward, a blood-like liquid began to seep from the ground, like there was something awakening beneath. Presumably, it was a genetic catalyst of sorts.

They encountered several scuffles where players and mutant creatures had fought each other. These monsters, being the frontline for the resurrection of the maleficent god, were becoming stronger and amassing in greater numbers. The players no longer killed each other, because there were enough of them dying without having to butcher each other. There was no need to worry about the issue of the zombie servants.

They ran into more and more people along the way. Everyone sized each other up and continued on their journey together in silence. It was not so much a team, but more like fellow travelers on the way to the venue of the final match.

By now, the maleficent god's character setting had already been passed down by word of mouth in the castle. Apparently, it would descend upon the human world through the Grand Duke's body and bestow upon him great power and eternal life. Going by the usual practices of the Killing Show, that definitely was not going to accomplished through special effects—it would be a BOSS that was the pricey product of a bio-studio. When the time came, the Grand Duke of Skymoat's mix of genes, chips, and biochemical products would

fly off the shelves in abundance.

That creature believed itself to be an overlord; one that had been schemed against and poisoned in the struggle for power. In its search for a cure, it discovered the temple of the maleficent god and offered up its wife and children as sacrifices. Prompted by the biochip implanted by the production team, it morphed into a terrifying, precisely-designed monster that went on to become the ultimate BOSS of the third round of the tournament.

The players had to find the perpetrator as soon as possible and kill off the maleficent god to restore order.

The crowd grew denser. All the survivors would gather here.

This was the deepest palace underground, the place where pools of blood converged. There was a huge sacrificial altar which looked like the center of the stage, and it was here that the maleficent god would awaken.

Despite going slowly, the group still made it to the final showdown. Like the other arenas, the underground palace was mobile. The producers definitely wouldn't let any players miss the ending because of minor hiccups, like losing their way or not wanting to come.

But going slow still proved to be helpful. They didn't make it in time for the opening; when they arrived, it was already pandemonium all around.

Bai Jing'an was utterly dumbstruck when he saw the creature crawling around the main hall.

The appearance of this man-made monster was unimaginable even in the deepest recesses of a nightmare—or it at least wouldn't be *this* detailed. Only god knew what mentality had led the GBC to design such a monstrosity.

A gigantic, deathly white human body crawled around the underground hall, grabbing living humans and stuffing them into its mouth. It...looked like a human, and even had the same facial features as Wei Ling, but it was gargantuan and naked with a deathly pale complexion. It had huge genitals, and a mouth with which it ate the people it grabbed with its human-like hands. Its belly was already round from all the eating. On its back there were a pair of fleshy wings; either degenerated or still growing. They kept flapping, looking extremely repulsive.

It crawled around on the ground, making sounds like it was crying. Its mouth was full of fangs, and there was a smattering of feathers sparsely growing from its skin. It no longer looked human, but like a giant, deformed chicken.

"I feel like throwing up..." Xia Tian said.

"You're not the only one who feels that way," Bai Jing'an said.

It was a critical situation, but quite a number of players began throwing up in the corner of the battlefield with no regard whatsoever to their images. This creature was really nauseatingly repulsive to an unimaginable degree.

It was still mutating. In theory, it'd only become even more terrifying, but Bai Jing'an only hoped that it'd look a little better when it really turned into the maleficent god. It looked way too much like a human being, so much so that the uncanny valley effect was at its most disturbing.

Amidst its wails and howls, its feathers extended as something grew from its tailbone—a long, revolting flesh-colored appendage that writhed up and down as if in pain. It dawned on Bai Jing'an that its cries didn't just *sound* like crying—it *was* crying.

He didn't know who would want to see this sort of thing, but then he realized that the scene unfolding before his eyes would not appear on the terminals in its entirety. There would only be a few quick clips to show that the metamorphosis had taken place.

In reality, these details—so sickening and lengthy to the

point it could make one suffer a mental breakdown—were only for the viewing pleasure of privileged members.

The "maleficent god" grew even more feathers, which turned black in the firelight. Eventually, it might transform into a giant version of those harbingers of death.

All of a sudden, it stopped what it was doing, trembled a little, and threw up. It vomited a mass of partially digested matter, in which were the human bodies it had chewed to pieces—some were in still recognizable shapes. Several battle-hardened veterans threw up in spite of themselves.

A ravenous hunger, paired with an inability to digest food, was most likely a side-effect of mutation... Bai Jing'an didn't want to know the details.

Anyone who witnessed such a scene would soon realize why every player in the Killing Show was all deranged. This was not an experience any human being should ever have to go through.

Eventually, it morphed into a bird in human shape. Crawling along the ground, it had the figure and limbs of a human, but was covered in black feathers all over. After metamorphosis, its tail unexpectedly grew into a snake with a triangular head and scales with spell-like patterns all over. It was bizarre and insane the way different creatures' characteristics had fused to produce such a chimera.

Several teams were engaged in combat with the monster, and there were many familiar faces from the Killing Show among them. Each of them was tough and nimble, having survived a life of danger and violence. There was no resemblance to how they looked on television when they played dumb and acted cute in interviews. Everyone was hysterically killing, their eyes ablaze with murderous fury. From time to time, one of them would drop dead.

In theory, this creature's terrifying appearance would be its main feature, so the organizers wouldn't make it too powerful; the stars should still be able to emerge victorious and become heroes. At least they couldn't be totally wiped out—could they? But right now, it didn't feel that way at all.

Dead bodies and vomit were everywhere. It was as if they had plummeted into a bloody and filthy hell from which they could never escape.

Bai Jing'an's head was throbbing with pain again. His irreversible brain injury was like a musical note that was intensifying to a crescendo, one which he could never shake off.

He knew it was better to stay as far as he could from the center of the arena as possible—just not so far that the producers would think he was slacking off—but when he saw the creature whip its head around and attack an unguarded player with its sharp beak, he pulled out an arrow and fired in that direction.

The organizers of the third round of the tournament were very stingy with weapons, but the bow he and Xia Tian got was pretty good. Bai Jing'an struck it in the corner of its eye.

The maleficent god trembled, and its sharp beak diagonally grazed past the player's right side. The latter went along with the momentum and dodged the attack, then he grabbed the slanting arrow and stabbed it in with all his might. The creature let loose a hoarse cry as the arrow went all the way into its eye. It hurled the guy against the wall before whipping its head around to glare viciously at Bai Jing'an.

Someone to the west shot at it with a crossbow, and it spun in response, exhausted from the attacks, but the moment it turned around, its viper tail came swinging at Bai Jing'an.

Ever since they got here, Xia Tian looked like he'd been dealt a great shock. Bai Jing'an thought he didn't throw up with the rest of them purely because he'd forgotten to out of fright, but when that creature attacked Bai Jing'an and caught him off guard, Xia Tian instantly acted. He rushed a step in front of Bai Jing'an and wielded his sword to block the tail. The snake coiled twice around the blade and tightened around it.

Xia Tian gripped his sword firmly as the blade twisted under the power of the maleficent god. The snake's fangs shone in the firelight, looking as if it could swallow the blade —but it couldn't. Bai Jing'an drew his own sword and hacked down with all his might.

The maleficent god screamed and whipped around. Its severed tail writhed on the ground, still trying to attack others. Bai Jing'an extended a foot and stomped down on it hard. He did not know where Doug and the others were, or if they were dead or alive; it was impossible to find anyone in this place. Only Xia Tian was always by his side.

Meanwhile, more and more mutant creatures were gathering here, foreshadowing a grand and bloody finale.

Just then, Xia Tian pulled him by the arm.

Bai Jing'an looked up. A...lizardman? It had crawled over at some point and was now staring at them. It was pale all over, with a figure that looked like a human's—but it was so skinny it looked like the ghost of someone who had starved to death. It also had huge, insect-like eyes that took up half of its head, as well as a mouth full of fangs. Not only did it have the characteristics of an underground creature, it also had a human-like face and cries that sounded like a child's.

Only GBC would go to such lengths to create such a monster, then relish in setting it loose to torture and slaughter humans.

The thing looked like the very embodiment of a creature from a nightmare. Its attacks, too, were sneaky and full of malice. Bai Jing'an and Xia Tian expended a lot of effort to kill it off, but another one stealthily crept its way over. Without the slightest hesitation, Xia Tian rushed over to Bai Jing'an and intercepted its blow with the sword he'd yet to put away.

At the same moment, a third, taller one with multi-colored patterns pounced. With his left hand, Xia Tian thrust a short sword into its shoulder. It let out a wretched cry and retreated, but the first one had deftly circled behind Xia Tian and lunged like a bolt of lightning.

Without even looking back, Xia Tian backhandedly plunged his sword into its abdomen. Its movements stalled, and Xia Tian jerked his sword out. He spun around nimbly and the blade of his sword penetrated its right eye and pierced through its head. Grabbing the hilt of the sword, he pulled it out with one foot against the corpse. In his hands, this mass-produced sword used by soldiers was wielded to its fullest potential.

Bai Jing'an had always felt that even though Xia Tian's combat style was not well thought-out, it was highly efficient and methodical. People often said that the warriors of the Lower City fought purely by instinct, but that was not the case at all. This was top-notch coordination, deeply ingrained in his very core.

In the dark, forest-like Lower City, where danger lurked close by like a shadow, one had to make timely use of whatever was at hand. Most of the time, killing wasn't done with a gun, but with a rusty fork, a shard of glass, a thin wire, or your own fists and brain. Xia Tian must have gone through many life-and-death battles in that school of darkness to develop such instincts.

The first time he met Xia Tian, Bai Jing'an had known just what kind of person he was: a young man full of rage and raring to go, one who refused to listen to anyone and was always thinking about killing *something*. Their temperaments were polar opposites. He didn't think he'd like Xia Tian, nor did he think the other guy would like him.

When the producers in the Upper City described people like Xia Tian, they always made them out to be lonely souls with heart-wrenching pasts. Eventually, they'd be healed in the bright and radiant sunlight of the Upper City—and there was usually a man or a woman who could fix it all.

But that would never come to pass. Every one of them had a sprawling dark history and foes whom they could never forgive. They'd meet with nightmarish deaths, one after another. The rules they learned in the Lower City would never ever change.

Such people couldn't be approached, nor appeased. But... going through all this together was enough to make a randomly selected fellow player feel like more than just a companion. More like a...friend.

Xia Tian naturally would not have become a better person under the influence of the Upper City. The Upper City didn't have any such capability to manage this, though it could make one go crazy. He was still himself—full of rage, burning with ambition, and burdened with severe emotional issues.

However, on the battlefields of the Killing Show, no one had any control over the formation of such a relationship. It was a meticulously designed man-made product for consumers' consumption. Yet there was no stopping it—it stemmed from human nature.

Even though he tried his best to keep his distance, Bai Jing'an still knew a lot about Xia Tian. He knew he had a younger sister, and he knew of his fighting style, his mercurial emotions, his edginess, the strength of his hand when he pulled him to safety, and the way he smiled.

There would never be another person like him, ever again.

The lizardman took a step back, whimpered, and readied itself to lunge again. Bai Jing'an had just finished off a bird-headed snake that had sprung out of nowhere when he noticed Xia

Tian looking at something, so he followed the latter's line of sight and froze.

It was that mutant rat.

Yup. That same one.

About an hour ago, Xia Tian had stabbed it in the eye with a spear. It'd wanted to pull it out, but had no success. The spear was still there. The rat had almost doubled in size, and more than a dozen different densely-packed eyes had sprouted on both sides of the punctured one. No doubt they were human eyes, and they all stared fixedly at Xia Tian with chilling hatred.

Maintaining his composure, Xia Tian shifted two steps to the left, and it dawned on Bai Jing'an that Xia Tian was hoping to distance himself from him—because it was only coming for Xia Tian.

Bai Jing'an didn't know where this strange kindness came from. Xia Tian was clearly a hot-headed tough nut with severe emotional issues. Fury blazed in him, and he had a tendency toward severe overkill during combat. Yet he seemed to possess a weird sort of kindness—he would spontaneously push him away or subconsciously block a heavy blow meant for him, even if it posed significant danger to himself.

Maybe it's because he's used to taking care of others, Bai Jing'an thought. Even if he'd never asked, he knew that in that city of darkness where everyone had to fight with their lives to survive, Xia Tian was likely the most outstanding one among them. He had no other choice but to look after others from very early on.

No matter how cold-hearted and merciless a person pretended to be, there'd always be someone special—parents, friends, a lover, or a sister who's too young.

Even if he didn't have that level of power.

No one did.

The mutant rat pounced, swift as lightning.

It swept past Bai Jing'an, emitting an intense, rancid stench. A thought flashed through Bai Jing'an's mind—it was no coincidence that it could find them. The organizers loved the theme of pursuit and revenge, so they hastened its evolution and drew it to this place.

This would be an exciting episode—the cunning rat on the hunt for the human who hurt it, tirelessly following his trail through the dark underground palace before it made a reappearance in the final showdown...

Meanwhile, in the maleficent god's palace, for all his first-rate skills, Xia Tian still couldn't even find a suitable sword.

It was the classic clichéd horror movie—bloody, bizarre, fatalistic. Especially when it came to Xia Tian; such a young man from the District N prison, who'd gone through untold hardships to make his way to the Upper City.

His hometown, having been through the greatest civil insurrection and largest massacre of the century, was a constant hot topic in the Upper City's entertainment circle. Mutant creatures still ran rampant through the area. There were even rumors that their intelligence was high enough to form a sewer kingdom, from which they hunted and preyed on weak human beings... He'd finally come to the Upper City, only to be trapped underground in the third round of the tournament and, in the process, encounter a giant, highly intelligent mutant rat...

How dramatic; like some kind of horrible destiny.

This had definitely been custom-made just for him. And it was worth a hefty bonus.

It all happened too fast. In the instant the mutant rat sprang, Xia Tian plunged his sword viciously into its skull. The blade went almost two-thirds of the way in, but the rat was using so much force and its momentum was so unstoppable that it slammed hard into him.

Xia Tian tightened his grip on the sword and ruthlessly thrust it in deep, pushing the rat back. But the next second, the sword in his hand broke.

The rat bit down hard on his neck and knocked him to the ground. He was a tall person, but even he seemed fragile under the claws of such a gigantic creature. Bai Jing'an wasn't sure if it had bitten an artery, although it looked like it had—

It then clamped down on Xia Tian's shoulder and yanked him backward so abruptly that it almost tore his arm off. Xia Tian gripped whatever was left of his sword and plunged it into its body from beneath its jaws.

The battle was extremely bloody. It was a hand-to-hand melee that demonstrated humanity's most pressing desire to survive. The fight lasted less than ten seconds, but it was enough to hit a five-star purchase rate.

After all that foreshadowing, they finally ushered in an ending for him. This would be a victory in viewership ratings. It was worth a win.

When it happened, Bai Jing'an knew he would be too late to do anything. It had happened too fast. It always happened so fast.

He felt his head hurting; it was probably still thanks to that blow by the river, but now, it was no longer dizziness. The distant pain from before had found him for real, turning into a scream that drowned out everything else.

He looked at Xia Tian in the pool of blood, knowing deep in his heart that this scene was all too common. Someone was about to die. His artery had been severed, and it would be a matter of minutes before he bled out... He'd seen this happen countless times.

He seemed to have never left that red-tinted darkness, where his mind was always a blank and his hands were always

stained with blood. Everywhere around him were people he couldn't save.

He looked up, knowing that countless hidden cameras were in the darkness, coldly filming. He couldn't see further in, but he knew innumerable eyes were watching it all.

There was no past and no future there—only fear and despair, dragging him down and down to the deepest abyss where he could never see the sunlight again.

Bai Jing'an walked over to Xia Tian. At the corner of his eye, a huge humanoid lizard flashed into sight and lunged at him. He didn't even look at it as his long sword pierced its throat. Without even stopping in his tracks, he grabbed its head and slashed down at an angle to the right, severing half of its neck. He moved with ruthless efficiency and a practiced ease that seemed deeply ingrained in his bones, as if he was born already knowing how to kill.

Bai Jing'an discarded the corpse with no letup in his pace. His white outfit was dirty, and as he passed through an area illuminated by the moss, his clothes reflected a faint glow—as if all the light in the arena was converging on him.

He was like a sharp blade just drawn from its sheath, stained with blood, dust, and the lives of countless people. And yet its glint was harsh and cutting, making it impossible for anyone to look away.

He walked to Xia Tian. The guy had fallen to the ground, and his eyes had already lost focus. It was as if he was looking somewhere else... Bai Jing'an wondered if it was that same expanse of darkness. When he tried to remember the past and the people he'd once loved, he couldn't recall a thing.

The darkness had consumed it all.

The mutant rat was dead. He kneeled, pushed its corpse aside, and hugged Xia Tian, as though he was all that was left in the darkness. It was chaos all around, but he didn't notice. He tried his best to press down on Xia Tian's neck, but the blood was still gushing out in torrents. The guy had lost his earlier murderous, untamed look; he looked lost and helpless, as if he was still unsure what had happened.

But he knew.

People like him always knew.

He opened his mouth and said to Bai Jing'an, "Dee Dee...my little sister..."

His voice was very soft and gentle, which was rare for him. The way he looked right now, so weak and innocent, fueled Bai Jing'an's fury. It had been a long time since he'd been this furious, and he didn't understand why it was happening now.

"I won't do a thing," he said fiercely. "Get out of this alive and go back for her yourself!"

Xia Tian looked overhead with empty eyes. After he spoke, Bai Jing'an realized that Xia Tian had never thought he could get him to agree—he didn't think anyone would do so much for another person. As he'd said before, she would be on her own if misfortune was to befall her. For him, disappearing without a sound in this kind of darkness was probably quite normal.

Death, destruction, and despair—these were all common occurrences. He wouldn't even feel incredulous about it.

An inexplicable rage in him blazed so hard that Bai Jing'an trembled. The one enraged was the person standing in the darkness in the deepest recesses of his soul; the weak, insubstantial specter of the old world, which he thought he'd buried deep.

Xia Tian flashed a smile at him. With his face covered in blood, his smile appeared all the more stirring, and still as blithe as ever.

"Don't make that face... You'll have other teammates," he said.

Bai Jing'an felt the pain in his head swell to intolerable proportions. This was a pain that would never go away, and his surroundings would always be pitch dark—a never-ending battlefield of bloodshed and carnage composed of dead bodies, killings, pain, and cameras.

All I want is to... save something, he thought, *...anything.*

But he'd never been able to save anyone. Nothing he did ever made a difference. Xia Tian's blood was still flowing between his fingers, his life ebbing away. No matter how important it was to him, no one cared. Death was humble and commonplace.

He tightly held the teammate who was always too energetic. The body in his arms was weak and compliant. He heard Xia Tian's voice saying, very softly, "So cold..."

And then he closed his eyes, at last finding rest, just like so many of his companions before him.

Lights suddenly flooded the area.

The oppressive sky vanished, receding layer after layer like sugared bricks to reveal the precisely calculated brightness and azure blue behind it.

The color of the sky. The color of the end.

Countless laser fireworks blossomed in the artificial sky, and Bai Jing'an heard the host's cheerful voice. "The third round of the 199th Killing Show Asaijin Team Tournament by the Gilded Broadcasting Corporation has officially concluded. Everyone's courage and wisdom has passed the test—"

He froze in place, unable to react. His hands were still trembling, and even his blood was boiling from the agony and pain. He couldn't react.

The host, dressed in a medieval-style costume, continued, "Injured players, please stay where you are and don't move. Our medical staff will provide treatment as soon as possible—"

Bai Jing'an went blank for two seconds before he felt for

Xia Tian's pulse in a fluster. His hand was shaking so badly he couldn't find it for a moment. He felt a beat so faint he couldn't be sure of it; it was so weak it felt like an illusion.

Then came the second beat.

Bai Jing'an fumbled to hug Xia Tian and bury his face in the sticky blood on his neck. He knew his expression was a terrible mess right now; he didn't want anyone to see.

Xia Tian would survive. No matter how bad the situation was, the medical department of the Upper City could bring people back from the brink of death if they wanted to.

Across from him where a darkness and madness beyond his comprehension lay, he could feel the cameras watching all of it coldly. They aimed at his face, capturing the most minuscule of his reactions to mass broadcast. Every single moment from now on would be captured and seen by all. It'd be replayed and discussed over and over again, dissected and ridiculed with indifferent amusement.

He felt utterly pathetic and terribly ashamed, and there was also that ice-cold rage.

But as he held his battle buddy, knowing he would survive, he was still crying, unable to control himself at all.

CHAPTER 12

NEW STAR

Xia Tian had to spend three days in the intensive treatment bay. The medical staff assured Bai Jing'an with a brilliant smile that it wouldn't be long before he was out and jumping around again.

The smile was way too enthusiastic, and Bai Jing'an just wanted to stay far away from them. He was covered in blood, and he felt like his expression wasn't cold and detached enough. But after a moment of hesitation, he followed them—he wanted to know how Xia Tian was doing.

It was very unlike the oppressive cold horror of the arena. The monsters had come to a standstill, collapsed to the ground under GBC's lights the moment the match ended. Stylishly-dressed staff entered the arena, bringing with them large amounts of booze, compliments, and medical equipment. Each of them wore a smile as they chatted excitedly about the battle. In no time, the terrifying underground palace turned into a banquet hall.

Bai Jing'an was drenched in blood from head to toe. He could see his own hands trembling non-stop. He clenched his

fists, not wanting the cameras to capture it on film.

The players around him fared no better. The ones who weren't lying on medical beds were battered and badly shaken.

Meanwhile, the cacophony of voices around him grew louder, with countless faces laughing and chatting. Booze flowed freely in generous portions, and the scent of expensive perfume and luxurious clothing permeated the air. But whatever was left of the battle's atmosphere didn't dissipate after the match, and the incompatibility of horror and merriment only accentuated the glaring difference between the two.

Bai Jing'an saw Doug as he was leaving. The latter had sustained an injury to his forehead, and blood was flowing over half of his face. His complexion was so pale it was startling. No medical staff had gone to him yet. Someone handed him a glass of alcohol; he took it with trembling hands, but didn't think to drink it. A person next to him was telling him loudly, "It's definitely a classic!"

He didn't catch sight of Feng Dan. He didn't know if the latter was dead or not.

Bai Jing'an followed the medical staff through the rainbow gate and stepped into the area outside the arena. The place had already been set up with decorative advertisements, mountains of booze, and trees of snacks in preparation for a grand dinner party.

He'd only just stepped out when he was pulled aside for a quick interview in front of a billboard. The journalists bombarded him with questions about Xia Tian's injuries and his feelings in those last moments when he thought Xia Tian was about to die. Bai Jing'an himself hadn't even figured out how he felt, but the media had apparently already let their imaginations run wild.

There were also some questions about his parents thrown into the mix. These people had obviously already dug up his past,

which was normal, and he was prepared for it.

If Bai Jing'an had been in a trance just now, the familiar atmosphere quickly snapped him back on guard. He couldn't cope with the darkness, chaos, and screams in his head, but he immediately regained his rhythm for something else. This world was deranged and ravenous; he had to shut it out and do his best to hide himself.

His expression instantly went cold—not the coldness of animosity, but the kind that shut down any display of emotion. He showed a model smile and answered the asker, "Xia Tian will be fine. I believe in the abilities of the Gilded Group's medical department—"

He said he felt bad about Xia Tian getting hurt, that he was an outstanding battle buddy, and so on. No one was going to dissect such an answer, repost it everywhere, and interpret it dramatically...well, hopefully.

The journalist also asked if he'd been a warrior before. His final blow had left a deep impression, stunning as it'd been. This made Bai Jing'an a little nervous, but he didn't let it show on his face.

"I'm glad I did well in the end," he replied with a smile. "I was anxious and didn't think too much about it. Maybe it brought out the potential of the human body—"

Someone was projecting a hologram not far away from him as he spoke. He glanced over and saw images of Xia Tian and himself in at least three spots. He tried his best to keep his expression neutral, but he could sense his palms sweating slightly.

They were famous now.

Bai Jing'an didn't want to attend the party. Not many people wanted to participate, but there was a stipulation in the contract that said you had to be wherever the GBC wanted you to be.

The medical department treated him quickly, then he showered and changed into his sponsor's clothing. It was a well-fitting, stylish formal suit that accentuated his figure. The top brass had even assigned him an image consultant; an elegantly-dressed young woman named Mo Huitian. Her exaggeratedly dyed hair couldn't hide the weariness in her eyes. She said he could call her Huitian or Xiaotian, and if he liked, he could also call her Xiaohui, but no one called her by her full name. No matter how she pretended to be bubbly, her eyes lacked life.

She handed Bai Jing'an over to some stylists, who quickly gave him a makeover. The entire process was as tense as a battle with mutant creatures, with a vocabulary of commands thrown all around and a quick tutorial on dealing with the dinner party.

After some fuss, Bai Jing'an saw a stranger in the mirror.

He wore a well-fitting, stand-up collar formal suit that accentuated his height and long legs. His facial features were dashing and gentle, and he looked much younger than he remembered. The chaos, pain, and killing from half an hour ago was cloaked under this makeover, revealing nothing out of the ordinary. He looked like a model in a magazine, seemingly oblivious to the suffering of the world.

This kind of celebration party would last for a week. It was a jubilant version of a news hot-pot. Journalists weaved in and out and asked all sorts of questions, embellishing the bloody and twisted events in the arena as something rare and interesting for broadcast to the world. Some journalists were friendly, while a portion tried to provoke him by asking questions that tested his self-restraint. Some even came with videos. Bai Jing'an couldn't estimate how many times he'd heard his father's screams before his death and seen his mother's funeral. These people hoped he would react so they'd have something to write about, but he handled it pretty well. All these years, he'd never said a word about it. After a short time in the arena, it became a standard question. Everyone was talking about it—his past was like cotton wool pulled out and tossed everywhere as they asked how he'd felt back then.

If he could handle it years ago when they asked a six-year-old him how it felt to lose his family, he could handle it now too.

Bai Jing'an answered these questions as nonchalantly and dully as he could. There was no hint of criticism in his words, which were just as polite as he appeared to be. It was as if he had not been hurt in any way, or did not take offense for whatever reason. He hoped they'd lose interest in him soon.

Among the questions he answered, two-thirds were about Xia Tian. They asked about his hometown, hobbies, living habits, who he'd bedded before, and so on, then they'd over-interpret every single one of his words and expressions.

Hope that guy doesn't have any painful memories, Bai Jing'an thought. These people could dig up everything and hype it up like mad, ripping open your scars before you to watch your reaction.

Amidst this extravagant mayhem, the thought of Xia Tian brought him some comfort.

After being released from the treatment bay, the guy would no longer need to steal food from dinner parties or swipe someone wallet. He was already a star; he'd be in high demand, and he'd become the darling of the world.

Bai Jing'an stayed at the dinner party for an hour—the minimum amount of time he had to put in an appearance as stipulated in the contract—before taking his leave. Most players tended to leave in a hurry after staying long enough, while others stayed behind to party. Alcohol and crowds could make one forget many things.

Oh, yeah. When Bai Jing'an was about to leave, he discovered he had a new car. It was typical for sponsors to hand out car keys after matches to players, like they were giving out candies. They handed him the keys to a luxury car and snapped a photo. He hurriedly took them, got into his new car, and drove home.

The car isolated him from the din outside. Bai Jing'an drove out of the main banquet area, braked to a stop, and stared at himself in the mirror. The air smelled of alcohol and perfume, and he looked like a young, talented man who couldn't tear himself away from the party. Everything that had transpired at the dinner party and in the arena an hour ago felt like they'd come from two completely different worlds, and the chasm between them was so unfathomably deep it was impossible to bridge and made him dizzy.

Bai Jing'an sucked in a breath and switched to autopilot. He used his terminal to connect to the GBC official website to check out the Killing Show's videos. He didn't want to see his face on the screen, but avoiding it wouldn't solve the problem.

The official website was so overcrowded that he couldn't squeeze his way in at all. With a frosty expression, Bai Jing'an thought about how insufferably stingy they were not to provide the players with a separate channel. Simply too horrendous.

And so, he decided to hack his way in from the side. But it was crowded here, too; there were probably many people entering through the backdoor. There weren't many hackers in the early years, but now, they were everywhere. Apart from civilian experts, there were also a large number of cyber support specialists who'd registered in the Killing Show.

It'd take some time to hack his way in, so Bai Jing'an took the time to read the columns on the official website. Their squad's header design was exquisite, depicting two guns leaning casually together. One was a Gretta Type III, while the other was a

Marauder Killer Edition. The design was quite fitting, and there was a line of text written at the bottom: *I'd take guns any day.*

The forum was rife with discussion about Xia Tian's injuries, and some were talking about just how deep Bai Jing'an's friendship with Xia Tian was. *Very deep, apparently, literally sworn friends ready to die for each other, like each other's better halves, and the final scenes had them all in tears*—so on and so forth. Latte was also mentioned because of the funeral, while the doctor had completely disappeared from their squad.

And then he saw the full version of the video of his and Xia Tian's final scene. Even though he already knew the situation was bad, he was still shocked at how terrible and raw it was.

The person in the video standing amidst the slaughterhouse-like showdown was a stranger. Younger than he'd imagined, and more helpless and furious. Wearing his emotions on his sleeve and clutching a terrible quality sword, wanting to kill anyone who dared to stand in his way because he couldn't bear another loss.

He remembered that distant diagnosis: *irreversible brain damage.* That was why the person in the scene was so unfamiliar. Too many memories had been lost to the damage... There were some terrifying things lurking in his mind, lying dormant in his subconscious, which would manifest any moment he lost control. He could never be rid of them.

This was a serious illness. The GBC medical department, who believed his claim that he was bitten by a mutant rat carrying the virus that had fled to the Upper City, once told him that this damage had greatly corroded his long-term memory, making him incapable of controlling his emotions... Which was why he was like that in the video.

He looked at Xia Tian's face in the footage. Covered in blood, the man smiled at him and said that he'd have another teammate soon enough. He felt a wave of stifling pain in his chest, like a blade twisting in his heart.

He couldn't return to where he'd been and remain unmoved as he watched him die.

He...was a friend.

Although not much of one.

He hadn't made a friend in so many years, but that massive net still caught him.

And then exposed everything to the cameras.

Sitting in a chair with screens hanging around him and empty bottles by his feet, Yakovsky felt just like a new-age sweatshop worker.

The celebration party was in full swing, and almost everyone in the office building had left. Sitting alone, he took out another bottle of booze.

From his position, he could see the illuminated banquet area. The producers liked seeing their stars; it was like going to meet their own creations. They'd fawn on them and be toadied up to, but Yakovsky never indulged in that... Uh, well, not exactly never, but one always learns from past mistakes.

At first, it started out okay. It was like a game then, and everything was "super cool"...but it turned into a nightmare. When that person died, he drank for about a month straight. He had no idea what he was doing. Consequently, he almost got himself fired by the GBC, and it wasn't the kind of firing that allowed you to go home and live a normal life.

Yakovsky did all he could to pull himself together, but this only made him despise himself even more. From then on, he tried to avoid meeting any of his managed players. However, given that they were in the same company, it was inevitable for them to run into one another. If that ever happened, he'd

pretend they'd gotten the wrong person.

One time, a star recognized him, but he insisted that he was a janitor and even started cleaning before he managed to get the person to leave. He didn't know if that guy thought he'd mistaken him for someone else, or if he thought he was mentally ill. Either way, he didn't care.

He couldn't talk to them and pretend that everyone was the same. He'd rather pretend those people didn't exist, weren't alive, had no kin or friends, no love or hatred, no emotions or feuds. He hoped they wouldn't have any sort of relationship with him.

In this business, countless faces would come and go. If you got to know them, some would lurk forever in your nightmares, never to leave.

He didn't need to boost those numbers further.

Yakovsky recalled the two young men—they were still the safest bets in his memory.

The moment Xia Tian encountered that rat, his fate had been sealed.

Yakovsky didn't like it at all; pandering to the audience made it out to be like some third-rate horror movie, and he harbored a particular hatred for the guy who submitted this plot. His name was Qi Xiashang, and he was delegated from *Deviant Lab*. When team tournaments began, all resources would be concentrated on the show. That guy had put in a direct call to Georg, and the new show producer, eager for the arena to be full of sensational highlights, immediately approved the storyline.

From a certain perspective, it was indeed fitting—a dark allegory about not being able to escape the world you belonged to. It'd make one's blood run cold even in a warm room.

But...he saw Bai Jing'an's fury during that final attack on screen, when Xia Tian moved away from him after realizing he himself was the monster's target. Yakovsky had never thought

Bai Jing'an would lose control; the medical data said Bai Jing'an had irreversible brain damage, and Yakovsky had only found out about that after Bai Jing'an became famous—that final attack had garnered him a lot of fans. Bai Jing'an didn't look like someone who would have a problem like this. He was more composed and apathetic than most normal people. He knew what he was facing. But these days, you couldn't avoid a mental breakdown even if you tried your best.

Yakovsky did a close-up for these tender moments and slowed them down. In these frames, the theme of darkness disappeared, and warm light blazed in this young man with a tragic destiny. An allegory of the darkness was thus turned into an inspirational story.

Three days later, Bai Jing'an went to GBC medical center to pick Xia Tian up. The higher-ups had issued a notice that he had to go, and apparently, there'd be a bunch of cameras following.

He arrived in the lobby, where countless journalists lurked. Advertising billboards for interviews dotted the place. Other stars from the Killing Show were also gathered here for a check-up or treatment. Some were here to pick up their own teammates, like he was.

Their image consultant didn't come, saying that she'd arrive later. After three days of grilling him with tests, she was pretty confident in his ability to handle interviews.

Bai Jing'an took on two interviews in the lobby; that was the minimum requirement as stipulated by the contract. All the questions had to do with Xia Tian. These people knew every word, smile, and tiny gesture he'd said and made to him, and they were relentless in asking him the meanings behind them. He was astounded how much these people had come to understand about his formerly little-known teammate in such a short

period of time, and most of it was stuff that even he himself didn't know.

Xia Tian's fans saw him as a hero who wanted to protect those he loved, only to get lost in the darkness as he did. Huitian candidly told Bai Jing'an that Xia Tian had just shown his most wretched and despairing moment before the cameras, and such moments had power.

Xia Tian was formidable, but in such a world, he was also fragile. Yet he once again returned to the world for the sake of the people he wanted to protect.

GBC was very clear about the direction in which his image was to be shaped. The production team was now looking around for relevant material, using whatever they could find and making up whatever they couldn't.

Xia Tian, who had once lost his way in the darkness and died, was about to reawaken. All the relevant websites and GBC did specials about it, so many that it looked like a celebration. The hero had left the battlefield alive and returned to the human world, a world where countless billboards flashed, and the producers, journalists, and technicians of the Upper City were engaged in a battle day and night for the sake of molding the hero's image.

Rationally, Bai Jing'an knew that this was just a cog in the massive star-making machine, but when he saw the details, he was still amazed at its powerful impact on human emotions. No matter how much he readied himself for it, this sort of fame still caught him off guard when it happened. It was so powerful it was incredible.

He tried to imagine what it'd be like for Xia Tian to leave the medical bay and step into this world. The guy had always fantasized about achieving success and fame, and now he had it all. Bai Jing'an wondered how he'd react.

When Bai Jing'an walked into the room, Xia Tian had already come out of the medical bay, having just taken a shower and put on his medical garb. He was wrapped in a thick blanket that had the medical center logo on it. It was warm in here, but he'd still bundled himself up tightly.

There was an empty cup of hot chocolate in front of him, and he was holding a box of marshmallows in his hand, having already eaten half of it. It was a while before he noticed Bai Jing'an, and his reaction was slower than usual.

He looked up at him with a slightly dazed expression. His hair had been haphazardly tied up, and he cut a pretty sorry sight.

"Xia Tian?" Bai Jing'an prompted.

The guy didn't respond, and the doctor at the side smiled as warmly as the spring breeze as he told Bai Jing'an that there might be issues with his reactions and emotions. This was par for the course. After all, his breathing and heart had stopped by the time he'd arrived at the medical bay; it was inevitable for a person to have all sorts of issues after dying.

Bai Jing'an moved closer to Xia Tian and noticed he was shaking a little.

"Xia Tian?" he prompted again.

Xia Tian looked at him for a while before responding. "Bai Jing'an?"

"Yup," Bai Jing'an said. "How much do you still remember?"

The familiar face looked at him again for another two seconds before flashing a smile that, given just how dazzling it was, didn't look like the smile of someone who'd just died.

"Everything," Xia Tian answered. "I remember a little about dying too. It was really fucking cold, man."

Bai Jing'an smiled at him too. Xia Tian set down the marshmallows and threw down the blanket. He made the medical center's white hospital gown look like some sort of fashionable outfit.

Bai Jing'an was about to say something more when the guy took a step forward and gave him a big hug.

Although his thought in that very instant was: *No hugs. There are cameras. And look at how gratified the medical staff looks, like they're watching a joyous reunion in a family drama...* But the hug still comforted him. His teammate's embrace was strong, and his body warm. It was a hug from someone who'd escaped death, a hug from someone alive. So he raised a hand and patted Xia Tian on the back.

The guy pulled back and happily took him by the shoulders. "I knew it! I knew we'd be fine!"

"Yeah, right, the hell you did," Bai Jing'an retorted.

Xia Tian paused and looked around quizzically at all the people in the room staring at them with smiles, not daring to approach.

Bai Jing'an patted him on the shoulder. "You're a megastar now. Now go and change your clothes."

Xia Tian went to do so. Bai Jing'an followed after him and closed the door behind them.

Xia Tian took off his hospital clothes nonchalantly. Bai Jing'an knew that the media would make an unwarranted fuss over him coming in directly like this, but he was in a hurry, and this was the only chance for them to talk alone.

As he picked up the clothes the sponsor had prepared, he said, "Listen. You're a star now."

"You said that before," Xia Tian said as he put on his trousers.

"An image consultant will be coming later. The company sent her to manage us and deal with any trouble."

"Is she pretty?"

"You just woke up, so don't think about that," Bai Jing'an

said. "Also, they know about your younger sister."

Xia Tian stopped mid-action, and Bai Jing'an continued, "They filmed that conversation after the funeral."

Xia Tian's face went cold. When a Killing Show star who killed without blinking made such an expression, the temperature in any room dropped by two degrees.

"You'll face similar questions when you go out," Bai Jing'an said. "Stay calm when replying. You can't call her from the medical center; there will be wiretaps. We'll plan on how to go back for her and get her up here when we return. It'll be impossible to keep it a secret; there'll be a bunch of journalists following. You have to..."

The door opened. The woman with the exaggeratedly dyed hair stood there and said coldly, "Are you guys getting it on in here or what?"

"This is our image consultant," Bai Jing'an said. "She will give you some guidance on answering the journalists' questions."

The woman introduced herself and gave her name. Xia Tian smiled at her, surprising Bai Jing'an at how quickly his expression changed. The coldness and indignation that had been there a moment ago had vanished in an instant. His smile was warm and cheerful, kind and amicable.

"I knew it. No way it wouldn't be a pretty lady," he said as he shook hands with her.

Then he picked up the shirt at the side and put it on, looking very handsome. Bai Jing'an smiled at Huitian—that's what they were calling her for now—and closed the door again. Once again, they were the only ones left.

"What else?" Xia Tian asked.

"They haven't gotten your house ready yet. You'll have to stay at mine for now," Bai Jing'an said.

"Wasn't it advertised that you can choose any house you

want in the Auspicious Light District as long as you survive the third round?"

"Yup, but they want to make it look like there's no vacant houses available so that they can make you stay at my place," Bai Jing'an explained. "They said it's not appropriate for you to return to an empty house after what happened to you, and me 'taking you home' will be a heartwarming topic of conversation."

Xia Tia glanced at him strangely, but couldn't think of anything to say, so he asked, "Then what about the house I rented at Starry Sky Condominiums?"

"The lease was canceled."

"Then what about the penalty for breach of contract?!"

"They paid for it."

"Well, at least they still have a bit of conscience."

"They will ask you about my past..." Bai Jing'an started, but hesitated for a moment. "Just say you don't know. Of course, you really don't. I just wanted to tell you."

"What is it?" Xia Tian asked.

"Look it up online when we get back. It's everywhere," Bai Jing'an said in a derisive tone. He looked at the time. "Also, don't touch me when we go out."

Xia Tian looked at him oddly, and Bai Jing'an replied, "We've been attracting too much buzz lately. I don't like being in the limelight so much."

"I like buzz. Regardless of whatever you're talking about, I think anything you don't like will be good," Xia Tian quipped and touched his hair. Bai Jing'an swatted his hand away. How could he ever forget just how annoying this guy was?

"Okay, I won't touch you," Xia Tian said with a smile. "So now I have to live in your house, and you won't even let me touch you?"

"This isn't funny," Bai Jing'an said as he handed him a coat.

Xia Tian deftly put it on. It was a new style of formal suit from one of the first-class luxury brands in the Upper City, and it perfectly accentuated his slender figure. It was the classic warrior figure. Even the expensive coat couldn't hide the danger and explosive power in his movements. On the contrary, he *added* a deadly charm, perfectly meeting sponsors' expectations.

Xia Tian didn't notice it at all, just like how he didn't notice his own nudity in the arena. He didn't button up, instead wearing those fine clothes like some dangerous undesirables. He turned to Bai Jing'an.

"So, I can touch as I please when I get to your house?"

An annoyed Bai Jing'an moved to help him button up. "Yup, on the floor or on the bed, whatever. Now, keep a low profile."

He pushed the door and went out. Discontented, Xia Tian followed behind him and quipped, "You aren't as easy to bully as you used to be."

They returned to the ward, and Huitian briefed the newly revived star on things to note during the interviews.

Other than touching on the format for answering certain questions, she also reminded him he didn't have to answer questions he didn't like. At the same time, she emphasized the type of image the higher-ups had designed for him and wanted him to portray. For example, his relationship with Bai Jing'an was that of good buddies—*very* good buddies. If one of them wanted to kill the other, they must never do it in front of the cameras; if one of them died, the other had to put on a touching display of overwhelming grief.

After a short media tutorial, they made their way to the lobby. Surprisingly enough, there weren't a whole bunch of journalists swarming over to surround them. Everyone merely turned their heads to look at Xia Tian.

Bai Jing'an suddenly realized that something was about to happen. Not like the ambush on the arena, but similar in nature—everyone here was prepared, knowing what was about to happen.

They were all waiting for Xia Tian to show up.

A woman with dyed orange hair walked out of the crowd with a large entourage following behind her. She was all smiles. Rainbow highlights framed her face at the corner of her temples. Very few people could pull off such gorgeous colors, but it was a cinch for her.

Most of the Killing Show players recognized her face; she was one of the official hosts of the GBC Asajin Team Tournament, responsible year-round for announcing the end of the match at its most devastating, tragic moment. She'd declare the cessation of killing and proclaim that the survivors had passed the test, and that for the upcoming period, they could dine, drink, and make merry to their hearts' content, receive their rewards, and embrace their loved ones.

"Xia Tian," she called and hugged him affectionately. They'd never met before, but they both acted like they were on familiar terms with each other.

Journalists gathered around them like piranhas, waiting eagerly.

"Miss Tangerine," Xia Tian greeted with a dazzling smile. "I often dreamed of your beautiful face in my long sleep after death, so I felt like I just had to wake up."

She giggled at his teasing words.

"From the way you behaved in the arena, I wouldn't know you were such a sweet-talker," she said, putting her hand on his shoulder as he flashed a pretty smile at her.

Bai Jing'an's gaze oscillated between the two. Had this been under normal circumstances, it probably wouldn't haven taken long for them to tumble into bed and get busy under the sheets. Showbiz in the Upper World was complicated. It was impossible to maintain a distance and keep to yourself. This place was a series of merry-making revelries that would squeeze one dry before discarding them in the sewers.

He didn't know what Xia Tian would do, and felt nothing would happen between him and her. She was setting him up, and he was vindictive and bad-tempered.

Just then, Tangerine's grip on Xia Tian's shoulder tightened. Showing a concerned expression, she said, "I don't want to appear mysterious, but I have to witness what comes next. You can think of it as a gift. We were surprised ourselves."

Xia Tian went momentarily blank as she gave him a gentle smile and stepped back. The people behind her also made way and cleared out a path.

It was then Bai Jing'an saw her.

The little girl, who looked much younger than six years old, was dirty all over, so much so that the original colors of her clothes were no longer distinguishable. Her hair could have been braided into a pair of pigtails, but locks of them were hanging loose over her shoulders. Her face was slightly cleaner; someone had helped her wipe it down in order to reveal her sweet and pretty facial features.

She stood carefully in the lavish and brightly illuminated lobby, tense and ready to flee. Bai Jing'an recognized the posture. This was a child used to hiding and running away.

Xia Tian froze for a moment on seeing her, and then she saw him too. Her eyes lit up. The dark clouds of gloom hanging over her dissipated, and she turned back into a six-year-old girl as she dashed toward him under countless eyes and cameras.

This was one of the rare, fully free videos from GBC, supposedly because such a touching, blissful scene ought to be seen by all. So for a time, an innumerable amount of people from the Upper City clicked to watch this new star's family re-union video. Thanks to the marketing campaign, a significant amount of attention was directed his way.

In the video, Xia Tian crouched down in that exorbitantly expensive formal suit and picked up the little girl in his arms, not minding her grimy appearance in the slightest. He did this with such natural ease it was apparent he was an old hand at picking up children, a very different impression than the one he gave others before. She immediately relaxed as soon as she was in Xia Tian's arms, as if this was a harbor that could shelter her from the world and allow her to be a child again.

At the same time, the show also inserted cool clips of Xia Tian in the third round of the tournament. The man who was ruthless and swift in killing and threw a flying kiss at the mirror was an entirely different species from the guy hugging this little girl. It explained to everyone why he fought, giving him a reason, an answer, and a happy ending.

In the bright sunlit lobby, the little girl from the Lower City pointed to the sun, emphasizing it several times to her older brother before she started chattering about her own experience.

Flame was dead—that sounded like the person Xia Tian had initially entrusted her to. He'd died on the streets, for reasons unknown. Poppa had already taken the buyer's money, and she realized the man was looking all over for her. She didn't dare to go home or go out on the streets. At a loss for what to do, her only options were to come to the Upper City.

She bribed the bus driver's son with a piece of fruit candy and snuck into the relay station by hiding in the back seat, then she hid in the luggage compartment to reach the District N21 central station, the only place with transportation to the Upper City.

It was sweltering in the luggage compartment, but she could handle the heat. She showed Xia Tian her arm, burned by the engine. There were many other wounds on it, some of which had festered because they'd gone without treatment for too long. She'd smuggled herself here, and the journey was nothing short of a thriller novel. Looking at it from this angle, she was not stupid at all; she was a prime model of intelligence.

As she was saying all this, the people around them wore moved and relieved expressions. As for the sudden death of the person who took her in, the buyer's proactiveness, and her sudden dire circumstances, no one other than a seasoned producer would notice anything odd.

Bai Jing'an maintained his composure as he moved in a little closer and pressed down on Xia Tian's shoulder. He could sense that his battle buddy was as tense as a bowstring stretched taut. But Xia Tian relaxed, and the gloom and fury vanished just as quickly it'd come. He smiled and sat quietly on the sofa, as friendly and handsome as he'd been earlier before the media, letting everyone see this family reunion play out.

He knew he had nowhere else to go, and he had a younger sister to take care of.

He introduced Dee Dee to Bai Jing'an. She carefully shook the tactician's hand, and the three of them sat on the sofa, looking the very picture of a happy family. The family of three put on a show for about twenty minutes, and Miss Tangerine even suggested they treat Dee Dee's wounds—live. Finally, they got in the car and prepared to set off for home.

As soon as they entered the car, the parties involved all fell silent. Only Dee Dee leaned against the window, peering out with astonishment, looking like she'd just come to heaven.

After a while, their new image consultant feebly said, "I had no idea this would happen."

Xia Tian smiled at her, indicating that it was okay. His smile was always so peaceful and tranquil, but Bai Jing'an noticed his hands were still trembling a little. The chill of death had yet to completely subside. Even his smile was barely discernible.

Huitian nodded and said nothing more about it. There was nothing she could say.

"I'll get Dee Dee's residency registration done before noon," she said, speaking quickly. "You probably won't be able to bring in any other relatives; the higher-ups wouldn't agree. The company wants your family members to go through a selection process so that they can accurately gauge their impact on your reputation."

She paused for a moment, then quickly added, "If there's someone you absolutely have to bring over, you'd best send me a list as soon as possible. The production team will look into it."

Xia Tian nodded. Huitian thought for a moment before continuing, "The family members of Killing Show players...have a high chance of getting drawn into the show. Because of the amplification effect of fame, they are already capable of drawing attention even as newcomers, which is exactly what the production team likes. So they'll think of ways to bring them in."

She glanced at Bai Jing'an with a hint of apology in her eyes, the kind expressed when someone had been subjected to something particularly uncivilized—this was rare; who could have expected that sentiment to still exist nowadays?

Xia Tian stroked Dee Dee's hair. He didn't seem particularly disappointed; possibly too used to getting his hopes dashed.

"She's the only one I have left," he said.

With a nod, Huitian opened the car door and left without looking back.

It was quiet all around again. Xia Tian gently brushed a dirty lock of Dee Dee's hair behind her ear, his expression gentle, just like that fleeting glimpse of Xia Tian in the corner of the training room, talking on the phone.

She kept talking to him about the trees, the clouds, and the sunlight. She said everyone down there said Xia Tian would surely die, but she was sure he'd survive, and she was right. Xia Tian merely nodded and smiled until they arrived at Bai Jing'an's house.

The house was pretty big, with a total of three floors—that could be considered affluent in the Upper World. Despite its size, the house's interior appeared rather run-down, with peeling wallpaper, broken chandeliers, and strewn advertising flyers from an unknown year. It seemed a large family had lived here before, but they'd left in a hurry and never came back.

Bai Jing'an entered Dee Dee's identity access privileges and told her she could go and familiarize herself with the environment. He also told her of the garden on the rooftop—if it could be called a garden. She was so excited that her whole body tensed up. As soon as Xia Tian gave the go-ahead, she dashed off like a shooting arrow taking leave of its string.

Xia Tian inquisitively surveyed the surroundings. The robot housekeeper slowly carried a glass of water to him, making creaking sounds as it operated. It was a model from twenty years ago.

"What's this?" Xia Tian asked as he scrutinized the residual stain left at the corner of the stairs. "Blood?"

"Maybe," Bai Jing'an answered.

"Did someone die here or what?"

Bai Jing'an said nothing, and Xia Tian continued, "The cleaning robot couldn't wash it off, so you just left it there?"

"I can't be bothered," Bai Jing'an said.

Xia Tian threw him a sidelong glance, and Bai Jing'an said, "I know what you want to say. You want to say that I don't look that lazy, but I am. If you want to get it off, do it yourself."

"I didn't say that," Xia Tian countered.

Holding the glass in his hand, he settled comfortably on the sofa. The way he looked sitting in this run-down house made Bai Jing'an feel like he was some inordinately luxurious ornament. His appearance, expression, and disposition made one feel unsettled, as if something was about to happen at any time—although the person in question himself was pretty carefree and at ease.

Upstairs, the little girl ran to another skydeck. Her footsteps, spry and cheerful, echoed throughout the house; they felt like they didn't belong here.

"I've cleaned up two rooms for you both," Bai Jing'an said.

"The robot housekeeper was the one who really did it, right?" Xia Tian remarked.

Bai Jing'an conceded that was indeed the case. All he did was choose the rooms and configure the program. Right then, the little girl flew down the stairs, her face flushed as she called out to her brother.

"Come and look at the clouds outside! It looks like there's a huge white mountain in the sky!"

Xia Tian smiled, stood, and walked over to pick her up in his arms. "But before that, you have to take a bath and have an ice cream."

The little girl let out a cheer, and the robot housekeeper creaked as it led them to the bathroom. Bai Jing'an watched as the duo disappeared from sight, wondering if he should find some clothes before he remembered that Xia Tian's complete set of new clothes had already been packed and delivered. He was sure there'd be children's clothing inside, also from the same sponsor. Looked like they had the intent for him to stay here for a long time.

This wasn't a pleasant house. It'd been a long time since anyone lived in it. He was the only one wandering around. Besides this place, he didn't know where else to go.

He surveyed the surroundings. For a moment, he felt vexed. He didn't want a close relationship with anyone. It was even worse than helping that guy dump the chief show producer's body.

But this was where his new life was, and he had no choice but to begin living it.

CHAPTER 13

WILD PARTY

While Dee Dee was eating her ice cream, Xia Tian browsed various information.

First, he watched the last scene of the third round, in which he died. It looked like a tragic blockbuster. Even he was moved watching it, despite looking quite the wretched sight back then.

He watched with interest as Bai Jing'an strode forth without pause and killed the lizardman with one blow of his sword; it was like the monsters could forget about trying to stand in his way. He was a warrior, and he was definitely an old hand. Xia Tian was familiar with such a sight. He knew of the rage that consumed you from all the killing on the battlefield. He didn't know what Bai Jing'an had done before, but this guy certainly didn't just undergo immersive simulation training in the Upper City.

He also saw what Bai Jing'an said was "everywhere online." Bai Jing'an had never spoken a single word about his past. Xia Tian guessed he didn't had a good life before. Some things were unpleasant even to think about, so all he could do was pretend it didn't exist. But now, it was really everywhere.

Bai Jing'an's father was named Bai Xiaoqi, and he'd died in the 182nd Killing Show. Xia Tian realized that he'd seen his face before in the Death Highlights Collection; Bai Xiaoqi was a regular feature there. A few thugs had tied him up in the bathroom, poured fuel on him, and burned him to death. There wasn't much fuel, so it took him a while to die. His killers even hung the charred corpse outside the building as a warning.

Bai Jing'an was six years old then, and he and his mother had watched this scene play out in front of the terminal. Medical records later revealed that he'd later developed severe anorexia nervosa and threw up everything he did eat.

Bai Xiaoqi had signed a contract with Gilded Group because of his wife's genetic disease. He obviously didn't think he'd die, but optimism on the Killing Show was unrealistic.

It was hard to imagine what Bai Jing'an, who was still a child at that time, had been thinking. But when he saw his father being burned to death alive, he must have realized that he would one day stand in that arena too. It was a fate he wouldn't be able to escape, no matter what.

His mother had a mental breakdown and often wandered the streets in a muddled daze. One year later, she fell into Sunward Lake, and they notified him to identify the corpse. At seven years old, Bai Jing'an signed the contract and went home. The GBC did a live funeral broadcast, but he didn't show up.

Xia Tian didn't read on.

The music in the video was extremely expressively lyrical and melancholic with an undercurrent of powerlessness, but for him, it was simple to understand. He remembered the way Bai Jing'an had grabbed him tightly at the end of the third round.

He touched his own neck. He still seemed to feel that warmth, a warmth that—just like the chill of death—was deeply imprinted in his body.

Xia Tian knew the expression he'd worn. It was the face of one who was all too acquainted with loss and despair.

He turned off the terminal, and the gorgeous colors of the homepage faded away. He turned his head and saw Bai Jing'an sitting on the sofa next to him. The latter was persuading Dee Dee to finish the ice cream, assuring her that there'd be more tomorrow, so there was no need for her to save it. Sometimes you just had to seize the moment and enjoy life. Conflicted, she started taking small bites.

Xia Tian thought about it, but he didn't know what he could say to Bai Jing'an. There were too many shitty things happening this year to put into words, so he reached out and patted his shoulder.

"We'll be fine," he said.

Bai Jing'an glanced at him. "That's an unrealistic statement."

"I know," Xia Tian answered, "but it's going to be okay."

Then he turned around to get another ice cream for himself, asking Bai Jing'an as he did so, "What time is the dinner?"

Not long into the night after they were done having their meals, Huitian came to visit, bringing with her their work arrangements along with various admonitions on how to conduct themselves now that they were stars. Then she took them to the dinner party.

Dee Dee had gone to sleep early; she was so exhausted that she fell asleep as soon as she hit the bed. Meanwhile, the Upper City's dinner party was only just starting.

Xia Tian's new wardrobe occupied two rooms, extending so far that he couldn't see the end of it. He'd been told it'd even continue to increase over time. At the same time, he also received a stylish designer car; a streamlined model brimming with killing intent. Allegedly, they designed it specially for him, and sales of the same model had already started.

This was absolutely incredible, he thought. He changed into a new tuxedo and drove his sports car with a look of arrogance to the dinner party with his two companions.

When he walked into the hall, he was greeted with a large sea of gazes, smiles, and cameras. Bai Jing'an walked beside him, looking happy that he wasn't drawing too much attention. He'd been regretting that scene at the end of the third round.

Compared to the disastrous dinner party of the second round, this place was much more luxurious, giving one the sense that the former party was merely to brush off the country bumpkins, and that this was the real venue where the folks of the Upper City came to live life. Alcohol flowed freely among the crowd, and the sophistication of the decor, drinks, and snacks had kicked up a few notches. Everyone was laughing; they appeared happy, surrounded by an endless supply of resources.

Xia Tian walked in and was immediately swept up in the never-ending lavish feast of the Upper World.

Compared to the cruelty of the Killing Show, there was a sense of disconnect at the dinner party. Xia Tian soon couldn't remember how many people had patted him on the shoulder, spoke to the two of them, and congratulated him on his accomplishments in the third round.

Here, savage killings were a remarkable achievement. They spoke of how a certain move was too cool, or which celebrity was fond of him and most likely willing to sleep with him. Someone also loudly said that he was very charming, which was good, since that was how he'd be able to survive. The Killing Show kept harping about strength and courage, but charm was the gospel truth in this line of work.

Here, the bloody and brutal events of the previous days became sidebar news belonging to the same category as someone's dress style or the decorations of the arena.

Huitian introduced several big names to them. At first, Xia Tian tried to remember them, but he soon got dizzy. It didn't take long for the image consultant to disappear into the crowd, and people followed him wherever he went. He caught a flash of Doug in this glittery world; the guy was in formal wear, looking very dashing. His wretched appearance in the arena seemed to be from a parallel world.

After saying hello, they hurriedly parted ways. The guy was downing glass after glass of booze, and he looked like he didn't want to have a conversation with anyone.

Xia Tian knew Doug was worth a lot now, all because of his stellar performance on the Killing Show. After they got separated from Xia Tian and the others, Doug and Feng Dan had encountered a...snake or some other kind of giant mutant creature with bony spikes on its head. It looked like a super huge spiked club. In one sudden move, it twisted its body and one of the spikes on its body came stabbing at Doug from behind. Feng Dan, who was engaged in a fierce battle, had seen it and took a sudden step forward to shove Doug away. The spike pierced him, shattering his ribs, grazing his heart, and perforating his lung.

Doug had leaped and thrust his sword into the giant snake's brain. It lunged forward abruptly, and Doug stepped aside. At the same time, he drew his sword again and stabbed it in its most vulnerable spot. This finally worked, and the snake had crashed into the stone wall and stopped, dead.

Doug had walked over and glared at Feng Dan, who was still hanging on the bone spike, then he moved him and laid him flat on the ground. He'd looked at him for several seconds, caught in a dilemma, before he dragged him to a safer spot at the side.

Two mutant creatures came by after that. He'd killed one and heavily wounded the other. All this time, Feng Dan remained unconscious. Doug only had to walk away and leave him there, and he'd die. But Doug kept standing there, saving his life.

Xia Tian had looked at the engagement rate of this scene when he reviewed the final battle of the third round. Doug said he didn't want to be entertainment for the others, but judging by the sales and comments, it was definitely worth a party and a substantial bonus for the production team.

They survived the final battle, and their worth rose rapidly. Xia Tian, however, didn't see Feng Dan around. Even after they'd saved each other's lives, they would still never appear in the same area.

He couldn't remember how much time had passed—this place made him dizzy—when Huitian dragged a small man over and introduced him, saying that he was a movie star who was very popular recently. His name was Wei Ling, and he seemed to have made an appearance in the third round.

This good-looking celebrity, already more or less drunk, hugged him with a dreamy smile. Xia Tian stiffened all over.

"I like the part where you took out...uh, Vosen. Too fucking creative," the guy looked all excited as he said to Xia Tian. "And by the way, his sailing game isn't all that good."

Wei Ling was a full head shorter than Xia Tian, and he looked even more delicate up close, but Xia Tian didn't want to see his face at all. However, for the next twenty minutes, this guy stuck to him like his life depended on it, acting like they were on very good terms. According to him, it was now the era of the Killing Show stars. He had to stick around him for long enough; otherwise, his manager would kill him.

Bai Jing'an had disappeared at some point. What an un-righteous fellow.

The star was the face of the third round BOSS, but was now no longer scary. He rambled on and on about a private party he had once attended; he'd met someone there and end-ed up on a bed somewhere, only for the other party to end up calling several people over. He only had a fuzzy memory of the event; all he could remember was that there were men and women, and he became the target of the merrymaking. When he woke up, his hands and legs bore traces of having been bound. It was pretty painful, and even now, he couldn't say for sure whether he'd been gang-raped. It was hard to be sure about that kind of thing.

Xia Tian listened in horror as Wei Ling recounted the experience like he was sharing gossip. Quietly, he took the glass with too many hallucinogenic drugs in it from Wei Ling's hand and traded it for a safer one. The star smiled goofily in front of him, like a defenseless child with no ability to protect himself.

He grabbed Wei Ling by the collar and hauled him to the man's manager, grousing about how people without the capacity to act shouldn't be running around as they pleased. It was really like entrusting a child to their parents.

After finishing with his babysitting job, Xia Tian stepped back into the party and looked around.

Before coming, Huitian warned him that many people at the party would be throwing themselves at him, so he had to be careful of any personal cameras on them. He shouldn't consume anything they offered, either; instead, he should get his drinks and drugs from sealed containers. These all felt like warnings to a completely defenseless child. The words made his heart itch, and he looked forward to having some romantic encounters.

He soon ran into one, but it was a disaster.

Xia Tian couldn't remember when he first got that drink in his hand, but for what it was worth, everyone here was eating whatever they wanted and guzzling alcohol. Doing as the locals did was as normal as it got, and he was the new star of the Killing Show, for god's sake. It wasn't like he was a lost little lady at this dinner party.

He couldn't remember when his mind started to haze over, either. By the time he realized it, he was lying on a couch in the corner. The drapes surrounding it were drawn, but he could still sense that he was in a corner of the dinner party. A heavily made-up, androgynous face was close by. If the folks of the Upper City so wished, it was hard for anyone to determine the gender. This person eyed him with a...covetous expression, like what lay before them was a huge plate of sumptuous food and they were ready to lick the plate clean.

Two seconds later, Xia Tian realized someone was on top of him. His coat was nowhere to be found, and someone's hands were groping under his clothes. There was definitely more than one pair.

He wanted to throw up, but he couldn't move. There seemed to be several people around him, but he was so dizzy that he couldn't piece the scene together. He attempted to move his body, but he was terribly weak. He'd never felt so powerless before, except for the time when he was dying.

Another face pressed in towards him from the right and stroked his hair. The expression in its eyes was malicious and ravenous. Xia Tian tried to dodge and heard his own voice saying, "No..."

His voice was hoarse and weak. He wanted to shove away the person who was leaning over, but his arm had no strength left in it. He heard someone laughing, as if his resistance was a joke.

"Go away..." he said.

Someone grabbed his wrist and pinned it above his head, while another hand groped between his legs. A mouth completely took in his ear, making horrifying sucking and swallowing sounds. Xia Tian tried hard to evade it, but a hand clasped his lower jaw and secured it in place. The sound of swallowing persisted in his ears.

Someone squeezed in between his legs. One of them laughed. "Such long legs."

Xia Tian desperately tried to extract his hand, thinking he needed a knife... As long as he had one...

A man tucked his hair behind his ear and said into it, "People like you who've just stepped out of the arena should be bound to a bed."

Xia Tian suddenly jolted awake. He was sitting in the car, and Bai Jing'an was beside him, driving them home. He wasn't wearing his coat, his shirt was fully unbuttoned, and his hair was loose over his shoulders.

He felt a little cold. Lowering his head, he realized he was barefoot. His shoes and socks were gone, and there was a deep bite mark on his right foot. A chill washed over him.

Bai Jing'an glanced at him. "You drank a glass of 'Fly All Night,' it's a kind of date rape drug."

Xia Tian looked ahead uncertainly before looking back at him. "What?"

"I've already injected you with a chemical antagonist," Bai Jing'an said.

"I don't understand..." Xia Tian said. "You're telling me someone fucking wanted to drug and rape me?"

"It's actually quite common."

Xia Tian sat there for a while, trying to piece together his fragmented thoughts, but he didn't have much success. Neurotically, he wiped his right ear, then tried to tie up his hair, but he couldn't find his hairband. He rummaged around in the car, feeling gravely furious but with nowhere to vent. He viciously grabbed Bai Jing'an's coat from the back seat and tore off a strip to tie up his hair.

He was cold all over and his hands were trembling, possibly because of the drugs. There still lingered the unshakeable sensation of someone pinning his wrist above his head. He suddenly gripped it so forcefully that it looked like he was killing someone.

He remembered...the sweet smell like animals in heat hanging in the air...someone ripping open his shirt, and someone pinching his right nipple with two fingers, rubbing it hard. A man made a joke, and laughter broke out around him... A man wearing purple contact lenses...the guy grabbed his chin, and he tried to dodge to the side, but the guy pried his lower jaw open and reached inside with his fingers... And then someone's tongue sticking in. The person who did it was wearing clothing that resembled fish scales, which felt icy cold to the touch and sent tingles through him. It was like a beast pressing down on him...and his grip on his lower jaw was so firm he couldn't move at all...

A man with dyed silver hair had whispered in his ear, *"Play with us, Xia Tian."*

"Stop the car. I feel like throwing up," he said.

Bai Jing'an braked, and Xia Tian stumbled out and bent over to vomit for quite a while. Bai Jing'an walked over and handed him a cup of water to rinse his mouth. Xia Tian returned to the car and tried to close up his shirt, only to realize that all the buttons were gone.

Bai Jing'an started the car again, and Xia Tian asked, his tone frosty, "How many of them?"

"Five," Bai Jing'an answered

Xia Tian subconsciously grabbed his lapels and glared ahead. After a while, he said, "I'm going to kill them."

"It's against the law to kill someone outside the arena," Bai

Jing'an cautioned.

"I'm going to kill them."

"Fine, let me know when you do. We'll have to come up with a plan."

Xia Tian remained expressionless and held his silence, and Bai Jing'an took it as a sign of his agreement.

Xia Tian didn't speak again the rest of the way. With a cold expression, he connected to the internet with the car's terminal and began his search. He hadn't been in the Upper City for long, but he'd always been a smart one, and he knew that someone was bound to share something like this. He found it in no time.

The organization that had done it was called "Honey&Sweet." They opposed the "glorification of criminals in the media" and believed that the Killing Show stars were just death-row inmates who should be shared by all. If honest citizens wanted them, they should get them.

Deciding to rebel against the despotism of the GBC, they chose the top favorites and most popular stars to "share." Their chosen venues were mostly dinner parties and the like; they'd use drinks enhanced with drugs and even set up temporary capsule spheres when carrying out the deed so that no one could get close. It'd taken Bai Jing'an about a minute to crack the password.

Xia Tian sat in the darkness, surrounded by large screens with rapidly changing numbers. Judging by the way he was fiddling around the computer, he would obviously make a pretty decent cyber support specialist. He was a fast learner.

Bai Jing'an took over one of the screens and helped him find those people's headquarters. The video couldn't be found in the public domain due to copyright infringement, so they had to dig a little deeper.

From the information, they could tell that Honey&Sweet

had been involved in seven cases, and the victims included both men and women. While their methods were not particularly sophisticated, they had succeeded in getting their way several times and were now quite the pros. It was like they were striving to make drugging and raping others a career.

Supposedly, there were five core members, which definitely included some pro hackers. From the information obtained online, there were also some influential figures, which was why they were always able to carry out their crimes. The police bureau had accomplished nothing to date, and they weren't all that concerned either. It was all good as long as the videos were not uploaded to the public network, as it'd otherwise infringe on GBC's copyright.

The duo found their discussion of the day's event in the cache. Some dude with the ID "The Groomer" said that God of Killing Xia Tian was as obedient as a kitty lying on the sofa after taking drugs, so much so that you could pin him down with one hand. Bai Jing'an was really a nosey parker; he was just a slave his parents sold off, yet he thought he could save someone. He really should be taught a lesson and put in his place.

"<3 Perverted Games" said that the problem was Bai Jing'an never drank alcohol, so he couldn't be drugged. He had irreversible brain damage. Someone after them ranted about how he was asking for death being a busybody even when he was in such a sorry state; some people just didn't understand their own circumstances. Then they started making lewd jokes about Xia Tian, saying that the way he looked crying as he pleaded must have felt particularly delightful.

In the "Celebrities Sharing Show" columns were exceedingly obscene videos. The members of Honey&Sweet kept narrating and describing the private parts of the victims' bodies as if they were introducing a product. They also shared the video of Xia

Tian from earlier; those people stroked his hair, describing the texture like they were reviewing it. Someone said that since he smiled so brilliantly, he ought to be played with until he cried.

Xia Tian expressionlessly watched these pornographic, obscene, and humiliating deeds, his eyes bottomlessly deep without so much as a ripple of reaction or emotion. He didn't seem to be all that outraged; he was used to being treated this way. He knew he didn't have any rights, and if he did, it was because it was in the GBC's interests. He was a felon, and countless people in the Lower City had told him so in various ways.

To him, this was not a matter of political opinion.

This was a personal grudge.

When both of them had been randomly picked to be in the same group, Bai Jing'an went to check Xia Tian's circumstances. He knew this guy had gone to prison because of a major murder case in the Lower City—he'd killed a john of his elder sister and clashed with the security forces of the local government.

The Lower City's administration and the local folks had always been in heated conflict with one another, and the massacre in District N back then had arose over a dispute between the locals and the administration. The enmity had not diminished over the years, but was passed down like a tradition.

Those men had ambushed him in an alley. Xia Tian was seriously wounded, and the friend with him died. He fled to a repair shop, and when those people couldn't find him, they killed his elder sister the next day. After Xia Tian recovered from his injuries, he returned and killed the five people involved in the incident, one at a time.

He knew it would cost him dearly, but he still did it anyway.

At that time, Bai Jing'an thought this person surely wouldn't be willing to take grief from anyone. He was never the innocent victim caught up in a disaster as portrayed by the media; he was a dangerous man himself, and he'd sought to pay back all he'd suffered tenfold. No one would dare to bully such a person as they pleased, even at the worst of times. He was strong and dauntless enough, and even if he died in the end, he'd make everyone who'd hurt him suffer.

But he'd finally realized just how vulnerable he was in the never-ending celebrations of the Upper City. He had always been able to control his own body, resisting and fighting regardless of the cost. But here, a tiny drink could snip his sharp claws and deprive him of his ability to move.

Thinking about what he saw when he opened the capsule sphere, Bai Jing'an's expression went cold. The people were pinning his teammate down on the sofa, and Xia Tian—his clothes in disarray—was saying "go away" in vain. He'd never seen him so helpless...other than the time he was dying.

Actually, Bai Jing'an had heard about this sort of thing happening many times. This was the Upper World, where non-consensual sex was so commonplace there was no need to make a fuss. Drugs obfuscated everything, and it was hard for someone to say if it had been voluntary or not. Pain ceased to be acute or important; it became dispensable. People didn't care much about their own pain, nor did they really understand the pain of others. They only demanded what they wanted.

But that wasn't the case for Xia Tian. If someone affronted him, he would exact vengeance at all costs.

Bai Jing'an felt he should personally keep a low profile, but he realized he was quite happy to partake in this revenge.

Give it to those bastards.

By the time they got home, it was already after midnight.

Xia Tian's expression was glum as he went to take a bath to wash away the smell of alcohol, drugs, and other people's

bodily fluids.

The drugs those people gave him were potent. He felt a wave of dizziness hit him when he turned on the shower, and he had to brace himself against the wall before he could steady himself. When he looked down, he saw the bite mark on his right leg oozing blood. He remembered someone grabbing his ankle...someone's tongue licking up his toe...

He threw up again, staying in the bathroom for an hour before he changed clothes and headed upstairs to take a look at Dee Dee.

The little girl slept soundly under the skylight, where she could see the twinkling, starry sky. He sat quietly beside her for a moment. Living in a place like this was her dream, as well as his.

At the party, the crystal chandeliers on the ceiling sparkled like the starry sky, while drinks and snacks flowed endlessly everywhere. The feast seemed like it would last until the end of the world. This was an opulent world of decadence and debauchery. Resplendence, bloodlust, and stimulation abounded in this eternal feast. There was no dignity, no future, and no personal destiny.

Xia Tian didn't treat his wounds. Medicine in the Upper City could make minor injuries disappear in the blink of an eye, as if they'd never existed, but the Lower City didn't have the same treatment habits.

He wanted the wounds to stay on his skin and burn like fire. It'd make him feel alive. He had to do something.

He had gotten what he initially wanted when he first came to this place, but he didn't feel any better. An indescribable rage blazed in him. He'd kill those people. He'd look them in the eyes and make them know the price they had to pay for what they did.

He sat beside Dee Dee for a while longer before he got up

and went downstairs.

Bai Jing'an was sitting on the sofa in the living room. There was a glass of...what seemed to be herbal tea on the table. He was looking down at his phone without using a speaker or headphones, and the light from it shined on his face like snow. He looked like he was out to kill, and it was almost an unfamiliar sight.

He glanced at the freshly showered Xia Tian, and raised his hand to project a hologram. It was of a man wearing a gray suit that resembled fish scales, and his hair was dyed a similar hue. His features were sharp and cold, possibly through some sort of non-surgical procedure, giving him an air of callous heartlessness. It dawned on Xia Tian that Bai Jing'an was watching a video from Honey&Sweet.

"This man," Bai Jing'an said. "There's something off about his clothes."

He zoomed in on the clothes.

"This brand is called Slow Velocity, and the particular style he's wearing isn't on the market yet."

Xia Tian stared at the floating screen. He remembered this guy. He'd pinned him down, grabbed his lower jaw, and forced him to open his mouth. Then...he'd even said to the camera, "He tastes like whiskey with 'Candy.'"

Candy—that was the name of a type of drug. Xia Tian felt sick to his stomach again, but he held back from dashing to the bathroom. There was nothing to throw up anyway.

"Either he's a VIP who can get the clothes directly from the designer, or he's someone inside the brand," Bai Jing'an said. "Slow Velocity is a niche brand; it isn't high-end enough to enter the circles of the rich and powerful."

Xia Tian nodded and went to the bar to pour himself an alcoholic drink. *He has an inside connection with Slow Velocity,*

Xia Tian thought. This was the first step.

He'd installed the temporary bar when he came here, and it was loaded with fine wines sponsored by various companies. Actually, he couldn't tell the difference, but it didn't stop him from being delighted when he learned they were all high-quality drinks.

As he removed the lid, his hand trembled, causing the bottle to almost fall. Carefully, he poured himself half a glass with both hands. He walked over to Bai Jing'an with the glass in hand and sat on the sofa.

"I'll recognize him if I see him again," he said.

Bai Jing'an shared the filtered information with him, and Xia Tian looked down to read it. The tactician turned his head to look at him and reached out to touch his chin. There were several purplish fingermark bruises on it.

Xia Tian dodged his hand, and Bai Jing'an said, "Aren't you going to take care of that?"

"I'll deal with it later," Xia Tian said sullenly.

For a while, they sat silently on this couch that looked like something out of a haunted house, drinking from their own glasses. There was a moment when Xia Tian wanted to make fun of Bai Jing'an's herbal tea, but on second thought, he dropped the idea. He was too depressed and drained to tease the latter.

"So," Xia Tian said, "this is where you grew up?"

Bai Jing'an looked up to glance at him, but he didn't say a thing.

Xia Tian continued, "Doesn't look like it."

"Need me to show you photos?" Bai Jing'an said.

"I mean, this place is like a haunted house," Xia Tian explained, "but you don't look like a ghost."

Bai Jing'an clutched the glass tightly. After a while, he said, "I haven't cleaned up since the incident."

Xia Tian nodded to indicate that he could tell.

"I...can't remember exactly," Bai Jing'an said. "I think I was happy for a period of time, but after that incident...nothing seemed right. I guess I just wanted to keep things as they were. Maybe I'll be able to find another suitable place."

"You won't be able to find one," Xia Tian said.

Bai Jing'an stared at the glass and said nothing for a long time. Eventually, he spoke. "I know."

"Sometimes you just feel like it's never going to get better," Xia Tian said in a hushed tone. "Pain is pain. There will be no answers to your questions."

He leaned back into a cushion at the corner of the sofa and finished his half glass of wine. It was so strong, it burned his stomach. When his stomach hurt in the past, his elder sister would cook him porridge and tease him, saying that he'd have the money to get sick when he'd really made a name for himself in the Upper City, and she wouldn't have to do this anymore— she could just sit back and enjoy some of his good fortune.

Beside him, Bai Jing'an took out a blue capsule, broke it apart, and poured the powder into his herbal tea.

Xia Tian looked at him quizzically, and Bai Jing'an explained, "It helps with sleep. Insomnia."

Xia Tian was still looking, and Bai Jing'an added, "Aftereffect of the Starlight Studio's Type 17-3 Genetic Virus."

Xia Tian nodded. He'd read about that in Bai Jing'an's medical history; the famous "District N Massacre Virus." The epidemic had been poorly contained—or perhaps the GBC let it spread intentionally—and cleared out the areas on the periphery of District N. Even the Upper City was affected, to a lesser extent.

The effects of this virus varied from person to person. With Bai Jing'an, it had almost wiped out his long-term memory. He couldn't even orientate himself after losing his parents. But if he hadn't seen the records, Xia Tian would never have guessed that Bai Jing'an had brain damage. This guy always seemed confident, meticulously planning every detail and knowing exactly where he was. He'd never let himself appear like a victim.

Xia Tian couldn't fathom how much effort it took for him.

Bai Jing'an glanced at him, as if he wanted to say a word or two, but ultimately he didn't. Instead, both of them just sat on the sofa in silence. Shadows weighed heavily around them, making it impossible to talk.

Eventually, Xia Tian merely reached out a hand to smooth down Bai Jing'an's hair that was sticking up. Bai Jing'an froze for a brief moment, but he didn't move. In the darkness of the night, the guy looked sad and gentle, as though a gust of wind could blow him away.

Xia Tian retracted his hand. It was still shaking.

Holding the glass of wine, Xia Tian walked through the party venue with a frosty expression.

He'd now put Huitian's suggestion into practice, which was to take nothing from a stranger's hand. If he wanted a drink, he would take it directly from a sealed container or from a waiter with an official name tag.

Like a little girl lost in the fucking forest.

As per the provisions stipulated in the contract, he had an endless number of "mandatory" parties to attend. This sort of dinner party that lasted for days on end was called a "Hardcore Rave," and by the time it'd stretched on to this point, there'd be no semblance of decorum remaining.

As Xia Tian kept walking, he found two people going at it right around the corner. One of them stared at him and mimed a blowjob with his hand. Sights like these were everywhere, and he later simply ignored them and walked past.

He was still looking at the filtered list of Honey&Sweet names in the terminal. This…"pornographic terror organization" had its own official website and fanbase, a sophisticated and comprehensive business, and certainly no shortage of money. Some people on the list didn't lack sexual partners, and they even kept celebrities as their sugar babies. Yet they still liked to drug and rape people during dinner parties, promoting the theory of "slave-sharing" and filming all the obscene details—pointing, commenting, even rating them.

Over the past two days, he and Bai Jing'an had reviewed all the videos and narrowed down the scope of the search to determine that the person with the ID "The Gourmand" was primarily active in the fashion circle. Back when Xia Tian was in the Lower City, he only knew that there were countless parties in the Upper City; only now did he know they were divided into themes and types. For example, the invitees of today's Killing Show party were predominately those from the fashion circle.

Xia Tian was dressed in an expensive tuxedo that stressed just how tall, handsome, and refined he was. He walked through the hall expressionlessly, though his eyes burned with murderous intent.

As Xia Tian passed by a group of stylishly dressed people from the fashion circle, he halted in his tracks. He turned his head and saw the back of a tall man. He didn't look like the man he was looking for, but Xia Tian remembered that scent…

It was hard to describe, but it was a sort of sweet and warm fragrance, but also a little sharp and invasive… It was a rare smell. It wasn't that of perfume, but more of like something picked up in a closed environment.

A part of Xia Tian's heart clenched. He turned around and

walked over to the group of people.

The fellow was discussing...*Son of Darkness*, the very same drama series that Dr. Xu really liked. The series was finally coming to an end, and it seemed that the female lead was going to bear the unfortunate Bai Lin's posthumous child, and live on with sorrow and hope.

A tall man with black hair seethed with indignation as he did all he could to refute the Upper City folks' misconceptions of Bai Lin: *"He wasn't an omnipotent god of war; let's be realistic here, okay?!"* He was quite handsome, sturdy but not bulky, and he was wearing a metallic-looking coat with a pretty cool style. These days, no ugly people among the Killing Show players could survive the season.

Xia Tian realized he recognized him. This guy was called Mo An. He and Luo Qingtian had supposedly been a couple, but they didn't end up on the same team this time. Many people, anticipating their meeting again in the fourth round, had made various predictions about it. But Xia Tian had wiped out Luo Qingtian's team right after the match had started.

At the dinner party last night, journalists had forcibly pulled them together for an interview, and this guy had behaved like they were sworn enemies. Had it not been for his companions, who considered the big picture and pulled him away, he'd no doubt have fought it out with Xia Tian and even killed his entire family. The journalists had a field day, gleefully capturing lots of photos and video materials of the exchange.

Looking at how engrossed he was today in chatting about a melodramatic drama series, he'd clearly forgotten the whole thing.

Xia Tian felt he should tactfully and inconspicuously join in the conversation and casually ask his questions, but...like, who the fuck even watches *Son of Darkness*?

He walked into the crowd and flashed a dazzling smile at

them, all of whom smiled back at him reflexively.

"Can I borrow him for a while?" he asked.

A chorus of enthusiastic responses came from all around.

"Who?"

"Of course, of course."

"You can borrow whoever you want."

Xia Tian grabbed Mo An by the collar and hauled him out of the crowd. The guy was completely stunned. He attempted to struggle, but Xia Tian wouldn't let go.

"Stop it!" the other guy cried out under his breath. "What do you want? You killed Xiaoluo, so I'm the one who should be angry... I didn't offend you, did I?"

"What's that scent on you?" Xia Tian asked.

Mo An wasn't listening to him at all. He looked around nervously.

"I can't be talking to you in public," he said, "and you can't drag me like this... Listen, I don't want to fight you, but if you keep it up and the journalists see, I won't be able to explain myself if I don't try to hit you—"

Xia Tian thought for a moment and felt that what he said made sense, so he grabbed him by the collar and dragged him away from the crowd. Behind him, Mo An yelped helplessly.

"Listen, I personally have nothing against you. I'm sorry about what I said to the media. My image consultant made me say it."

Xia Tian thought the public image this guy portrayed was that of an impulsive warrior with high combat prowess who would go to great lengths for Luo Qingtian. As it turned out, the reality was the complete opposite.

"Uh, while I still have the chance, I'd like to thank you," Mo An continued from behind him. "Really. When I came out of the arena and heard of Xiaoluo's death, I thought I was just hearing things because I wanted it so much."

Xia Tian finally couldn't help but ask, "Weren't you a couple?"

"Nah, we met in the last season, and that was the start of the disaster," Mo An said. "He was a tactician, so I naturally had to defer to him. I don't understand why everyone thinks I worship him.. I was just trying to be friendly!"

Xia Tian opened a door and saw a few naked bodies tangled together. Had this been in the past, he would have surely taken a few more glances, but now, he slammed the door shut with an annoyed expression.

"And now I'll never be able to rid myself of that freaking loyal hound label!" Mo An continued, "My image consultant said I should be prepared to get blacklisted if I couldn't protect him at all costs. What could I do?!

"You know, I got high scores in all the tactic strategizing courses. But just because I met him, I had to act out the role of an all-brawn-no-brains dumbass who constantly tries to toady up to him, sacrificing my dignity to highlight his intelligence! Please. He's not even my type at all. I couldn't get hard even if you delivered him to my bed on a silver platter!"

He paused for a moment. "Uh, please keep what I said today a secret, okay?"

Xia Tian finally found an unoccupied room and pulled him in.

STILL WANNA PLAY?

Mo An turned his head and said solemnly, "Listen, I'm totally straight."

"Where did you get that scent on you?" Xia Tian said.

"What?"

"You know what I'm talking about."

The guy glanced at him and lowered his head to sniff the smell on his sleeve.

"I'm not sure…"

Mo An looked at him tentatively. Xia Tian returned the look coldly. The metallic cufflink on his right wrist flowed like liquid into his hand, where it turned into a long, slender blade.

Weapons were not allowed at dinner parties, but everyone had their own ways of sneaking them in. Guns were harder, but it was a piece of cake to swipe a knife. After all, GBC would love for people like them to cause a commotion.

"Okay, you're probably talking about the 'Kinky Hollow,'" Mo An eventually said.

Xia Tian glared at him, waiting for him to continue.

"The Kinky Hollow is an illicit organization involved in

erotic entertainment," Bai Jing'an said in Xia Tian's earpiece, his voice calm and icy. "They offer sexual services using unauthorized celebrity images. Sometimes, they also facilitate personal sexual transactions with the stars themselves. Their operations are highly secretive, and they only cater to familiar clients."

He'd slipped away from the dinner party half an hour ago and was now probably in that luxury car in the parking lot. He'd rather stay in his car than show up at the dinner party venue. Xia Tian envied his ability to disappear silently under the gaze of so many people. He couldn't do that at all. It was like he came with his own spotlight.

Mo An sniffed his clothes again and made an expression of disgust.

"This is a specially formulated signature fragrance. It's hard for the smell to fade once it gets on you," he said. "When I first came out of the arena, a friend suggested finding a place to relax, saying Xiaoluo was dead anyway... So, I just went to take a look."

On the other end of the earpiece, Bai Jing'an snorted.

Xia Tian didn't know what he did, but in any case, his actions were swift and efficient. Three seconds later, the holographic screen of Mo An's mobile phone suddenly popped up, with the "Kinky Hollow" app prominently displayed.

It was aesthetically beautiful. The landscape of city lights and glitzy buildings were transformed into a sheer veil guiding visitors into a lavishly decorated area. The words "highly confidential" were written on the entrance, while naked limbs were everywhere inside, giving it a vibe that wasn't unlike an erotic den.

"You can't enter without registering as a member," Bai Jing'an said.

Lewd noises and lascivious talk permeated their surroundings. Mo An raised his eyebrows and watched the app open without batting an eyelid. For someone who'd been painted as an impulsive warrior with high combat prowess, his mental fortitude was top-notch.

Xia Tian stared intently at the app Bai Jing'an opened. His tactician directly opened up the administrator panel, where three people were listed. One of them had an emblem of fabric that resembled a fish scale, and his ID was "Man-eating Shark." Xia Tian now knew it was a special fabric called "shark skin"— it had protective, camouflage, and memory functions, and was generally used as a restraint in bed.

He turned to look at Mo An, who'd always looked sincere and guileless. Even now, he merely just shrugged nonchalantly.

"I don't know why I lied to you." He smiled at him, but something in his expression had changed. "Perhaps I've been brainwashed by my lovestruck character setting. Yeah, I went to the brothel, but so? Are you going to slap the death penalty on me? Okay, Xiaoluo probably would. Thank god he's dead."

Xia Tian glared viciously at the promiscuous holographic program. "Where is it?"

"No specific location. Wherever there's that fragrance, that's where the Kinky Hollow does business," Mo An said. "Their business is illegal, it infringes on hundreds of copyrights; there might also be stuff like drugging and raping of minor celebrities and the like. I don't concern myself with it. That's just how the Upper City is."

He leaned against the wall. Just like most Killing Show players who could survive a season, he was wary and apathetic as the gears turned quickly in his mind

"I want to know where it's operating *tonight*," Xia Tian said.

Mo An narrowed his eyes at him.

"I don't believe you got that scent on you a few days ago," Xia Tian said coldly. "Why would an illegal business give itself a signature scent that can linger for a week? It's not like it's an ink marker."

Mo An looked at him for two seconds before he stood up straight and said, "I'm not obligated to answer any of your questions."

He turned and made to leave, and Xia Tian grabbed him by the arm from behind. Mo An shook him off, and Xia Tian threw a kick toward his lower abdomen. Mo An hurriedly took a step back, but Xia Tian's boot still grazed his side, causing him to stumble. He hit back, and Xia Tian seized the opportunity to twist his right arm, bringing him down on one knee. At the same time, the bracelet on Mo An's left wrist slithered into his palm like a snake and transformed into a hilt.

A blade grew, and he counterattacked without so much as a pause. It took just an instant for the blade come within milimeters of Xia Tian's neck, but he didn't get to deal the finishing blow.

Xia Tian stood there, looking down at him with his long, slender, and sharp blade pressed against Mo An's neck. To people like them, victory or defeat was decided in a matter of moments.

Xia Tian pressed on the blade, and blood oozed from Mo An's neck. The guy was a sorry picture as he kneeled once again.

Mo An stared at the floor. He retracted his blade reluctantly, like shattered building blocks coming back together. After five seconds of silence, he blurted, "I went to Kinky Hollow because it was private. I have nowhere else to go. For so long, I couldn't have sex with anyone because of him. I couldn't even say a word more than necessary. I need someone...I don't care if it's fucking legal or not. Did someone claim to be an unwilling party?"

"Where are they doing business tonight?" Xia Tian asked.

"Luo Qingtian went nuts," Mo An blabbered on. "I just flirted a little with that girl, and he saw us. That night, he brought her to my room, and then...he...he had his way with her for an hour. At the end of it, she..."

He stopped for a moment.

"He said if I betrayed him, he'd kill me first, and disguise it so that it looked like I'd died for him..." he said. "I told him this was just a show, and he said he didn't care. He wanted to trample me under his feet for life."

On edge, he started laughing.

"You know," he continued, "I had to use twice the amount of drugs as usual to have sex with him!"

Xia Tian was at a loss for what to say, and Mo An continued, "If I reveal the location, I'll be blacklisted."

"Luo Qingtian is dead."

"Yeah. The production team wants me to avenge him. I'm supposed to be fucking heartbroken and devastated until the fourth round and then die for the cause! He said I couldn't break free of him even when he's dead, and he was right!"

He laughed again, and blood trickled along Xia Tian's blade.

"If we run into each other next round, I'll look like I've gone mad with fury because I lost my 'most beloved person'... But I promise you, I have nothing against you personally. In fact, I should buy you a drink," Mo An said.

Xia Tian said nothing. After a few seconds, Mo An sighed.

"The Hall of Silence on the twentieth floor. They're all bastards who only know how to fuck. Business should be done by now; you won't be able to find anything," he said as he glanced at him. "What are you planning on doing?"

Xia Tian released him and turned to walk out. The blade in his hand was still dripping blood.

"Just going to 'play,'" he said coldly.

The place Mo An told him about was in the west wing. Xia Tian walked through the banquet hall, and his blade transformed back into a cufflink and lay quietly on his wrist. A tiny blossom of blood bloomed on his shirt.

It was indeed over.

When he came to the side hall, he could still see traces of the capsule sphere in the corner. It was a mess inside, with sex toys strewn all over. An orgy had apparently just taken place. There was a large bloodstain on the carpet, and a corner of the wall even had a chain secured to it. Who knew what that was for?

Xia Tian surveyed his surroundings with a frosty expression. A sweet scent reminiscent of animal rut pervaded the room. These people didn't even clean up the venue. Xia Tian wondered if they came with their own cleaners, or if they had some clandestine connection with the official organizers that had emboldened them to brazenly and blatantly leave the aftermath behind for the hotel to clean up.

On the official app, people could even request the person they wanted to bed the most. The administrator would take the orders and collect money according to the situation.

Xia Tian picked up a champagne glass. The liquid inside was still bubbling. He took a sniff; there were quite a lot of added ingredients.

It was silent all around. The fragrance of "Kinky Hollow" lingered in the air, along with the smell of blood and human bodily fluids. Xia Tian told himself to calm down. It was impossible to catch them right away. It wasn't like no one had ever tried to find them before...

He suddenly smashed the glass against the wall. Glass shattered all over. His body tensed. He wanted to clench his right fist, but then he spread it open again. The fury consumed him, so much so that he didn't know what to do.

He heard Bai Jing'an's breathing on the other end of the earpiece. He sucked in a breath, letting his breathing synchronize with the latter's as he told himself to stay calm.

He turned and walked out, then came to a sudden stop and turned to look at a thin, transparent item on the table. It was someone's mobile phone, and it was still unlocked. When he picked it up, the screen illuminated. The wallpaper on the home screen...was him.

A certain shot from the show, probably from the start. Shirtless, he sat under the sunlight, smiling brilliantly at someone— probably Bai Jing'an—with a completely unguarded expression.

The camera work of the Killing Show was very steady, but this one had been clearly remastered in 3D, giving the footage an added pornographic quality. The camera slid down his back, lingering at the tips of his hair, before wandering to his chest... Truly a fully unobstructed 360-degree view.

Xia Tian watched it expressionlessly. No one would discard their mobile phone and leave it lying around these days. Either the guy would come back for it, or he was still here.

He took the phone and treaded lightly through the place, pushing open the partially opened doors one room at a time with his blade in his hand.

He found him.

He was in an inexplicably large, brightly illuminated bathroom. Steam rose from the floor and the water was running, but no one was using it.

Xia Tian heard the slurred voice of someone who wasn't clear-minded.

"Where is this place? I wanna go back... Go away..."

Another voice answered, "It doesn't matter where this is. You only need to know that you and I will be getting up close and personal very soon."

There came the sounds of a struggle and rustling clothes.

"Stop, I... I don't wanna..." the first voice slurred. It was a voice that'd previously made a deep impression on Xia Tian: Wei Ling.

He walked over. The middle was partitioned by a curtain with starburst effects. People here even made building bathrooms convoluted.

Wei Ling let out a slurred moan, and the other guy said, "Don't move. Let's play..."

With a frosty expression, Xia Tian yanked the curtain open and saw the scene before him.

It was an inner room designed to resemble a hot spring, with alcohol and snacks on exquisite trays everywhere. Wei Ling sat against the wall, pinned. His pants were off, and he was dead drunk.

The guy pinning him down was already ready and raring to go. One of his hands was inside Wei Ling, expanding his entrance. He was even making obscene remarks like how he was already wet, and how people like him were meant to be used for fun.

Xia Tian saw his face. It wasn't the face he saw at the dinner party, but he knew it was him. No matter how much surgery he had to alter his appearance, the filth deeply ingrained in his bones would never change.

Wei Ling was trying in vain to push the guy away, but then stopped and looked up at Xia Tian. The rapist was about to penetrate him when he finally realized something was amiss and turned to look.

Holding his blade in hand, Xia Tian flashed him a dazzling smile.

Startled, the rapist froze for a moment. "Xia Tian?"

He stared fixedly at Xia Tian, and it took about five seconds for his mind to clear up a little. He then looked around, realizing the situation did not look good for him.

There wasn't a single other person here—it'd been cleared out early for a "business event." They didn't even leave a single surveillance camera behind. The one the rapist had placed on the table was probably being used to film footage to keep as a memento.

He flashed Xia Tian a smile, probably thinking he was still safe after he'd masked his appearance with those procedures.

"I spent a lot of money on you, Xia Tian. I bought the full set of your holographic videos and even ordered the spin-off sexual services under your name. But the real person is still different," he said. "No one has the same..."

He paused for a moment, like he couldn't find the right word. When he saw the blade in Xia Tian's hand, he laughed.

"Especially when you're holding a blade. No one can take their eyes off you!" he said.

He finally released Wei Ling. The famous star shrank back powerlessly and tried to close his legs. The rapist shoved him away in irritation, as though he was dismissing a bag of trash. He looked at Xia Tian, completely unconcerned about baring his lower body—his penis showed no sign of softening.

Xia Tian didn't move a muscle as he stared back at him. The bright light from overhead fell upon them like snow. Even the temperature seemed to have turned cold.

"I found him in the rest area," the rapist said as he stroked Wei Ling's hair without realizing it. "He won't remember what happened tonight at all. Lots of people want to screw people like him. We can share if you like..."

Xia Tian didn't think he was all that clear-headed, either. Noticing Xia Tian's expression, the Honey&Sweet bastard laughed again.

"You're new here, so you don't understand. This kind of thing is normal; it's just having fun. There are lots of things to play with in the Upper City. You'll find out soon."

"Is that so?" Xia Tian said.

The guy looked at the blade for a few seconds, finally realizing something was off. To him, it was like a faint shudder running through his body. Even though the room was warm, the chill seemed to penetrate deep into his bones. The Upper City was like a giant greenhouse where springtime pleasure never waned. Here, death was merely a hallucination brought on by drugs.

He slowly rose to his feet and put on his trousers. Wei Ling curled up in a corner by his feet and fumbled to find his own pants, but didn't succeed.

The inside of the bathroom was exquisite, with murmuring water flowing at one side that was spotted with pink, red, and blue blooming wildflowers. It perfectly replicated the delights of a mountain hot spring during the Terrestrial Era.

The rapist walked over to Xia Tian, and for a fleeting moment, he wanted to reach out and put on a show of patting him on the shoulder. There was something about this person that made him want to touch him, but he wasn't sure what to do once he had him in his hands—probably just enjoy him to his heart's content. In any case, it'd all be destroyed soon.

But in the end, he didn't dare to do it. A day ago, this guy was quite a stunner when he was sprawled on a sofa after consuming that drugged drink, but the vibe he gave off when he was awake was completely different.

He brushed past against Xia Tian's shoulder. The vague sense of foreboding in his heart told him that he had to leave as soon as possible, that this was no longer a cozy den of debauchery...

But at this time, Xia Tian suddenly strode forward. Like a heartless player at a dinner party, he wrapped his arm around the guy's shoulders and said in a breezy tone, "Don't go, man.

Weren't you having a good time?"

The guy tensed suddenly when Xia Tian touched him, and he reached into his pocket for the weapon he'd sneaked in. The main city was a gold mine of opulent debauchery, but there was also danger lurking everywhere. People like them were bound to run into trouble.

A thin, icy sensation swept across his neck.

He froze for a moment. It happened so quickly that it didn't yet occur to him what'd happened. All he felt was a slight pain. Some kind of warm liquid spread across his neck. He reached out to touch it, and his hand came away covered in blood.

Vosen did the same thing when he died, and Xia Tian had found it incredibly thrilling at the time. Now that he'd become the protagonist, the sight of blood was shockingly startling.

The rapist staggered a step and collapsed to the ground. His open shirt revealed half of a gun handle, but he'd forgotten all about the firearm. His first reaction was to fumble around in a panic, trying to find something.

It took Xia Tian two seconds to realize he was looking for his mobile phone. He took it out and shook it in front of him as he looked at the fear and desperation in that guy's eyes.

The guy groped for something on his chest with his feeble right hand. Bai Jing'an's icy but composed voice rang out from Xia Tian's earpiece.

"It's an emergency medical call device. The second button."

Xia Tian squatted in front of him. The guy was about to grab the button on his chest when Xia Tian ripped it off.

The rapist—the guy with the ID "The Gourmand"—glared at him with eyes wide as his fingers twitched feebly. That hand had once pried his jaw open, inserted its fingers, and described how he tasted. He'd said that the greatest value of people like him was to let rich people have their fill of fun.

Now, the deep crimson-red in his arteries spewed out, staining the luxurious bathroom a stark, startling hue. Its color was no different from the blood of any of the Lower City criminals in the Killing Show, with their worthless lives.

Xia Tian kneeled on one knee before him, with one hand holding his weapon. Blood trickled down along the blade and dripped onto the floor. The sensation of blade slashing through the man's carotid artery still lingered on his fingertips—a truly tangible memento.

He looked deep into the guy's eyes and smiled at him. Then he bent in close to his ear and said, "So, still wanna play now?"

The guy stared at him, his eyes full of shock and disbelief. Eventually, he went completely still, becoming the very thing Xia Tian had seen on the Killing Show and on the streets of the Lower City.

He looked into those eyes for a few more seconds, then withdrew his hand and stood. The fury that had gripped him tightly subsided; death seemed to have appeased something within him. Only death had the power to bring that kind of peace.

He felt a lot better.

Xia Tian turned around, opened the window, and dragged the body over. Bai Jing'an had already cased out a dumping site for the corpse. If he threw him down from this spot, he'd most likely land on the hotel signboard below, where he'd be discovered after a night or so. Even if he were to fall directly onto the ground, it'd also take the police some time to find this room.

He grabbed the corpse by the collar and threw it out the window with practiced ease. As he turned around, he picked up the camera on the desk and stuffed it into his pocket. The device was set to sync and upload to the cloud, but Bai Jing'an had already cut off the transmission channel before Xia Tian entered the room.

All this time, he listened attentively—it seemed the corpse didn't land on the ground.

Looking left and right, he walked over to the stone-shaped faucet, turned on the water to the maximum, and kicked over two boxes of detergent. The cleaning tools in places like these were extremely strong, especially targeting bodily fluids and the like.

Xia Tian threw the mobile phone into the water too. Ten minutes or so from now, this place would turn into a large hot pond. Everything would vanish in the stream of water.

If the police really wanted to investigate this case, they might be able to find out something with reagents, but places like this had definitely seen a lot of action, and there would be no shortage of other blood traces left behind. And now, it had one more notch on its belt.

Xia Tian turned around, ready to leave. The long blade in his hand transformed back into a small cufflink and lay quietly on his cuff, oozing a little more blood.

Xia Tian looked at the time and realized that he had already been at the dinner party long enough to meet the requirements stipulated in the contract. What an enjoyable three hours.

"I love this kind of dinner party," he said to Bai Jing'an on the other end of the earpiece.

"Buttons," Bai Jing'an cautioned.

Xia Tian quickly looked over his clothes and found his shirt had three buttons undone. Perhaps his movements had been too strenuous. He buttoned up and straightened his collar, now the picture of an outstanding young man. He walked to the door, stopped, and looked back at Wei Ling, who was huddled in the corner.

The famous star was sitting on the ground, looking dazed. Under the influence of the drug, his behavior seemed to regress

back to his early childhood. He'd even forgotten how to put on his pants and was instead clutching them helplessly with uncontrollably shaking hands.

Xia Tian hesitated for two seconds, wanting to just turn and leave, but...eventually, he sighed, walked over, pulled him to his feet, and helped him put on his pants.

The guy's pupils were dilated; he was still not quite clear-headed. He was very handsome, but there was something crazy about his expression—it was the kind that belonged to a person who'd long given up on himself. This type couldn't survive a week in the Lower City, but with the drugs and medical treatments in the Upper City, it was probably not easy for him to die even if he wanted to.

He looked at Xia Tian, his eyes unfocused. On the upside, he probably wouldn't remember anything tomorrow.

Xia Tian dragged Wei Ling outside. The man grasped at his cuffs, asking in a feeble voice where a person named "Xiao'an" was. It sounded like said person was his girlfriend, and that she was dead. He was very persistent with his questions, as if Xia Tian would know.

Xia Tian didn't dare to send him back to the dinner party, so he placed him in the rest area of the west wing. He asked Bai Jing'an for the number of Wei Ling's manager, then called to inform him that he'd chanced upon Wei Ling and the guy didn't look too good; so he'd better come and pick him up.

Other than that, he didn't know what else he could do.

After he was done with the kid's handover, he headed downstairs and said to Bai Jing'an, "I've exceeded the minimum required attendance for this dinner party by an hour."

"You can come back now," Bai Jing'an said.

Xia Tian happily headed for the parking lot, quite ready to go home together with Bai Jing'an. The dinner party below was noisy, but here, it was silent. The cleaning had just concluded, and the snacks and booze had not been served yet, so it looked a little desolate.

The two of them chatted sporadically, with Bai Jing'an explaining to him over the earpiece the procedures the police would follow if they found the body. He truly was an expert in committing crimes.

But as soon as Xia Tian stepped into the banquet hall, he bumped into Huitian. The image consultant looked nervous, and the moment she saw him, she dragged him by the arm to a spot without further ado and said, "Interview with GBC Channel 2's *Sky's Perspective*. Hurry up."

"What?" Xia Tian asked.

"Interview with the ace show," Huitian answered.

She looked at him with a complicated gaze, as though she was looking at a dangerous person.

"They're all prepared to laud you to the skies," she said.

Huitian dragged Xia Tian to a sofa area in the banquet hall, which was inlaid with gold foil. They had already set things up with luxurious decorations and bright lighting, making it look like a tiny shrine. They ushered Xia Tian onto the sofa, and under such lighting, he looked as dashing as a young god.

Huitian looked around. "Where Bai Jing'an?"

"No idea," Xia Tian answered.

He knew he was in the parking lot downstairs, but he would never betray a battle buddy.

Three stylists swooped in simultaneously to spruce Xia Tian up, and someone else shoved an interview outline at him. Before Xia Tian could look, the other person was already rattling on about all the key points, probably thinking they couldn't trouble a star to read the document.

Under the dazzling lights, Xia Tian, without even batting

an eyelid, discreetly tugged at his cuff to cover the tiny splotch of blood.

Xia Tian had just sat on the sofa when someone immediately coached him on his sitting posture so as to appear cool, dashing, and harmless. Xia Tian wondered why he needed to be "harmless" as a Killing Show player, and Huitian answered expressionlessly. "Gap moe."

Bai Jing'an had obviously sensed the danger. As soon as the words "GBC Channel 2" were out of her mouth, the guy had mercilessly cut off communication. He had all sorts of opinions when killing people, but when it came to interviews, he'd go silent and pretend he didn't exist.

In just a matter of moments, dozens of people circled around Xia Tian. Everyone was talking. A small man beside him—supposedly his assistant—quickly informed him that the one interviewing him was a representative of the news TV station GBC Channel 2's ace program, *Sky's Perspective*.

The interviewer was the ace host He Yu, and the man behind her, who looked overworked and displeased, was the ace producer Xu Changxin.

Xia Tian had been very popular as of late, which was why resources had been so tilted in his favor. *Sky's Perspective* hoped to show the fans his strong, gentle, and protective side.

Miss He was elegant and beautiful, with an imposing presence, and she hurried over as if she was about to face off against a formidable foe. Surrounding her was a large retinue of people passing around juice, patting cushions, and carrying the interview outline.

There was also a bunch of them around Xia Tian, who sat there confused and disoriented and feeling like they were at war. The photographer claimed he was so heartbreakingly handsome that anyone would fall in love with him at first sight. Everyone was busying around, yelling, and doing something extraordinarily important.

In the floating cities, entertainment was indeed the top priority, affecting the lives and deaths of countless people.

Across from him, Miss He looked even more gentle and pure after a battle-like styling process. The show producer of *Sky's Perspective*, Xu Changxin, briefed Xia Tian.

"You met her by chance at the dinner party and decided to do a spur of the moment interview. It will seem more realistic this way."

Before Xia Tian could nod, the guy had already started lashing out at the lightning engineer. Oh well; any response was inconsequential anyway.

Fifteen minutes later, all the staff were in place, their expressions serious. Miss He sat across from him, looking relaxed and laid-back as she chit-chatted with him.

Miss He said, "It's a shame I didn't get to meet Dee Dee. She's the sweetest kid I've ever seen."

"She's at home sleeping. It's long past her bedtime," Xia Tian answered.

"I don't think you'd like her attending this kind of occasion."

Xia Tian smiled at her and said nothing. On the camera, he leaned on the bright, luxurious, and slightly decadent sofa. He looked vibrant and radiant, yet also sad and resigned.

"You want to protect her," He Yu sighed, "but protecting family has never been an easy task. You're from District N, so you should be keenly aware of this. There, countless people die in their own hometown."

Xia Tian said nothing and subconsciously grasped his right sleeve.

The host stared at him and continued, "The insurrection in District N was so extensive that, despite being in an area on the periphery, you were undoubtedly a first-hand witness to that nightmare."

She paused before adding, "I've always been a little curious. Do you know the legendary leader of the resistance force?"

Xia Tian had been reflecting on the sensation of slashing that guy's neck in the bathroom earlier; it was still just as thrilling thinking about it again. At her words, he gave a start.

"Bai Lin? But he's from District N7," he said. Seeing He Yu still looking expectant, he explained, "I'm in District N21. Do you know how far apart those two are?"

He Yu frowned, and the ace producer waved his hand irritably to call for a pause. To Xia Tian, he snapped, "Didn't you read the interview outline? You have to say you know him!"

"But I don't," Xia Tian said.

"Then make it up!"

Xia Tian glared at him, and he glared back. Xia Tian had a feeling that Xu Changxin would probably lose his temper had he been just an ordinary starlet, but since he was on the Killing Show, they were naturally more cautious when talking to him.

"Listen, the turnover rate in the entertainment circle is high. One year and there'll be a generation gap, three years and it'll be an era. Once creativity and stars are past their prime, they're as common and as meaningless as debris. Except for the massacre in District N," Xu Changxin said patiently. "That's an evergreen topic, and Bai Lin is the guy standing at the apex of the entertainment circle in the Upper City."

Xia Tian looked at him. The guy's expression was unusually serious; he didn't look like he was joking.

"You came from District N, so you have to have some connection with him," the guy continued. "Everyone here wants a piece of the massacre, and you have a natural advantage in that regard."

Xia Tian listened to him in horror.

"*Son of Darkness* is approaching its finale, and the recent massacre-themed game, *Lockdown Zone VII*, is about to be released," the guy continued to say to him." You absolutely need this."

"What?" Xia Tian asked.

"The halo of the massacre!"

The staff from *Sky's Perspective* were afraid Xia Tian wouldn't be able to make it up, so they listed several versions for his reference. Xia Tian took a look, feeling like they were weaving a novel instead. It was even more ridiculous than *Son of Darkness*.

He looked up at the person across from him again. The ace producer's gaze was firm. He Yu was swiping her mobile phone in a race against time. It seemed he had no other choice but to have some connection to Bai Lin.

"I'll make it up, then," he said drily.

He returned the stack of materials. The group of people prepared for another two minutes before they restarted the interview.

He sat on the sofa. The lights were so dazzling they made him dizzy. Here, everything bloody and cruel turned into strong lights that enveloped him.

"I've seen him once," Xia Tian said in a hushed tone.

He Yu leaned forward, looking expectant. When Xia Tian didn't make a sound, she prompted encouragingly, "And?"

"I once helped deliver goods to District 7. Someone pointed him out to me, saying that the guy over there was Bai Lin," Xia Tian said. "He was quite far away from us. However, he's very famous in District 7."

"What was he doing?" He Yu asked.

"Playing pool with his buddies," Xia Tian said.

"What did he look like?"

"He looked..." Xia Tian thought for a moment as he looked

past the icy cold lights of the Upper World to the vibrant Lower City of bygone times. "Very happy."

Xia Tian wasn't sure why these people were bubbling with excitement, as if he'd just spilled some gossip about a superstar.

He'd indeed seen the legendary leader once from a far distance—the one who, of all young people, was particularly good at stirring up trouble in those days. It'd been just a distant glance, though; he didn't get a clear look at his appearance.

Looking back now, the one who was very happy had probably been himself, because of that always joyous girl and her smile. Those days had been his happiest and most carefree times.

He knew calamity would come calling sooner or later. This was what life had taught him. Although he was still a child then, you didn't need to grow up to understand these things—but at the time, he still naively believed that everything would be fine and nothing bad would happen.

The people from *Sky's Perspective* kept bombarding him with questions. With finesse, they dug up his old wounds as well as much rotten flesh and blood for all to see. Xia Tian felt he should act indifferent like Bai Jing'an and not provide any entertainment for these people, but he simply couldn't do it.

The person across from him said, "It must be heartbreaking for those happy times to be gone for good."

Xia Tian looked down at the blood oozing from the edge of the cufflink and silently tugged the sleeve of his coat over it again. He flashed her an icy cold but extraordinarily dazzling smile. "Yeah."

Under the spotlight amassed by money in the Upper World, his smile was like the most resplendent jewel on the crown of the entertainment industry. He was the dazzling newly born God of Killing in the Upper World.

Xia Tian left the dinner party in style. He got into his luxury sports car and went home with all eyes on him. The rough cut of his interview was very quickly sent over, with a video of the massacre affixed to the opening credits. Xia Tian turned it off in annoyance.

Bai Jing'an had already slipped back home when the interview started. When Xia Tian opened the door, he saw the guy sitting on the stairs talking to Dee Dee.

Next to Dee Dee there was a brush and cleaning solution, seemingly for cleaning the bloodstains on the carpet. It was a good habit she'd developed when she lived under someone else's roof in the Lower City—she simply had to clean whatever she saw.

Later, Bai Jing'an said that he'd seen Dee Dee cleaning the carpet when he got home. When he told her she didn't have to do that, she launched into a spiel about how a person should help out with chores when living in someone else's house—and that he shouldn't lecture her about how there's no need for that between friends. Xia Tian told her that friendship is nothing but a lie.

Xia Tian greeted them and proceeded to take a shower. They looked very...safe sitting on the stairs. It was what he'd vaguely imagined he would see when he returned home.

Bai Jing'an might have grown up alone in a big house, but he got on well with Dee Dee. Xia Tian couldn't do that; he was pretty sure she was mentally challenged and needed special care.

When he left the dinner party, Producer Xu had flashed him a brilliant smile, saying that the interview turned out pretty good. The viewers loved to hear about anything to do with the massacre, so they would be conducting a follow-up interview tomorrow and sending him an outline in advance.

Xia Tian felt sick to his stomach, though he couldn't pinpoint why. He'd pulled a glum face all the while, but that gang

of people chased after him, taking a never-ending stream of photo after photo.

He felt better after a shower. Before, he didn't understand why Bai Jing'an was always trying by every means possible to flee the dinner parties, but now he had some inkling.

He wiped his hair as he walked out of the bathroom and saw Dee Dee sitting in the doorway, waiting for him.

Seeing him stepping out, she immediately stood up straight. Solemly, she said, "I've officially entrusted you to Bai Jing'an. He promised to take good care of you."

Xia Tian's hand that was wiping his hair paused mid-action, wondering how that conversation had come about.

After his elder sister's death, Dee Dee seemed to feel that she should take over the heavy responsibility of taking care of him, worrying her little head off about his future. Xia Tian wondered if she'd revealed all his shenanigans in the Lower City to Bai Jing'an, like a parent of a worrisome child who just had to dig up all his embarrassing details as a token of sincerity when entrusting him to another.

"I like Bai Jing'an very much," Dee Dee said in all seriousness. "I thought about it for a bit, and I think I can entrust you to him."

"Well, thanks then," Xia Tian said.

"I told him that I hope he can look out for you," Dee Dee said. "You're not very good at taking care of yourself. Who knows how many times you've messed things up? He said he's probably not very good at taking care of others either, and he's messed up a lot too."

She shrugged. "I thought about it and understood. After all, the world is a tough place."

Xia Tian made a noise of agreement, then said, "Life's so difficult these days; let's not make things harder for Bai Jing'an."

Dee Dee replied that she thought the same. Probably because she looked so worried, Bai Jing'an had assured her that if things got messed up, it'd be both of them in the mess together—he wouldn't leave Xia Tian in the lurch. She thought that two people in a mess together was indeed better than one, so she agreed.

Xia Tian thanked her again for her help and sent her upstairs to bed.

TO BE CONTINUED...

Killing Show
Volume 01
An imprint of Via Lactea Ltd.

Copyright © Fox

ISBN 9781774085240